THE SHADOW PATRIOTS

A THRILLER

WARREN RAY

"This is a war of unknown warriors; but let
all strive without failing in faith or in duty."
Winston Churchill

"Americans don't give up."
Douglas MacArthur

CHAPTER 1

Without hesitation, Cole Winters jumped out the back of the slow-moving American military transport then stumbled and rolled on the sandy ground. He picked himself up and ran after his hat, which had blown off his head. At fifty-two, chasing a hat blown about by a swift spring wind wasn't an easy task, especially for an out of shape bookkeeper. After a couple of futile attempts, he finally stepped on it and then took a moment to catch his breath before picking it up. Winters put the hat back on, turned around, and saw his friends waving at him as the last of the three-truck convoy disappeared over the crest of the hill. Contemplating the remaining half-mile trek to the train station, he wondered why he had impulsively jumped out of a moving truck all for a hat.

Winters stood a couple of inches under six feet, with narrow shoulders and thinning salt and pepper hair. His facial wrinkles had deepened with age and gave him a serious look. He didn't drink beer but carried excessive belly fat. This was a result of infrequent exercise and indulging in too many vending machine snacks.

He walked down the center of the road, which was bordered by barren Iowa cornfields. Not wanting to be thought a slacker, Winters picked up his pace and reached the top of the hill. He squinted his eyes and spotted his friends standing beside the parked trucks up ahead.

Loud crackling sounds rang out. Those, mixed with loud screaming sent a chill up his spine. Confused, he ran towards the tree line to his right. More popping echoed through the air.

It was gunfire.

Reaching the cover of the trees, he fell to the ground and focused on the source of the screams. His mouth dropped open as he realized it was his friends.

"Die ya old geezers," shouted a skinny man with an AK-47.

"That's enough, stop wasting your bullets, can't you see they're all dead," yelled another who's nose appeared to have been broken more than once.

"Hey, did you hear that one big feller begging me not to kill him?" asked the skinny one.

Both men checked over the dead. "Bunch of idiots, thinking they could actually fight," said Crooked nose.

"Well, they did die for their country, just not how they figured," said the skinny one.

Both laughed.

They turned around when Bill, their boss, yelled at them. "Get those bodies out to the field and clean up that mess, pronto."

Crooked nose gave a half-hearted salute. "Oh yes sir, pronto, right away sir." He turned to his friend. "Never see him do any of the dirty work."

Two more men joined them and added to the jovial banter.

Frozen with fear and shock, Winters stared at his lifelong friends lying dead on the concrete platform. The scene started to sink in making him sick to his stomach.

The three big transport trucks pulled out of the parking lot and headed home. The four men started to throw the dead bodies into the back of a pickup truck.

"Hey, I only count twenty-nine, shouldn't there be thirty bodies?" said the skinny man.

"Are you sure?" asked another.

"Yeah count 'em up."

"Two, six, ten, fifteen, twenty, twenty-two, twenty-nine. Damn! One's missing alright."

Winters kept his eyes on the four men as they started looking around in the distance. They appeared to be searching for something.

The skinny one yelled across the parking lot. "Bill, looks like we're missing one."

The boss walked over and counted. "Get these bodies over to the field then go check the surrounding woods. You two take the other pickup, see if our missing man isn't walking home."

The second pickup peeled out and took off south. The rest of the workers finished loading the lifeless bodies in the truck. They then drove into a field, where they dumped the corpses into a large pit. Minutes later, they left the field and made a beeline towards the woods. The truck pulled up within forty yards of where Winters hid. Two men carrying AK-47 rifles slid out of the vehicle and walked into the woods.

Winters shimmied backward before getting up to run. His legs turned to rubber and shook uncontrollably, which made him stumble after a few strides. Desperation forced him to crawl on his hands and knees across the pine needle covered ground.

Winters tried to get up once more, but his legs failed him again. His panic-stricken breathing came in short rapid spurts. He dragged himself over to an old fallen tree and hid behind it.

Twigs snapped a short distance away, and faint voices grew louder as the two men closed in. They moved within yards of Winters, who scrunched himself tighter into a ball trying to disappear. He fought to control his breathing as the two men walked right past him.

Winters' eyes locked on them. He recognized the skinny one and Crooked nose. With their backs toward him, the two stopped and ceased talking. They stared into the empty woods looking for any signs of life.

Winters' chin trembled while sweat began to bead on his forehead. The

3

woods were quiet except for a gentle breeze whispering through the pines, and he worried his pounding heart could be heard.

The skinny one fished out a cigarette out of his pocket and flicked open his lighter. After lighting the smoke, he puffed on it a couple of times, and they continued walking.

Winters smelled the smoke as it wafted toward him. He waited for them to go over a hill before getting up and moving to the other side of the moss-covered log. He didn't dare peek over the tree, so he sat and waited for time to pass. During which, he pondered how he might be caught and killed like his friends. The thought sent shivers through him.

The sun started to set and made the heavily timbered woods darker, giving him a slight sense of relief as less and less of the sun's rays penetrated the woods. A half an hour later, the truck engine roared to life. Wheels spun in the dirt as it pulled out of the woods.

Winters let out his breath when the sound of the engine faded. He sat on the cold ground struggling to figure out what had happened. His eyes welled up as he thought about his friends. All of whom he'd grown up, worked, and gone to church with. They had been his lifelong friends and now they lay dead in a field.

Now alone, Winters wondered what to do. He knew better than to return to the Patriot Center. The men running the place had to be involved. He couldn't trust them, but still, he needed to find out who was behind this and prevent them from killing anyone else. He owed that much to his friends.

Winters waited over an hour before getting up and bolting out of the woods. He kept running until he ran out of breath. It didn't take long before pains shot through his stomach. He stopped, bent over, inhaled the chilly air, and waited for the pain to subside.

Minutes passed before he could stand up straight. He stared into the darkness, barely able to make out anything in front of him, but was able to see the distant lights of the train station.

Like a warning, the sound of a bad muffler echoed in the night air. He jerked around and saw bright lights coming around the bend.

CHAPTER 2

Winters dove to the side of the road and fell into the tall grass. He rolled a couple of times before the same pickup from earlier sped by him. He watched the taillights of the truck growing smaller and smaller.

Winters did an about face and started walking on the road again, his thoughts wandered to his deceased friends and their murderers. An internal battle began in his mind, should he risk his life and kill the bastards or tell the authorities. What if the authorities already know and are involved? He decided to keep running.

Ten minutes later, an overwhelming sense of guilt washed over him. He stopped walking and stood still. He tried to get rid of the guilt by making excuses that there was nothing he could do. He shook his head knowing that wasn't a good enough reason. The urge to do something wouldn't leave him alone, so he finally gave in and decided the only way to alleviate his guilt was to avenge the deaths of his friends. With his mind made up, he started walking toward the train station all the while wondering how he was going to do it.

Having no weapons, Winters set out toward the burial pit with the plan of scavenging through the dead in the hope of finding a weapon.

As he got closer to the pit, the odor of rotting bodies floated through the air. Upon arriving at the edge an unbearable stench caused him to vomit. He was thankful the darkness did not reveal the butchery.

He slid down into the pit and stopped after touching the first corpse. He pretended the dead were asleep as he dug into jackets and pants pockets. He yanked his hands back each time he touched flesh and whispered an apology for disturbing them. After a few minutes of scrounging, he discovered an eight-inch blackened steel knife. It was perfect for what he needed, not too long but incredibly sharp. Cole Winters climbed out of the pit, said a quick prayer for the dead and goodbye to his friends.

Keeping to the safety of the woods, Winters headed toward the main building. He surveyed the grounds and soon determined this was where the men lived. Working up the nerve to get in closer, he scurried to a shed, which sat to the left of the station. Chatter from inside became obvious. It was a mixture of laughter and yelling. The men were drinking and it sounded like the booze was to do its job.

If they were already this drunk, then a couple more hours would give him an edge. An edge he desperately needed. He sat on the ground and leaned back against the shed thinking about how he got here.

He had come to the Iowa Patriot Center to volunteer to help fight in the disastrous war being waged against the Chinese in California. For the past year, China and America had been arguing over trade disagreements, encroachment by China in South America, and the U.S. debt.

This was happening during a worldwide economic depression that included a complete collapse of the American economy. Tens of millions of Americans were out of work and out of hope.

Up until six months ago, negotiations had been going smoothly with both countries coming to an agreement. Then out of nowhere, China attacked southern California.

At first, U.S. forces made progress against the enemy but the momentum shifted, and now they were losing fighting men and women in droves. America needed anyone and everyone to help.

The government, in need of more volunteers, formed recruiting stations called Patriot Centers. They contracted private companies to operate them. At first, the centers recruited men and women in their thirties and forties. As the war continued to escalate, they asked anyone to join.

Winters woke up shivering. The temperature had dropped so much that his breath turned into a frozen mist. A bit groggy, he stretched his arm out and looked at his wristwatch. To his surprise, it read three in the morning. Before getting up, he listened for any sounds from the building. Silence. It was time. He snuck across the parking lot to the entrance of the building.

He paused and eyed the door, giving himself a chance to back out. He found his adrenaline had given him the unusual strength to carry forth. He reached for the door handle. It was unlocked. His pulse quickened as he slipped inside the building and crept through the dimly lit hallway.

He opened the first door he came to and tiptoed into a room that reminded him of a dorm room. Beds sat on either side of the room, each occupied. The men slept with their heads toward the entrance. A floor heater sat between the beds and created white noise as it blew warm air through the room. The only other sound came from the snoring man on the right, who Winters saw to be Crooked nose.

Winters inched the door shut and pressed himself against it. He knelt down, wondering which man to kill first and decided to leave the snoring one for last. He was much smaller than the other one. He crawled across the vinyl floor to the man on the left. The man was big and bulky with broad shoulders. The stench of booze rose up from his breathing and stung Winters' nostrils.

He stared at him wondering how he should do it. He didn't want the man to make any noise or yell out to his colleague across the room. As an avid hunter, he had killed various kinds of animals, but this was different. It was up close and this was a person.

Thankfully, it appeared they had all been drinking heavily and had passed out drunk. This gave him a shot of confidence that he could do this. Still, he was about to kill a man and he started to rethink what he was going to do.

His thoughts turned black thinking about his murdered friends. His best friend was now lying in a pit out in the field. Winters' heart began to race faster the more he thought about it.

His breathing became rapid.

Remembering the ghastly sight of his slaughtered friends, Winters covered the man's mouth with his hand and threw his full weight down on him while forcing the knife into the side of his neck. Anger poured out of him the deeper the blade sank into the fleshy double chin. Blood spilled over the man's chest and onto the dingy white bed sheets.

The man's eyes opened in complete surprise but Winters bore down harder. He watched life fade away, as the man hopelessly struggled for a brief moment.

Winters let go and leaned back. A sense of accomplishment swept over him as he stared at the dead man. The tightness in his chest loosened as he contemplated what he had done, but the euphoria was fleeting and the knife in his hand seemed heavier now.

He kept his attention focused on the dead man for a few more seconds, but then realized that Crooked nose had stopped snoring.

The smaller man rolled over on his side facing Winters. He opened his eyes and blinked a few times. He was groggy from drinking giving Winters that needed edge.

Without hesitation, Winters zipped to the other side of the room. As he did, his foot hit the heater sitting on the floor between the beds. The sound was just loud enough to startle the man awake.

Winters jumped on top of him swinging the knife down into his stomach. The man let out a breathless gasp and grabbed Winters' wrist. He tried in vain to stop the attack and swung at Winters.

The blow hit his jaw but it was too little too late. Ignoring the pain, Winters plunged the knife again into his stomach. The second strike took the fight out of the smaller man and he stopped struggling.

Winters took a long breath and exhaled slowly. He rubbed the side of his jaw and was glad the blow had been a glancing one. He grabbed a towel from the floor and wiped the blood off his hand.

A voice from the back entrance made Winters jump. "Johnny-boy, wake up, it's your watch. Johnny, get your ass up."

Winters froze not knowing if Johnny was one of the two dead men. He stared at the door expecting it to open. He felt like a gladiator thrown into a pit of lions. His heart raced ahead of his lungs, and his knees began to shake.

Winters let out a breath when he heard, "I'm up. I'm up. Gotta take a leak first." He sucked in a gulp of air and held it trying to calm his racing heart.

While he waited for the guy coming off-duty to fall asleep, Winters began to question his judgment and wondered if he'd made a mistake. Not knowing they had a guard on duty outside was amateur hour. Not getting spotted was pure luck. Of course, if he left now the guard might see him. He had no choice but to finish the job.

Winters continued sitting on the bed for thirty minutes before tiptoeing out of the room. Back out in the hallway, he opened the next closed door. A squeaky hinge forced him to stop.

He peered through the crack and could make out a figure lying on a bed. He carefully pushed the door just enough to fit through the opening. Again, the smell of alcohol hit his nostrils.

There was no floor fan, which made for a quieter room than the first. The two men slept the same way as the last two, their heads toward the entrance. He glared at the skinny one on the right and strove to remember the sound of the man's voice. He wanted to take out the off-duty guard first and didn't think it was the skinny one.

The guard, who lay before him, had a full beard, which made it difficult to determine where exactly his throat was in the dark. Though having killed two men gave him a bit more confidence. Winters angled the blade under the beard and repeated the same action he had taken on his first kill. Pushing down with all his weight, he covered the man's mouth while driving the blade into the throat.

His eyes opened up as he grabbed Winters' arm in a futile attempt to stop him. He struggled for only a few seconds before dying.

Without waiting, Winters scrambled over to the skinny one. The one who had been making jokes about his friends. He slept on his side with his back toward Winters. He grabbed the man's shoulder to turn him over. As he did, the man rolled over holding a gun.

Even in his drunken stupor, the skinny man seemed to sense something was wrong and pulled the trigger. Winters jerked his body sideways as the gun went off. He grabbed for it with his left hand as he started stabbing wildly at anything with his right. He wasn't sure if any of the blows hit their mark until the man began screaming.

The skinny man let go of the gun and Winters took control of it. Swinging the weapon around he fired twice. The first round entered the man's nose. The second struck just below his right eye. He fell back in his bed dead.

Winters' heart was pounding against his chest knowing that Johnny-boy would be storming inside. The only upside was that he now had a gun of his own.

The back door opened and Johnny-boy yelled out.

Winters shuffled to the back of the room and waited for the door to open. He stood still. A light in the hallway came on, spilling under the door. He could hear the man going into the other bedroom.

"Son-of-a-bitch," huffed Johnny-boy.

Winters tightened the grip on the pistol as the door started to creak open. Faint light spilled into the room. He didn't know how many rounds he had and didn't want to waste them. He needed to see the target before firing.

The door flew open and Johnny-boy started firing wildly into the room.

The quick move surprised Winters but he dropped to the floor as the room erupted in muzzle flashes and loud thunder.

A bullet ripped across Winters' left arm. His increased adrenaline level blocked the pain. He raised his gun and fired three times in rapid succession.

Johnny-boy collapsed to the floor and crawled down the hallway.

Winters cautiously crept to the door. He kneeled at the entrance and listened. Johnny-boy was breathing heavily, almost gasping for air.

Winters peered around the corner.

A shot rang out and hit the wall.

Before taking cover, he saw Johnny-boy's shirt was bloody. Winters took a moment to gather his thoughts. The man was wounded but he didn't know how bad it was, which meant he might survive until morning. He had to finish the job. He was trapped in the room and couldn't afford to wait.

Winters checked the magazine of the 9mm. Two rounds left. With one in the chamber, he had three.

He couldn't think of any other way but to rush out into the hall while firing. He inhaled a couple of times to calm his nerves. Gripping the gun tighter, he jumped into the fight. Johnny-boy was waiting.

They both fired.

CHAPTER 3

Both of Winters' shots were dead-on and hit Johnny-boy in the chest. They knocked him over before he could fire a second shot. The dead man's only shot was hurried and had hit nothing but the ceiling.

Winters fell back against the wall out of breath. A flood of emotion overwhelmed him knowing he had killed five men. He got up, stumbled down the hallway and into the kitchen. His stomach began to rumble and within seconds, he vomited into the sink. His face flushed with sweat.

The pain in his arm was now throbbing. He took his jacket off to tend to the wound and grabbed a towel hanging from the stove to begin wiping the blood from his arm. The bullet had grazed him and had taken out a small chunk. It wouldn't be too serious if he could stop the bleeding. Using his knife, he cut the towel in two, fixed the ends together, and wrapped it around the wound. He pulled it as tight as he could before cutting off the circulation and tied it off.

He turned on the faucet to wash the remaining blood off his arm and splash cold water on his face, which helped clear his head. The tap still ran as he grabbed another towel and dried himself off. He stood in a daze watching the water rinse his vomit and blood down the sink. He shut the faucet off, moved over to the kitchen table, and sat down to think about what he'd done. Killing people was not in his nature and he wondered how it would change him.

After putting the towel down, he noticed a piece of paper with a list of names. Picking it up, his heart sank as he read the names of his friends. He studied the whole list, remembering moments with each one of them. Tom, his friend and best man at his wedding was on the list. He had been the closest to Winters; their families had even shared camping trips. His eyes welled up trying to make sense of what was happening. He looked down the hall at the dead Johnny-boy. "Bastard! You got what you deserved," he yelled out.

Winters got up and paced back and forth, then sat down on a couch to try and figure his next move. He reread the list and realized his name was on it. The hairs on his arms suddenly rose straight up, as if charged with electricity. Winters realized his knowledge of these murders would make him a liability and seeing his name on a list, told him they could easily figure out who had killed these men. If they knew who he was then it would only be a matter of time before they found him.

CHAPTER 4

The sound of engines rumbling woke Winters. He was in a state of confusion and had to look around for a few moments to remember what he had done. After last night's rush of adrenaline had worn off, exhaustion overtook him and he had fallen asleep on the couch.

Feeling the vibration of the ground, Winters ran to the window. He peered through the glass and saw three transports roaring into the parking lot. Were they already searching for him? There was nowhere to run and hide, so he hustled back down the hallway. Reaching for the 9mm from last night, he remembered it was out of ammo. He bent down, picked up Johnny-boy's gun, and checked the magazine. Empty.

He didn't have time to hunt for where they stashed their weapons. So, he grabbed a camouflage jacket off its wall hook and carefully put it on trying not to disturb his wounded arm, which had become stiff and painful. After discarding his hat, and opting for another he found sitting on a table, he went to the bathroom mirror to check his appearance and pulled the What down to hide his face.

Winters hurried down the hall to the door window and looked out. "Damn, more recruits," he said to no one.

He cursed himself because he had no choice but to kill these three drivers. He couldn't let them kill all those men out there. He tried to formulate a plan. Although being outnumbered three to one, he had the element of surprise on his side, but he'd still have to find a gun.

The three drivers stood together obviously waiting for someone to come outside and take over.

Winters' legs started to shake when one of the drivers moved across the parking lot toward the building. He backed away remembering Johnny-boy was still lying in the hallway and ran over to move him. The man was heavy and now stiff. Winters grabbed the legs and using as much strength as he could muster, dragged the body into the first bedroom and shut the door. He hurried to the kitchen as the front door opened.

"Guys, is anyone up?" asked the driver.

Winters took a deep breath to calm his nerves.

"Yeah, down here. We tied one on last night," said Winters in a low scruffy voice.

"You got any coffee ready?" the driver asked as he came down the hallway.

Winters bent down behind the open refrigerator door and pretended to reach for something. His pulse was at the breaking point. The door shielded his body as well as the knife in his hand.

"Just made a pot."

The driver, who was tall and skinny, entered the kitchen.

"Is that you Bill?" he asked.

Winters backed out of the refrigerator keeping his face from the driver.

"Thought you said there was coffee?"

In one continuous motion, Winters turned towards the driver and drove the knife into his gut. The man bent over as he clutched his stomach screaming in agony. Winters pulled the bloody knife out, grabbed him around his neck and sank the blade into his throat. The driver stepped back and crumpled to the floor.

Winters stood staring at the man and realized he had blood all over himself. He tore the jacket off, threw it on the floor while rinsing his hands at the kitchen faucet. He looked down at the dead man and reached for the Colt .45 in his holster. He pulled the magazine out. Full.

He scrambled back down the hall and grabbed another jacket from a coat rack by the door. While donning the jacket, he glanced out the window and saw the two remaining drivers walking toward the building.

The rumbling sound of the diesel engines idling got louder when Winters stepped outside. The two drivers stopped dead in their tracks as he came walking out holding a gun.

Simultaneously, they reached for their side arms.

Winters reacted first. He fired at the driver on the left hitting him in the chest and killing him instantly.

The second driver was stilling fumbling with his holster when Winters fired. The bullet hit the man in the upper right chest, knocking him to the ground. Winters second shot penetrated the man's upper right leg. The driver writhed in pain and yelled at the top of his lungs begging for his life.

"Ahhhggg, please don't kill me," screamed the driver.

"Why not, you murdering son-of-a-bitch?" yelled Winters.

The driver cried. "I'm not the one killing them. I'm just a driver."

"So that makes you completely innocent of this?" asked Winters

Winters rifled through the driver's clothes to check for any weapons.

"I'm just doing what they tell me to do."

The volunteers had taken cover and were now all staring at Winters. He realized he probably looked like a raving lunatic and would, somehow, have to explain all of this.

A few of the passengers had gotten the courage to move out from behind the truck and come toward him.

Winters waved to them. They must have been from another part of the state because he didn't recognize any of them. They were all about the same age as him, and more than half as physically out of shape.

Winters needed to convince them not to fear him. After subduing the driver, he tucked the weapon into the small of his back and walked toward the volunteers.

Winters took a deep breath and began. "My name is Cole Winters, and I'm not gonna hurt ya. Yesterday, I was on one of these trucks but jumped off and had to walk the last half-mile. I saw my friends lined up on the platform there and murdered in cold blood, the same as you would have been this morning."

The men stood silent. They looked at one another, not knowing how to take this news or to even believe it.

"There is a mass grave across this field," Winters continued, pointing across the parking lot. "It's filled with hundreds of bodies."

One of the volunteers shouted out. "How do we know you're not one of them?"

Winters didn't respond.

"What are we supposed to do now?" yelled one.

"Where are those men now?" asked another.

"I killed them last night," said Winters.

Winters filled them in on last night's events. After he finished, a couple them walked across the field to inspect the open pit while a few more ventured inside the building. The rest went over to the wounded driver and peppered him with questions.

"What the hell are you doing this for, why kill us?"

"I don't know why," he replied.

"Who are you and who's in charge of this?"

"Is the military involved with this?"

"I don't know anything, I'm just a driver."

One of the men kicked the driver in the leg. He screamed out in pain. "I told you I don't know anything."

"Kick him again, Nate," yelled his friend.

Nate kicked the driver again in the same wounded leg. "Listen you son-of-a-bitch, we're going to get some answers out of you, even if it takes us all day. Do you understand?"

Winters stood off to the side as the volunteers interrogate the injured driver. He was relieved to see someone else doing some of the dirty work. Even though those men had deserved to die, his actions sickened him. Now that he had killed two more, it made Winters wonder what kind of a man he really was. He didn't have a bad temper and considered himself pretty laid back. It gave him chills to think maybe he was like Dr. Jekyll and Mr. Hyde only he had never before experienced being Mr. Hyde. Winters snickered to himself remembering that Mr. Hyde wasn't scared of anything and didn't recall him vomiting afterward. Whoever he was last night, he hoped that would be the last of him.

He looked across the field at the burial pit and where two men had fallen to their hands and knees and were throwing up.

The door to the building opened and two of today's recruits walked out.

"Elliott, it's like he said. There's a bunch of dead people in there," said one of them.

Elliott was a tall, burly man in his mid-fifties and wore a ball cap over his thinning gray hair. His skin was dark and leathery from spending many days outside. He was a good ole boy and everyone seemed to like him. He spoke with a friendly tone in his voice.

He turned to acknowledge his friend and then walked over to Winters.

"I'm Rich Elliott, most folks just call me Elliott," he said as he extended his hand.

Winters shook Elliott's big hand and received a firm grip around his smaller one. "I'm Cole Winters."

"Nice to meet you, Cole. Kind of weird what's happened here, I'm not sure I'm even able to believe it."

Winters tilted his head. "Had I not seen it with my own eyes, I don't know if I would have either."

Elliott said with a slight smile, "You sure you're not a crazy man?"

"Starting to wish I were, be a helluva lot easier I think."

After a few more well-placed kicks, the driver had enough and told the men volunteers had been killed since the beginning of the program and thought it might be going on at a few other places in the Midwest. He had been told these volunteers were troublemakers and by getting rid of them, he'd be doing his country a great service. He also acknowledged the pay was excellent.

The volunteers were in shock. They had signed up to help fight the Chinese. Instead, a different enemy was leading them to slaughter. An enemy they never would have dreamed existed.

"We need to figure out what we're going to do," said Elliott turning to Winters. "What do you think, Cole?"

Winters looked at him in surprise. "Why are you asking me? I don't know what to do. I just wanted to get these guys for what they did to my friends, and make sure they would never kill anyone else."

"Gosh darn Cole, you heard the man say they're doing this in other places. We need to stop them," said Elliott.

"He said it might be going on in other places. I don't know why you think I could be of any help. I don't have any military experience. I'm just a bookkeeper."

Elliott raised an eyebrow. "Bookkeeper? You don't look like no bookkeeper to me."

"What's that supposed to mean?"

"Well, you're not nerdy looking."

"Thanks, I guess. I'm just good with numbers, is all."

"Well, if you're good with numbers, then you, as in one person, in the last five hours, have killed seven men by yourself. Adding those numbers together tells me you have more experience than any of us."

Winters stood considering this while the men gawked at him like he was some sort of leader. This was not what he envisioned when he decided to come back and take revenge for his friends.

He realized his options were few. Even if the authorities weren't involved with this, and he wasn't sure about that, he would have to explain why he killed those men. It had not been an act of self-defense, but more like that of a vigilante. So, either way, they'd arrest him. At the same time, he still needed to find the list of names. Then an idea struck him. These guys can help him get the file and then he could bolt out of there.

He looked at the men. "If you'll remember when we signed up, they recorded all of our names, which means they can find out who did this. So, we don't have much choice but to go back and search through those records."

"What should we do with our prisoner?" asked Elliott.

Winters winced at the question. A prisoner?

He wondered what that even meant. It's not like they were an army or band of kidnappers, but yet they had a prisoner, a wounded one at that. He didn't want to have to deal with this.

"Let's bring him inside and tend to his wounds," said Winters feeling a bit awkward giving out orders.

They helped the wounded driver up and took him into the building. Some of the volunteers went inside while others walked over to the trucks to grab their belongings.

A stern looking man approached Winters. "I'm Nate Foster."

Winters shook the hand of a man who appeared to be his own age and height. The man carried his beer gut quite well. His black hair had streaks of gray running through it. Dark, thick eyebrows framed eyes.

"I'm Cole Winters."

"Cole like Cold Winters?" asked an amused Nate.

"I was born at home, during a blizzard. My parents had a sense of humor. I'm just glad they decided on the letter E instead of a D, on Cole."

"Well, I think the name fits, we might have to call you Ice Cold after what you've done here," said Nate.

"It's not like it was a fair fight. They were all passed out from drinking," said Winters not wanting to tell him about his wound for fear of needless pity.

"Yeah, but still, it was a bad-ass move."

Winters shrugged. "If you say so."

The two men stepped inside the building, walked up the hall, and into the kitchen. Some of the men had moved the body of the first driver into one of the bedrooms and laid their prisoner on the couch. They also applied bandages to his wounds. Speculation filled the room as to who was behind this operation. They made coffee and ate the food found in the refrigerator.

Winters sat at the table. "Here's that list of names I was telling you about. All they need to do is go through the pit and figure out who's buried and who's not."

Elliott grabbed it. "Then they'll come looking for us."

"Yes, they will. These people will keep looking till they find us," said Winters. "We've stumbled onto something devious here. I'd imagine whoever is behind this wouldn't want the knowledge of it to spread around."

"So, we're just supposed to waltz right back there and storm the place?" asked one of them.

Nate spoke up. "Why the hell not?"

"How are we going to do that?" asked another.

Nate raised his eyebrows in disbelief. "For crying out loud guys. We just walk in and shoot up the damn place."

"We can't just stroll in there, those guys were carrying guns," said another.

"These idiots here left us their guns," argued Nate.

"We've got their three trucks," said Elliott. "They're gonna be expecting them back, plus there weren't that many men running the darn place."

"Then what?" asked another.

Elliott replied. "Like Nate said, we shoot the place up and kill 'em."

"Who exactly is going to do that?"

The room fell silent with that comment and all eyes fell on Winters. He wondered if they thought he was some kind of a cold-blooded killer. They might think differently, if only they knew how afraid he had been out in those woods, his legs shaking so bad, he had to crawl on his hands and knees. How he had run away before the guilt of not doing anything turned him around, or how he vomited in the sink after killing those men.

"I'll volunteer," said Elliott.

Nate spoke up. "Hell, count me in. I'd love nothing more than taking these bastards out."

No one else said anything. Eyes turned toward the floor. Winters knew they were afraid, and so they should be. Pulling a trigger was easy. Taking a man's life was not.

He spoke. "I'll go. We'll just walk in like we're the drivers."

Suddenly, chills rushed through his body. A radio sitting unnoticed in the corner of the room had come to life: "Train station Alpha, come in. Train station Alpha, come in, this is Bravo Patriot Center, come in."

CHAPTER 5

VICTOR IOWA

The radioman turned to Decker and asked. "They're not answering the radio. I've been trying to contact them for twenty minutes now. Should we call the colonel?"

"No! Last thing I need is that guy up my ass. We'll wait. They're probably having a problem with a truck or something."

Decker was in his early thirties and wore his greasy, brown hair shoulder length. For a diminutive man, he was a smug bastard. He was in the transportation business, and the cargo didn't matter to him, so long as he got paid. In these trying times, it was every man for himself, and he was all about looking out for number one. He wasn't fond of the volunteers and thought they were a bunch of self-righteous old men thinking they could be the saviors of the American dream. For him, that dream was dead in the water. He thought it better to get rid of them, rather than having them around making trouble for the new government. Besides, it would be fewer mouths to feed.

"Maybe we should send someone and see if anything has happened," said the radioman.

"Don't worry, they'll be along soon enough. You worried about a bunch of old men who don't have a clue what's going to happen to them?"

LUCAS COUNTY IOWA

The radio sitting in the corner of the room fell silent again.

Some moments passed before Winters spoke up.

"I think we need to leave."

"We should burn this place down," suggested Elliott.

"Probably a good idea. Try and hide what I did here."

"Well, I was thinking so they wouldn't ever be able to use it again."

Winters grimaced. "Yes, of course, that too."

"What about the prisoner?"

Winters turned to him and noticed he had grown pale. "Well, we can't leave him here. Better to take him with us."

A few of the men hopped into the transports and moved them closer to the building. The remainder scattered around in nervous excitement.

Fifteen minutes later, everyone was out of the building except Winters and Elliott.

"You ready?" Winters asked.

"Yep," said Elliott as he backed down the hall pouring diesel fuel on the floor. When they walked out the door into the parking lot, Nate came over to them.

"He's dead," said Nate.

"Who's dead?" Winters asked.

"The prisoner…little prick got what he deserved anyway."

Winters rolled his eyes. He thought about the dead driver and how he represented yet another man he had killed. He didn't necessarily want him to die, but on the other hand, they wouldn't have to deal with a prisoner anymore. He instructed them to carry the driver inside with the others.

Elliott lit the torch he had put together with old rags soaked in diesel fuel.

"You want the honors?" asked Elliott.

Winters shook his head.

Elliott threw the torch into the building. Fire immediately ran through the hall and into each room quickly spreading throughout the old building. The place began to crackle and smoke poured out of the windows as they gave away to the heat. The men watched the orange flames dance high into the air as the building began to collapse.

Winters formed a small smile. "Let's go get that list," he said.

The trucks pulled out, leaving a billowing cloud of smoke behind them. Winters sat up front with Elliott who drove the lead truck.

"Everyone's real thankful for what you did," said Elliott.

"Well, we got lucky I suppose," said Winters.

"You married?"

Winters flinched at the question. He had just buried his wife a week ago. "Widower."

Elliott turned to Winters. "I'm sorry. What was her name?"

"Ellie. She, ah, got cancer. Took her real quick."

"That sucks. You got kids?"

"Got a daughter, Cara. She's off in Florida."

Elliott decided to change the subject. "So, where you from?"

"Sabine Iowa."

"Oh yeah, I know a couple of farmers over that way," said Elliott. "You know the Nelsons or Clarks?"

Winters shook his head. "Can't say I know any of them. All these guys here your friends?"

"Pretty much, we're all from the Fairfield area, and know the same people, or what's left of them."

"You and Nate good friends?"

"I've known him ever since we were kids. We're both fifty-three, so we went through grade school and high school together. His family had the farm next to ours, and there were plenty of times we helped each other with the chores. He didn't like farming much, which is why he became a mechanic. Boy can fix just about anything."

"You a farmer Elliott?"

"Yep. Daddy left the farm to me after he died. About the only thing I know how to do is farm. That and fish."

"You married? Any kids?"

"Oh yeah, my Amy and I been married thirty years now, got myself two grown girls, neither married yet."

"Nate?"

"Nate never did marry, he never wanted to get tied down, although truth be known, no girl could ever slow him down. Nate is a bit on the aggressive side, got a wild streak in him. I always thought he'd settle down by now," said Elliott chuckling to himself.

"How many of your neighbors headed south to the camps?" asked Winters referring to the FEMA camps set up to handle the mass migration into the warmer climate. Since the crash, the nation's inadequate power grid caused major blackouts. The shortages spread around the country, forcing power companies to ration electricity.

"Some did. Most of us don't trust the government anymore. Look at the way they threw out the Constitution."

Winters scoffed at that. It was beyond comprehension how that happened. During the chaos of the economic crash, people started protesting by the tens of thousands. These protests turned violent and the military was ordered to regain control. Unfortunately, they made the situation worse by opening fire. Hundreds of Americans died. Everyone blamed the president and under pressure from Congress and the media, he resigned.

The new president wasn't the Vice President, because he was embroiled in corruption scandals of his own and had resigned as well. The Speaker of the House became president, but he was just as corrupt as the Vice President. With help from wealthy power players, a willing media, corrupt judges and other politicians jockeying for power, the new President with the excuse of restoring control, nationalized the government.

After using the Constitution to get in the white house, the new President threw it aside and all power now resided with him. Besides eliminating states rights, the President put a ban on free speech and outlawed firearms.

Elliott turned to Winters. "Hell, I wouldn't be surprised to find out that they're somehow involved with these killings."

Winters took off his hat and scratched his head. "Damn I hope not. I'd hate to think the Army would do something like this." He paused for a moment before continuing. "If we can't trust them, who can we trust?"

Elliott shrugged his shoulders.

Winters sat quietly and went through the plan they'd put together for when they got back to the Patriot Center. He tried to think of the name of the little guy in charge. Winters remembered him as an annoying little bastard who continuously yelled and barked orders like a Chihuahua. At the time he couldn't wait to leave but now, couldn't wait to get back.

"What was the name of that annoying little bastard?" Winters asked.

"Oh, you mean Decker."

"Ah, yes, Decker."

"Quite a character that one."

"I didn't like him from the get-go."

"Well, Mr. Decker is going to have a very bad day today."

As they bounced along the highway, the wind whistled through the open windows. Winters pulled his hat down, which reminded him of yesterday and the friendly banter among his friends when a heavy gust whipped through and blew it off his head. He had gotten up and started climbing over the tailgate. His friends were flabbergasted that he was going to jump. They immediately started razzing him, but Winters retorted with a single phrase, "It's my lucky hat," and then made his fateful jump.

Elliott turned to Winters. "We're getting close."

Winters recognized passing landmarks and knew they were coming up on the outskirts of Victor, Iowa. A few more minutes and they would be there.

"Okay, here we go," said Elliott.

As the three big green transports entered the north end of town, the rumbling sound of the trucks echoed off the houses on either side announcing their arrival.

Elliott slowed down as he approached the entrance. They saw two guards, who were both carrying AR-15s, standing in the parking lot waiting for their return, and staring at them as the transports pulled in.

"Real easy, Elliott, real easy," said Winters.

Elliott took his time pulling in. Fortunately, the sun reflected off the truck's windshield and prevented a clear view of who was driving. As Elliott pulled in to park, Nate was right behind him in the second truck. He shifted the truck into neutral and engaged the parking brake. Neither of them spoke as they glanced at each other while grabbing their weapons.

Elliott climbed down keeping his back toward the guards. He lifted his boot up onto the running board to tie the shoelace.

Winters hopped out and scooted to the front, staying out of sight. The diesel engine sat rumbling, radiating heat and making Winters sweat while he waited for Elliott to make a move.

Elliott's big move was to come around the front. He looked so panicky that his hands were shaking.

Winters asked him. "Are you alright?"

He nodded hesitantly. "I didn't know what else to do. Is he following me?"

Winters peeked over Elliott's shoulder. "Yes, steady now. Give him another few seconds, he's passing Nate now."

The guard raised his head while moving past Nate's truck. Nate pretended not to notice him and the guard kept walking toward Elliott. Nate kept his eye on the side mirror and saw the second one coming toward them.

"Where the hell have you been? Decker is pissed off," said the first guard as he came toward them.

Winters placed his right hand on Elliott's shoulder pushing him to the side, as he stepped forward and shoved his knife into the guard's stomach, withdrawing and stabbing him again. The guard yelped, dropped his rifle, and clenched his stomach as he collapsed to the pavement.

The sound gave the second guard pause and he raised the AR to his shoulder. He slow-walked toward the front of the truck.

Nate jumped down with a knife in hand and hit the ground running. He raced up behind him and grabbed the collar of his jacket. He pulled the guard back while swinging the blade around stabbing him in the stomach. He caught him falling to the ground and dragged the limp body to the other side of the truck. He looked at Winters and Elliott with a hint of a smile curling around the edges of his lips. Nate moved to the back of the vehicles, some of the guys jumped out and ran toward the windowless building to wait for Elliott and Winters.

"What now?" Elliott asked.

With an intense voice Winters said, "We go in like we own the place."

"Heck fire, I was just here this morning, won't they recognize us?" asked Elliott in a nervous tone.

"It won't matter. You know he's just sitting behind his desk."

Elliott agreed.

"I'll go first," said Winters. "You guys stay here and cover the entrance."

Elliott pulled the door open for Winters and followed him inside. Decker sat behind his desk. Elliott and Winters strolled into the office and pointed their guns at Decker, who looked up and froze.

Winters gestured for Elliott to cover the hallway door. He turned his attention back to Decker.

"Why?" asked Winters.

"Why what?" responded Decker.

"Kill the volunteers. Why?"

"Don't know what you're talking about," replied a nervous Decker.

"Yes, you do. It's written all over your face," said Winters.

Decker shrugged and then smirked. "So, you're the one who escaped yesterday, huh? Well, lucky you."

Winters raised his gun higher and closer to Decker. "Why?"

"For the money of course," said Decker.

The answer infuriated Winters and his anger so clouded his mind it diverted his attention from Decker who calmly reached under his desk for his gun. In one quick motion, Decker pulled out a small Beretta .380.

The movement didn't register right away and took Winters a split second before he fired his gun, striking Decker in the chest. The impact hurled him and his chair against the wall, where the man drew his last breath.

Someone from the back of the building yelled out. Elliott flattened himself up against the wall and waited. The man stepped through the doorway and saw Decker in his chair. He turned to Winters while reaching for his sidearm but was too late. Elliott took aim and fired. The man's head exploded in a shower of blood, bone and flesh before collapsing to the ground.

The corpse on the ground represented Elliott's first kill. He examined him on the floor, lying in an ever-widening dark red pool of blood. Elliott gave Winters an uneasy glance. Winters responded with an encouraging nod understanding the surreal moment.

Neither spoke as some of the volunteers rushed in. Several ran to secure the back of the building.

Nate walked over to where Decker still lay in his chair. "Not much of a bad-ass now, are you?"

Winters grabbed the chair and wheeled Decker out into the hallway. He noticed Elliott had not spoken yet and asked him if he would go and see if any of the neighbors could tell them anything.

Everyone followed Elliott outside, while Nate and Winters moved over to the desk, which had files stacked on top of each other. They set their guns on the table, grabbed chairs and started digging through the paperwork.

"Don't really see anything here, mostly receipts and truck log records," Nate said.

"It's got to be here somewhere."

Winters opened the desk drawers and looked through the files. A minute passed before he found the folder with the names of the recruits.

"There's hundreds of them," said Winters thumbing through the pages.

He handed some to Nate. The two men poured over the names, each recognizing some. Winters' heart sank when he saw his name and those of his friends. While reading them, he felt the urge to grab the papers and take off running. He shut the folder.

Winters found a business card taped on the wall above the desk phone. He tore it off and read the name aloud.

"Colonel Nunn United States Army, Commander of the Midwest Region."

"Colonel Nunn? Never heard of him," said Nate.

"Neither have I."

They stopped sifting through the files when Elliott returned to the office.

"Everything's secure, some townspeople were asking questions," said Elliott.

"What did you tell them?" asked Winters.

"I told them the truth."

"Did they know anything?"

"No, and none of them liked Decker. I guess he strutted around like he owned the place."

"How many people are still in town?"

"Not many and after what's happened here, they're leaving as we speak. Can't say I blame 'em. Who knows who might show up and ask questions," said Elliott.

Winters thought the same thing.

The three of them went out to the parking lot, which was full of vehicles abandoned by the volunteers who had come to serve. Winters' own beat up car sat by the street. He thought about getting in and taking off.

A couple of pickups heading toward them interrupted his thoughts. The tension elevated as the men looked at one another and then started to scatter in different directions. Everyone took cover as the vehicles drove in.

They waited anxiously as the two pickups pulled up. Both were loaded with men. The lead vehicle stopped when the driver noticed the two bodies lying near the transport trucks. Winters saw the hesitation in their eyes. They were volunteers.

Winters and Elliott both walked toward them. As they approached, some of the guys jumped out of the back.

"What's going on here?" asked one of them. "Isn't this where the volunteers are supposed to go?"

"It is. We're volunteers like you." He pointed to the two dead guys on the ground. "And these scumbags were here to kill us."

They started murmuring and seemed unsure of the story. One of them recognized Elliott.

"Elliott."

Elliott turned to the voice. "Oh hey, Scar, how the heck are ya?"

"Great, I think. What's going on here?"

"These sons of bitches have been killing off the volunteers. This is Cole Winters. He stumbled onto this whole thing yesterday and saved our lives this morning."

Elliott gave them a brief account. They stood dumbfounded listening to the story. They looked at Winters, who wasn't sure how to respond and felt uncomfortable with all the attention. After Elliott finished, everyone walked over to shake hands with Winters to thank him.

"Hell of a thing you did, Cole. I'm Scott Scarborough, but call me Scar." A big right hand came toward him and Winters put out his own.

Scar, a retired Marine was a big man with a heavy frame and stood a few inches over six feet. He was in his early fifties and kept himself in shape. He wore a camouflage ball cap bearing a Marine emblem. His blue eyes lit up whenever a big smile formed on his wide face. He loved to laugh and joke around. He put his hand on the shoulder of his friend Meeks and introduced him.

"This here is my good friend Stephen Meeks. We like to go with one-word names. So it's just Meeks," said Scar.

"Don't let that big ole Jar Head fool ya. One word is all he can handle," Meeks said with a smirk. He extended his hand to Winters. "Hey, nice to meet you."

Meeks, back in his youth was a running back and played football for the University of Iowa, he was of average height, though the same age as his friend, he was in better shape. He always wore a Hawkeye ball cap. Like his friend Scar, he was a jokester and always seemed to have a sly half smile on his face. If he had any gray hair, his blonde hair kept it hidden.

"Nice to meet you. Hawkeye fan?" asked Winters.

"Played for them back in the day," Meeks answered.

"Way back in the day," laughed Scar.

Meeks smacked his fist into Scar's shoulder. He nodded to Winters. "Who do you think is behind all of this?"

"The only name we got so far is a Colonel Nunn."

Meeks shook his head. "Never heard of him."

Scar turned to Winters. "What are we going to do about this?"

Déjà vu, Winters thought, remembering Elliott asking the same question. "What do you mean? We already did something. We took out the train station and this Patriot Center."

"Yeah, but someone needs to pay. Maybe even this Colonel Nunn. You don't think they're going to just stop do ya? They'll have this place up and running again in no time. We can't let them do that."

Winters felt like he was being sucked into something he didn't want any part of. "We don't know if Colonel Nunn is involved. Maybe he's the one we need to be telling this to."

Scar crossed his arms over his big chest. "You sure you want to go up to this guy without knowing for sure. I mean you did, just killed a bunch of their guys. You think he might be a little-pissed off?"

Winters sighed. "Yeah, I'd already given it some thought and I still don't know. I'm not even sure how we can distinguish the good guys from the bad ones."

"Well, the bad guys will be pointing guns at you," said Scar.

"Really, thanks for the heads up." Winters was starting to dislike this guy.

"No seriously, we'll have to watch them," Scar said. "It's the only way we can tell who's who. We'll just have to see who comes after us. Hey, if no one comes for us, then we'll know you got them all. Until then, we don't have much choice in the matter. I mean it's not like any of us can really go home now," said Scar.

Winters gave him a quizzical look.

"If they're willing to murder us, then what are they going to do next? At some point, they'll come after our families and neighbors."

Winters let out another sigh. Damn. He hadn't thought about that.

CHAPTER 6

Cole Winters had signed up to help fight the war against the Chinese. Instead, he was now fighting an unknown enemy. It was an unsettling thought, not knowing who the other side was. Not knowing what or where an item was, made the bookkeeper in him stress out.

After listening to the retired Marine, his guilt for wanting to run away had returned. Would he be able to live with himself if he ran off and did nothing more? He felt pressured into taking this fight further than he had intended.

Winters studied the volunteers still standing in the parking lot. He envied them because most of them were friends. He desperately missed his friends and being able to confide in them. Their advice would be appreciated right now.

The men gathered in small groups, some were talking to one another, and others were staring at Winters. He wondered if they thought he was some kind of superhero or a cold-blooded killer. He wished he had the nerve to jump into his car and drive away.

Considering his situation, Winters decided to stay with this group of volunteers, at least until they got some answers. He wondered where they could go to get them, and how long would the journey last.

Ever since the economy collapsed everything was in limited supply, especially fuel. Also, there were no more cell phones or Internet service. The regular phone lines were spotty at best. All the conveniences you took for granted were gone. It was like living in the seventies again.

"What's next?" asked Meeks.

Winters looked at him trying to remember his name. "We should probably find out who's coming with us."

"Who's us?" asked Meeks.

Winters remembered he played football for Iowa. "Our group."

"We can't just be called us, we need a name for our little band of merry men," replied Meeks gesturing to Scar for an answer.

Scar started thinking aloud. "We have an enemy we're planning to find and probably kill, and they don't know we're coming for them. So, we're like in the shadows trying to avenge our friends and neighbors."

Meeks interrupted. "We're Avengers then."

"Avengers…no that's taken and it doesn't sound right. We're more than Avengers, I mean we came together as patriots." Scar clapped his hands. "I got it…we're the Shadow Patriots."

The name hung out there for a second before everyone started nodding their heads and smiling.

"Shadow Patriots it is then," replied Meeks patting his friend Scar on the back. "You always come up with something good."

Scar acknowledged the compliment.

"Now let's figure out who all want to be members of the Shadow Patriots," said Winters who then remembered Meeks' name.

"You got it, Captain," said Scar, looking at Winters.

"Captain?" Winters asked.

"Take it from an old Marine, every group needs a captain. From what

I've seen and heard about you, you're him."

The other men nodded in agreement and came forward to congratulate Winters and shake his hand. He wasn't pleased but couldn't turn them down at this point.

Scar jumped up on the bed of the pickup. "Listen up. Captain Winters here needs to know who wants to join the Shadow Patriots and go kill the sons-of-a-bitches that are behind all of this."

In unison, they yelled out, "Hell yeah!"

"Well, I'd say you have an enthusiastic group, Captain," said Scar.

Winters flinched at being called Captain.

"Don't forget there's more coming in right behind us," said Scar.

"How many?" asked Winters.

"I know of a few coming up from my area."

Winters meandered back into the building and looked at the two dead bodies bleeding on the vinyl floor as he contemplated their predicament for a moment. If this Colonel Nunn is in charge that probably meant the military was somehow involved. This meant they could trust no one.

More importantly, how would they be able to fight them? Most of them were out of shape, they had no supplies, limited weapons and they were about as organized as a shoebox full of receipts. "Shadow Patriots, yeah, we'll be keeping to the shadows alright," Winters chuckled to himself.

Then an idea hit him. The name, Shadow Patriots, gave him an idea for subterfuge. As of now, no one knew of their existence. Why not use it to their advantage?

He headed back outside.

"Whatcha need, Captain?" asked Elliott.

Winters shook his head after being called Captain. He hoped he wouldn't have to put up with that for too long. "I've got an idea on how to keep us in the shadows. Let's load up the dead and clean this place up like nothing happened here."

Elliott gave a knowing nod.

"Whoever is in charge might think Decker and his men just took off. Maybe just because the train station burned to the ground."

"Good call," said Scar. "Hey, also, some of us live close enough where we can go home and bring back our own weapons."

"Yes, great idea."

"I know of another Patriot Center up in Minnesota," said Elliott.

"Oh?"

"Yeah, we should head up there and check it out," Elliott said. "So, we can keep an eye on them."

Winters liked the idea. Being in northern Iowa would make it an easy drive to Minnesota. He gathered the men together and instructed anyone who lived in the vicinity to go home and grab any weapons they owned and get back as quickly as possible. They could then leave for Minnesota and check out that Patriot Center.

After most of the volunteers took off, Winters decided to tend to the wound he'd received at the train station. Finding a first aid kit, he headed to the bathroom. Slowly taking his jacket and shirt off, he started to remove the kitchen towel he had hastily used to stop the bleeding. He unwound the cloth, which had gotten heavier from being soaked with blood. The last bit of towel stuck to his arm, so he gently pried it off trying not to rip open the wound. The towel fell off to show he was missing an inch-long strip of flesh, but not too deep. Some of it had started to dry, scabbing up in the process. Blood still oozed out in other parts. Stitches were in order but he knew that wasn't going to happen. He cleaned the wound by gently dabbing it with a wet towel. He grabbed a brown bottle of hydrogen peroxide and poured it on his arm. The liquid began to bubble up into a foam as it cleaned the wound.

Better than rubbing alcohol, he thought to himself.

He laid a three-inch white pad over the wound, wrapped gauze around a few times and taped it on. He opened a bottle of aspirin, shook a bunch out and swallowed them, stuffing the bottle into his jacket pocket.

Within two hours, everyone had come back bringing with them quite an assortment of firearms. It included everything from shotguns and rifles of varying calibers to an amazing variety of handguns.

With everyone back and the dead buried outside of town, the Shadow Patriots were ready to leave for Minnesota. Winters glanced around at the vehicles filled with men eager to start their adventure. They all stared at him with excitement in their eyes. He began to walk across the lot as he contemplated various ways to ensure they would be able to recognize who the enemy was. Reaching the street, he looked at the empty houses lined up in rows and while staring at them was struck with an idea.

He turned around and searched the maze of vehicles to find Scar. Winters spotted him and Meeks alone in an F-150. He navigated his way between two cars full of men and finally reached them.

"Hey Scar, you said we've got to watch these guys right."

"Yepper, which is why we're headed to Minnesota."

Winters grabbed Scar's arm. "I've got a little something else in mind for you."

CHAPTER 7

ROCK ISLAND ILLINOIS

Sergeant Owens knocked on the open door of Colonel Nunn's office and waited for permission to enter. Colonel Nunn waved the young sergeant in. The office was uncharacteristically sterile, no family pictures on the desk, no awards on the walls, only a map of the Midwest and a lone American flag standing in the far corner. The one thing that gave it any character was an umbrella stand, sitting by the entrance and holding two umbrellas. Owens had been working for the colonel for three months now. Not only did he not know anything personal about the man, but he also wasn't comfortable talking to him.

Colonel William "Champ" Nunn had a barrel chest and was in his late sixties with short white hair and bushy black and gray eyebrows. His droopy eyes told a story of the many years he had spent in the army. Not all of them were stellar, especially of late. He was court marshaled for black-marketing excess supplies. The charges warranted a dishonorable discharge and jail time, but this happened during the calamity which had befallen America. Once the government had been nationalized, he had low moral friends in high places who were able to pardon him and in exchange, order him to Rock Island Illinois to oversee the Patriot program in the Midwest. His fall had been especially hard for a man with the nickname, "Champ," which was a play on his last name. At first they had called him "Second to Nunn," but if he was second to none, then he was always the winner henceforth the name, "Champ." It was a perfect fit for a man who had always won in his early days.

However, Nunn was far from his early years and figured he didn't have too many left. Running this operation not only got him out of jail, but his employer also paid him handsomely. Supervising the Patriot Centers was much easier than wheeling and dealing in the black market. The workers at the centers were scum, but he was used to those types in his underworld trade. You just had to know how to handle them. They were useful, provided they kept their mouths shut about the centers' real purpose. He figured a few would more than likely get a little loose with the lips, and this meant he'd be required to step in and eliminate them. Since secrecy was priority one, that wouldn't be a problem for him.

"Colonel, we haven't been able to reach Bravo Patriot this morning and they didn't check in last night either," said Owens.

Colonel Nunn looked up surprised, "Bravo Patriot, that's Decker's place, right?" he asked.

"Yes, sir."

"Has he ever not called in before?" he asked.

"No, sir."

"Seems a bit odd, are the phone lines down?"

"We haven't had any problems with any of the other centers sir, plus we've been trying to contact him on the radio as well."

"Okay, get Major Green in here," he ordered.

Colonel Nunn did not think highly of Major Green. He thought the man to be a squirrelly ass kisser and Nunn didn't like ass kissers. Over his career, he'd dealt with people like him. They would take no responsibility for any screw-ups and would maneuver others to take the blame. All they wanted were promotions and a cushy office job in Washington where they could hobnob with the important people.

Five minutes later, Major Green knocked on the door of Colonel Nunn's office.

Green was in his mid-thirties, average height, with a muscular build that indicated he worked out consistently. He wore fatigues and a sidearm. He had an eagerness about him that had not been beaten down by the rigors of working for Colonel Nunn.

"You wanted to see me, sir?" he asked.

"Yes, Major Green. We've not heard from Bravo Patriot this morning or last night, so I want you to go and check it out," said Nunn.

"Yes sir, I'll leave right away," replied Green.

"Yes, you will," said Nunn not looking up at him and shooing him away with the back of his hand.

Green turned on his heel and left the office muttering to himself. "Yes, you will. Friggin jackass. The man doesn't deserve this position."

Major Green marched over to the mess hall to locate Lieutenant Crick, his friend, and right-hand man and instructed him to round up some men for a trip to the Iowa Patriot Center.

Twenty minutes later, they took off with his men a couple of transport trucks. Green, along with Lieutenant Crick, led the way in a Humvee.

CHAPTER 8

VICTOR IOWA

Scar looked over at Meeks. They were hiding in the attic of an old two-story house. It sat opposite the Patriot Center where they would have met their fate, had it not been for the bravery of their newfound friends. Winters asked them to stay behind and keep an eye on whoever showed up.

"You hear that?" Scar asked Meeks.

"Sounds like we got company."

Scar looked out the small window. "Ah, LMTV's," said Scar.

"LMTV?"

"Light Military Transport Vehicles, just like the three sitting across the street," said the retired Marine.

The two leaned closer and saw a Humvee and two LMTV's, come up the street and park a block away.

"So, the Army is involved. Boy that about fries my ass," fumed Scar.

"Well, we can't say for sure they're directly involved."

"Oh really?" asked Scar in disbelief.

"Not positively," said Meeks peeking out the window.

Scar shook his head.

"They sure are taking their time," said Meeks.

"Probably want to make sure there's nothing wrong not having heard from Decker. So, they're being cautious," said Scar.

"One of them is getting out."

Scar grabbed his binoculars and focused in. "Got ourselves a major."

Soldiers jumped out of the vehicles and ran to the back and front of the building.

"This will be entertaining," said Meeks.

The soldiers entered the building and several minutes later, a few stepped back outside and waved to the major. He walked to the entrance and they took a moment to talk to them before walking inside.

"Wonder how long they'll stay," said Meeks.

"Well, there's nobody home so I wouldn't imagine too long. Surely, they'll want to check out the train station right away."

Some of the soldiers came out and lit cigarettes. Three others moved the vehicles up the street closer to the Center. More strolled out to smoke and await further directives. Ten minutes later, the major walked out and issued orders to his men. The soldiers fanned out in different directions.

"This doesn't look good," said Meeks.

"No, it doesn't. They probably want to question some of the townspeople," said Scar.

"Two of them are coming this way," said Meeks.

They heard a loud knock on the front door. Meeks gave Scar a concerned look. After more banging, there came a crash, as the front door was broken in.

Scar and Meeks stood still, listening intently as the soldiers moved around the house, opening and slamming doors. The sounds got louder as they climbed the staircase.

Each step made a thumping sound under the heavy boots of the two soldiers. Reaching the top, they began checking the rooms. Scar and

Meeks listened to them, as they talked loudly right beneath them.

Scar motioned to Meeks to move across the crowded attic, filled with abandoned toys, boxes of clothes, and furniture.

Moving away from the light of the window, made the going more difficult. Meeks bumped into a cardboard box with a tall vase on top of it. He quickly grabbed it before it hit the floor. He gave Scar an apologetic expression.

A screeching sound made them both stop for a second before scurrying into a hiding spot as the attic ladder was pulled down.

Light poured through the opening and washed onto the ceiling in a square block. The old ladder squeaked as a soldier climbed up.

Meeks and Scar got down, each reaching into his jacket for their own pistols.

The soldier stood on the ladder and waited a few moments for his eyes to adjust to the darkness so he could search the old attic. He then grabbed his flashlight and made wide sweeping searches of the dark room.

The light made a pass by the box of clothes where Meeks hid. The position he had taken was uncomfortable and his right leg started cramping. Desperately needing to stretch it, he slowly unfolded the leg. As he did, it hit a cardboard box, which made a sliding sound. Meeks froze. The beam of the flashlight whipped back in his direction.

The soldier took another step up on the ladder and put his hands on the attic floor. Just then, the hot, dusty air hit him, triggering a sneezing frenzy.

After his sneezing stopped, he complained. "Hell, there's no one up here and this dust is killing me." He descended the ladder not bothering to close it.

The two made as much noise going down the stairs as they had coming up. Seconds later, the front door slammed shut. Both Scar and Meeks let out a big collective sigh.

"Damn," said Meeks.

"What the hell were you doing over there?" asked Scar.

"My leg was cramping up."

"Thank God, he started sneezing. One thing's for sure, we'll never forget this."

"Hell no, we won't. Little too close for comfort."

The two crept back to the window as the Humvee pulled away, and headed out of town.

"They're not all leaving," said Scar.

"No, they're not," responded Meeks. "I see the major is staying."

"Why put yourself in danger," chuckled Scar.

Meeks sat down. "I hope these guys leave pretty soon. Why are they even staying?"

"That Humvee can travel a lot faster than those transports."

"I want to get the hell out of here."

For the next couple of hours, they continued to sit there keeping an eye on the activities below. The soldiers stood around as they waited for the return of the Humvee.

The day had turned into a long one and Scar remembered he had brought some food. He pulled out packets of cheese and crackers and threw one, intentionally high, to Meeks, who nimbly reached up and made a spectacular catch.

Scar grinned knowing he failed yet again to make Meeks miss.

Meeks played football throughout his youth. He had been instrumental in helping his high school win a state title and ended up getting a full scholarship to play for Iowa. As a running back, he broke into the school's top ten for rushing yards. Unfortunately, he blew out his knee his senior year, which ended his playing days. He did stay in the game by coaching high school football where he was able to coach his own sons. Once the economy collapsed and the war started, money dried up and the small town dropped the football program. After moving his family to his parent's house in Florida, Meeks came back to Iowa to volunteer with his friends.

"What do ya think about Winters?" Meeks asked ripping open the package.

Scar popped a cracker in his mouth. "I like him. Brave son of a gun, though you'd never know it by looking at him."

"Yeah, I was thinking the same thing. Sneaking into that train station, and killing those bastards…that was a gutsy move," said Meeks.

"Doesn't give himself much credit for it though."

Meeks nodded. "Right…seemed almost embarrassed."

"Push comes to shove, how many of us would really do something like that."

"Like to think I would."

"One thing's for sure, we all owe him our lives," said Scar.

Scar understood honor and duty having spent four years in the Corps. He had enlisted right out of high school. Having combat experience, he knew what it took to do what Winters had done. After his discharge, he came home and married his high school sweetheart. He learned to build houses and eventually started his own contracting business. He and his wife raised a son who was currently out West flying as a Marine Aviator.

A subtle vibration began in the attic floor as the Humvee pulled back into town.

Scar and Meeks both hastened to the window as the soldiers including the major poured outside.

"He doesn't look like a happy camper," grinned Scar.

"Can't say I would be either."

"Maybe now they'll leave."

"Please," begged Meeks.

Scar and Meeks continued to keep an eye on the soldiers from the attic window. The major yelled out to his men. Some of the men went inside while others moved the LMTV's further up the street.

A minute later, men carried out wooden stakes. The soldiers started wrapping strips of cloth around them. Scar had a bad feeling when one of the soldiers took out his cigarette lighter.

CHAPTER 9

BLUE EARTH MINNESOTA

Elliott was familiar with another volunteer station in Minnesota which was just across the Iowa border. The uneventful drive ended as they stopped five miles away from their destination. They pulled into an unused cornfield, which had gone to seed and was filling up with weeds. It would soon be unrecognizable as a place where crops once grew.

They came to Minnesota to see if that operation was like the one in Iowa. They had to either witness them shoot the volunteers or see another burial pit. Unfortunately, they only knew where the Patriot Center was. What they needed to know, was the drop-off location.

Everyone exited their vehicles and gathered around the lead truck occupied by Winters and Elliott.

Nate spoke up first.

"I'll volunteer Captain," said Nate.

"Volunteer for what?" asked Winters.

"To go in and find out where the drop-off is."

"How are you going to do that?"

"I'll walk right on in there and pretend like I'm volunteering."

"Just like that?"

"Yeah man, I mean how else are we going to find out?"

"Well, we can follow the trucks."

"Listen, I can't wait around for them to kill again," sneered Nate.

"We don't know if that's happening."

"Exactly, which is why we should go in and get a heads up on where the location is. It'll be simple. I'll take Rogers with me," he said pointing to his friend. "He's pretty quick on his feet, aren't you buddy."

Rogers shrugged.

Winters didn't particularly like how Nate had pushed himself into this assignment but gave in. "If that's what you want to do."

"Don't worry man, we'll be alright."

Nate and Rogers hopped into a pickup.

"We'll find a place where we can keep an eye on what's going on, so look for us as soon as you find out where the drop-off is," said Winters as the pickup pulled out of the cornfield.

Winters stewed over Nate's action. He wasn't in charge. What was the point of making him Captain if they weren't going to listen to him? If this kept up, he'd gladly hand over the reins over to someone else, maybe even leave and travel south to search for his wayward daughter, Cara. She had taken off with her boyfriend before the invasion and he hadn't heard from her since. She didn't know her mother was dead.

His thoughts turned to Scar and Meeks. Despite his initial assessment of Scar, he actually liked him. He had a big personality and was quite entertaining. Winters thought Scar and Meeks made a great team and planned to use Scar's military experience regularly. That was why he had asked them to stay behind.

Winters prayed nothing would happen to them and they would be able to find their way back to the group. They had a pre-planned meeting spot, but he wasn't sure how long they should wait.

Now Nate and Rogers had gone to pretend to be volunteers. Regardless of Nate's hasty decision, Winters still felt responsible. He never had to make decisions like this before. Balance sheets and payroll were his biggest responsibilities for most of his life. His wife even made the decisions on what they did on the weekends. His new duties began to grow as weighty as an anchor around his neck.

Elliott must have sensed Winters' tension. "Don't pay him no never mind, Captain. I told ya he's a bit strong-willed, but he's a good ole boy, with a big heart. He just doesn't always think things through is all."

"That's what I'm afraid of."

Elliott slowed down as they approached the town where the Patriot Center was located. "Don't look like anyone lives around here," said Elliott

"Just thinking the same thing, take your first left," said Winters.

Elliott turned left and then right. They drove a couple of blocks and parked in front of a wide two-story house, which looked to be about a hundred years old. The other vehicles followed and parked behind them. Winters told the others to stay put. He and Elliott ran through the back yard staying close to the house, got comfortable and waited.

"This might take a while, hope you got some patience in ya," whispered Elliott.

Winters gave Elliott a half smile. "Yeah, I do, we bookkeepers are known for our patience."

Elliott chuckled. "Still can't believe you're a bookkeeper."

Winters understood the confusion. Most bookkeepers were a bit on the nerdy side. He just happened to be good with numbers and knew where things should go.

They kept themselves hidden behind a row of bushes. Sitting on the ground, the only noises they heard came from birds chirping high up in the trees, and squirrels running around the branches. They both waited in silence, which suited Winters. He had too much on his mind to be a good conversationalist. He wondered how Scar and Meeks were doing and if they had seen anyone come to check on the Center.

Soon a couple more pickups arrived, each carried two or three men in the back. After a while, many of the volunteers were hanging around outside.

"Hey, Nate's coming out," said Elliott.

"Sit up a bit, try and get his attention."

Elliott got up and waved his arms but to no avail.

"He must think we're further down," said Elliott.

Winters stood up and started to walk toward the Patriot Center.

"Captain, whatcha doing?" asked Elliott in a hushed voice.

"Stay here." He walked through the side lawn to the street. Staying on his side of the road, Winters waved to get Nate's attention. After getting a nod, he then took a left at the next house and walked behind it. Nate crossed the street and found Winters waiting for him.

"Captain."

"Hey, how did it go? Did you find the location?"

"Everything's real cool. One of the drivers told me where the place is. Get on the interstate go west, take exit 50 go north on 71 and then a right on 60. It's an old implement dealership. You'll run right into it."

"Excellent. We should get going. Where's Rogers?"

"He's still there."

"Why? Is something wrong?"

"We decided to go with them. This way, if they're killing them there too, we can get the drop on them."

Winters tilted his head slightly. "I don't think that's a good idea. What if we can't get to you?"

"They won't be expecting anyone to shoot back."

"They'll have automatic weapons. You guys only have pistols. It's not as easy as you might think when you have a gun pointed at you."

"Maybe for you, it wasn't, but it won't bother me."

Nate's response stung, but Winters suppressed his anger.

"I don't mean to be insulting, but the difference is, we'll be ready for them."

"Okay, well, you've got your mind made-up anyway."

Winters watched Nate shuffle across the street to join the others. He shook his head and rejoined Elliott.

"Where's Nate and Rogers?"

"They've decided to stay and go with them."

Elliott rolled his eyes. "I told ya, that boy's a little head-strong. He'll be okay."

"More like bull-headed," smirked Winters

The two of them hustled back to the others and tore out of town. Winters tapped his fingers on the cloth console, which was between Elliott and himself. He remained quiet for most of the ride deep in thought on how Nate and Rogers were doing.

Elliott glanced over at him. "They'll be okay, Cole."

Winters found some comfort in being called by his name, first time he's heard it since they nominated him, Captain. "I'm not so sure about that."

"Being Captain, I know puts some extra burden of worry on ya, but it'll be fine. They'll be fine," said Elliott not expecting a response.

With Nate and Rogers staying, they could afford no errors. If they failed, someone would die.

CHAPTER 10

VICTOR IOWA

Major Green walked into the building, sat down in Decker's chair, and mulled over what he had learned. He prepared himself for Nunn to blame him for what happened at the train station. He couldn't be responsible if, in all likelihood, they got drunk and burned the place down. Green questioned why the government subcontracted this program to a bunch of incompetent drunks. He also wondered why they even bothered with the recruitment of a bunch of out of shape old men. No matter, Green knew better than to question the government on why they did anything, especially in the current political climate. He would follow orders like a good soldier even if they came from a criminal like Colonel Nunn.

He reached for Decker's phone, dialed the number and waited for the connection, which took forever, because of the inadequate telephone system.

"Colonel Nunn's office."

"Owens, it's Major Green, is he in?"

"Hold on Major, I'll transfer you."

Green sat on hold for quite a while. He thought the colonel purposely took his time, his little way of being a jackass. Another minute later, the colonel got on the phone.

"Major," said Nunn.

"Colonel, I'm here at Bravo Patriot."

"And?"

"Something's happened here, Colonel. The train station is burned to the ground and all the men are dead there."

"Where's Decker?"

"I couldn't say. There's no one here. The transports are still here but everyone is gone."

"How did the station burn down?" asked Nunn.

"My guess is they got drunk and caught the place on fire. I got eight charred bodies in there. They might have died in their sleep. Decker might have been up there himself or he didn't want to stick around and have to explain what happened."

Nunn paused for a few moments. "Major, I want you to torch the houses on the main street."

"Sir?" Green said, taken aback by the order.

"You heard me. Decker lives there. He and his men have screwed up our operations. A strong message needs to be sent."

"I'll get right on it," said Green shaking his head in disbelief.

"Bring back our transports," ordered Nunn, hanging up the phone.

"Yes..." began Green as the phone clicked off.

CHAPTER 11

ROCK ISLAND ILLINOIS

Colonel Nunn sat at his desk giving some thought to what happened. He figured someone must have found out about their operation. "This can't be an accident like this idiot Green thinks. Of course, Green has no idea what is actually happening at the Patriot Centers so why would he suspect anything was wrong. Probably someone from town found out and took revenge. That may, or may not, explain why they burned the train station and not the Patriot Center, which was located in their town," he thought.

In any case, Nunn had decided to send a message to whoever did this. Mess with us and this is what happens.

He opened a drawer and pulled out a bottle of single-malt Scotch, one of the few luxuries still available to him. This was supposed to be a very low-risk operation and kept very quiet. With over thirty years in the Army, he should have known better. Word will get out now and plans will have to be changed. Nunn poured himself a drink while he mulled over the situation. He inhaled the aroma of the Scotch for a moment before letting the liquid wet his lips. He had been drinking single-malt since he could remember, and the smoky liquor went down as smooth as ever.

Operation Wildflower, the operation of eliminating older volunteers, was now at risk of being discovered. If this happened they would be out of business. His bosses would assume him incapable and have little further use for him. The only thing he'd miss was the vast sum of money they were paying him. He hadn't particularly liked the killing of American citizens, but he knew that most of these volunteers would have been involved in more protests and more trouble for the new government.

Older Americans hadn't been as thoroughly indoctrinated as the younger ones. Consequently, they protested about every little thing. It was the last thing the fragile new government needed. The protests were having their desired effect and were starting to put a strain on the new regime. It started off on shaky ground to begin with and immediately weakened its position by trying to eliminate the private ownership of guns.

The wails and cries were endless and very few people voluntarily gave up their guns, which led to the disastrous Weapons Reclamation Program. The Government ordered local law enforcement authorities to confiscate all firearms. Not only were gun owners not complying, but many local Sheriff's departments across the country didn't agree with the act and wouldn't enforce the law. Those departments that did try to enforce the law found themselves getting into lethal conflicts and people were dying on both sides.

The Government learned some valuable lessons from this program. The foremost was; they couldn't always count on local authorities to enforce their new laws. This lesson launched the nationalizing of all police departments across the country.

The second lesson was; they now realized just how passionate gun owners were and the third was; they would have to figure out another way to disarm the citizenry. For the time being, they decided to disregard the strict enforcement of the law. This did little to quell the protests but once the Chinese attacked the country, the issue dropped out of sight.

Nunn leaned back in his chair and took another sip. With Decker either missing or dead, Nunn decided to report to his superiors. He didn't necessarily want to, but they'd eventually find out and he'd rather control the conversation instead of being on the defensive. He leaned forward in his chair, reached for the black phone on his desk, and punched the numbers.

"Director Reed's office."

"This is Colonel Nunn, is he in?"

"Hold on," came the response.

Nunn waited for Lawrence Reed, his civilian contact to pick up the phone. Reed was a man who ranked high in the new government and was in charge of Operation Wildflower. He had been the one to put Colonel Nunn in charge of the Midwest; figuring they would need someone who had no choice but to follow orders. Reed, the ever-master politician, had been instrumental in collapsing the previous government. He, with his many influential friends in Washington, unabashedly did the dirty work for the new government.

"This is Reed."

"Lawrence, Colonel Nunn here."

"Colonel, how are things going in the Midwest?"

"Not a good day today. We've had an incident." Colonel Nunn filled him in on the events.

"You think this Decker was among the victims?" asked Reed.

"I can't say for sure."

"Well, you need to find out. If he's alive, we don't need him running his mouth off to anyone," said Reed.

"I don't think we'll need to worry much about that."

"Oh, why not?"

"He lived in that quaint little town he worked out of, so I sent a message not to screw with us. I had my men burn down the houses along the main street."

"Nice. How long before you can have the place up and running again?"

"Probably two or three weeks at a minimum." He didn't want to bring up the obvious subject. Word will spread around the area and this location would be a waste of time to reopen.

"Call me if you need anything."

Reed hung up the phone, leaned back in his chair, and gazed out the window over the Potomac River. Streetlights began to turn on all over the city as the day turned into night. Washington was one of the few cities in America with no power shortages and no curfew, so the streets remained alive with people bustling about, tending to their business, and not letting the woes of the world get in the way.

He grabbed the phone to call his boss, to relay the news.

"Larry, it's important this operation continues as planned. You think Nunn can keep things under wraps?"

"He's got a lot riding on it, so yes," replied Reed.

"If he doesn't, we'll have to send someone else out there."

"Let's see how things progress."

CHAPTER 12

VICTOR IOWA

Major Green's soldiers wrapped scraps of cloth around long pieces of wood and dipped them into a container of kerosene, One of the soldiers then lit the combustible rags.

"What the hell are they doing?" asked Meeks.

"They're lighting torches," said Scar.

The soldiers fanned out in different directions with the flaming torches.

Scar grabbed Meeks' shoulder when a soldier approached the house. He heard faint footsteps as the soldier moved around setting the house on fire.

"What the hell they doing this for?" asked Meeks.

"Probably payback for us setting their precious train station on fire," said Scar. "We're stuck here till they leave."

"Let's hope they don't fancy watching fires for very long," said Meeks with a sly grin.

They stood at the window to wait for the soldiers to leave. Some of them did hang around to watch the fires.

Meeks shook his head. "I reckon they're enjoying their handiwork."

A long moment passed before Scar responded. "Let's get out of here before we can't."

The crackling fire relished the dry lumber of the old house. The living room was consumed in no time. The fire then danced its way into the kitchen. Flames shot up walls to the ceiling and started burning the second floor. Hot, black smoke rose up through the still open entrance to the attic cutting off the air supply.

Scar hopped over to the opening and dropped down the ladder. Meeks followed right behind him. The second floor was filled with so much smoke that it felt as though you were swimming in it. Scar got down on his knees to try to get under the choking smoke. Breathing became a painful exercise. What air they inhaled burned their lungs. Bright orange flames leaped up from the stairwell in front of them. The heat seared the skin on Scar's arm. Meeks pulled his shirt up over his mouth to try to filter the air. They turned around and headed toward a glimmer of sunlight. A beacon of light pierced through the haze of smoke and led them to the end of the hallway. Scar put his hand on a door to his right, turned the knob and opened it into a bedroom. They both rushed in and slammed the door shut. The room still had fresh air and they both greedily sucked it in. They coughed and gagged while trying to catch their breath.

"You okay?" asked Scar.

"Yeah, I'm good. Didn't see that one coming, did we?"

"Nope," coughed Scar. "Not on the top of my list."

"You had a list?"

"Left it up in the attic, you want to see it."

"No, I think I'm good." Meeks looked down from the window. "Looks like a bit of a drop from up here."

"I didn't figure you to be afraid of heights."

"I'm not. What I am afraid of is breaking my ankle."

"Yeah, can't say that'd be a good thing. Let's tie these bed sheets together. I'm pretty sure the fire department isn't coming to rescue us."

The two ripped off the sheets and tied them together. Then moved the bed to the window and fastened the sheets to the bed frame. While doing this, the big engines of the army transports revved up and shook the walls as they pulled out of town.

Scar opened the window and instant relief came from the fresh air rushing in. The two stood at the window for a moment enjoying the breeze. The whole house creaked, as the old girl got ready to collapse in on herself.

Scar climbed out first and slid down the bed sheet rope, with Meeks heckling him to hurry up because his fanny was catching fire. This only encouraged Scar to take his time. Once on the ground, they ran away from Main Street to where they had parked their pickup. Scar started the engine and drove back toward the destruction. He stopped at the edge of the small town to watch the flames consume the houses.

"So, you convinced now?" asked Scar.

"Of what?" replied Meeks.

"Army being involved."

"Yeah, I'm convinced, just can't say I'm real happy about it."

"Don't know how it can get any worse."

"Knock on wood, buddy," said Meeks pounding on the dashboard.

"Wait till we tell the Captain about this."

"I wonder how they're doing?" mused Meeks.

CHAPTER 13

JACKSON COUNTY MINNESOTA

Winters sat in the passenger seat of the pickup admiring the passing scenery, as Elliott drove them to the drop-off location. He was reeling over the insulting way Nate had implied he wouldn't have a problem having a gun pointed at him.

They finally reached the drop-off location. The place sat in a wide open valley with woods on the far side of the road. The building had once been used to sell farm implements and accessories. It had a big parking lot and still had a sign out front advertising John Deere. They stopped, got out and looked over the area. Seeing the woods gave Winters an idea where they could set up and hide. They all drove off the road and down into a field.

The Shadow Patriots tramped through the woods as the gentle breeze swept through the trees and whispered its song to the men. Within minutes, they were able to see the building and the several pickup trucks parked close to the entrance.

"Perfect place to be killing volunteers, out in the middle of nowhere," said Elliott.

"Yes, it is," agreed Winters.

"If they are, they've got to be taking the bodies somewhere close, we should try and find the burial site."

"The ground is too open, if someone came outside, we'd be spotted in no time," said Winters. "We could have someone climb one of the trees to get a better view."

"Good idea," said Elliott as he turned to his friends and asked one of them.

The Shadow Patriots watched one of their members, who at forty-two was their youngest, climb the tree carrying a set of binoculars around his neck. He negotiated the branches to low cheers and jeers from the guys. There wasn't any sign of a burial pit, but he was not able to see behind the building.

Winters started to pace, trying to come up with a way to keep Nate and Rogers safe. Elliott walked over to him.

"I can't sit around and wait for something to happen," said Winters.

"Looks like a little of Nate is starting to rub off on ya," said Elliott with a sly smile.

Winters half rolled his eyes. "Funny you should say that because I do have a crazy idea."

"Going to be dangerous?"

Winters nodded.

Elliott hesitated for a moment. "Well, count me in. I can't let you have all the fun. So, whatcha got in mind?"

After telling Elliott his idea, he gathered everyone together and informed them.

"You're going to walk on in there and ask them if you can volunteer?" asked one of the men. "You competing with Nate for the dumbest person award?"

Winters made a sour face. "No, I'm not. If these guys are doing the same thing, as in Iowa, then we're too far away to help them."

Everyone nodded in agreement.

After giving out instructions, Winters and Elliott walked to the vehicles. They hopped into an F-150, with Elliott in the driver's seat. After starting the engine, he backed up a little before shifting it into low drive.

The truck bounced up the incline, then headed back in the direction from which they had come. He drove for a few miles on the empty country highway, and then stopped at the top of a hill. This gave them a broad and deep panoramic view. Elliott turned off the engine. They sat silently while Elliott scanned the horizon with binoculars.

A crisp breeze blew through the open windows and Winters leaned his head back to catch a nap. This proved difficult with so much on his mind. Between what they were about to do, and the questions as to why this was going on, sleep would evade him.

At last, Elliott spoke up. "They're coming." He handed the binoculars to Winters. He spotted the three big green transport trucks, which carried Nate and Rogers, coming over the horizon. Elliott put the truck in gear and headed toward the drop-off location.

Winters glanced over at Elliott. "You ready for this?"

"You were right, this is damn crazy," said Elliott.

Winters re-checked the Colt .45 he had absconded back at the train station. He had a full mag with one in the chamber.

As soon as Elliott pulled the truck into the parking lot, three guards rushed out with rifles at the ready. They spread out and waited for him to park.

"They don't look too thrilled to see us," said Elliott.

"No, they don't. This might not have been such a good idea."

CHAPTER 14

Elliott closed the door to the truck and waved at the approaching men. "Is this where you volunteer to go out West? My friend and I want to join the fight."

"Yes and no," said a short, stocky man as he lowered his weapon.

"Whatcha mean?" Elliott asked.

"Well, first you have to go sign up at the Patriot Center and then you get transported up here," he responded.

Winters acted ignorant. "How far away?"

"Blue Earth, it's about seventy miles."

Winters shook his head. "We don't have enough gas to go another seventy miles."

"That just don't make much sense. Can't we just sign up here since we're already here?" asked Elliott.

The short man ordered his friend to ask the boss for instructions.

Winters looked at him pleadingly. "Just doesn't make any sense to go somewhere else and then have to come all the way back, when we're already here."

The short man shrugged his shoulders. "I'm not in charge."

They all turned when the guard who went inside came out with the okay to go ahead and line them up with the others.

Winters glanced at Elliott with a troubled stare. He turned to the short man. "Well, isn't there some paperwork you said we needed to fill out first?"

"We'll get to that, don't cha worry."

"So, do we go inside for that?"

Everyone turned around at the same time and looked up the valley as the three transports came over the hill. Winters gave a nod to Elliott who asked one of the guards. "Is there a bathroom I can use?"

"Yeah, hang a right when you get inside."

"What time do we leave? Will there be anything to eat?" Winters kept asking them questions trying to gauge their intentions. He only got short answers out of them.

The three transports drivers pulled in, parked and turned off their engines as three more men walked outside. With the drivers, nine potential bad guys were now outside waiting for the volunteers to disembark. The drivers got out and instructed the passengers where to stand. The middle-aged volunteers including Nate and Rogers jumped out of the truck.

Nate gave Winters a slight nod and began to walk over to him. One of the drivers stopped him.

"Where do you think you're going?"

"I need to use the bathroom," Nate responded.

"You can use the field," said the driver.

"I can't do that man," said Nate walking past the irritated driver.

Winters glanced toward the entrance looking for Elliott. He hadn't come out yet, and Winters didn't like the odds of him against six armed men plus the three drivers. One of the guards turned toward him. Winters stood at his pickup pretending to get something. He looked in the mirror to watch the approaching guard.

The other guards stopped Nate from coming any closer to the building. At that point, Winters knew they were getting ready to shoot the volunteers. He kept pretending to get something out of his truck as he waited for the approaching guard. He needed him to be closer before he could strike. He took a deep breath to control his nerves.

"Hey, let's go. You need to get with the others," said the guard

Winters turned. "What about that paperwork I'm supposed to fill out?"

He watched the guard try to form a response to the question. Winters stared past him, at the other guards who were lining themselves up in front of the volunteers, and figured he only had seconds before they opened fire.

He couldn't wait for Elliott.

Winters angled the blackened steel knife and plunged it into the man's stomach. He gritted his teeth as he pulled the knife out. Blood poured out and soaked his victim's shirt. The guard's eyes filled with abject terror trying to figure out what had just happened.

Winters felt the rage of Mister Hyde flow out of him when he shoved the knife into the man's stomach again. It released all his pent-up stress. Winters yanked the knife out as the guard fell to his knees. Winters moved to the side letting the man fall forward.

This attracted the attention of a volunteer who pointed at him and yelled out. Then all hell broke loose.

Everyone turned and saw the guard lying on the ground not moving. One of them raised his rifle, pointed and fired at Winters. A bullet whistled by his head and slammed into the side of the truck.

Winters let the knife fall out of his hand and reached for his Colt when a shot rang out dropping the man who had just fired at Winters. The shot had come from Nate who was already aiming at his next victim.

Gunfire erupted from both sides. Winters crouched down and fired several rounds hitting one of the guards. Everyone scattered in different directions. Some of the volunteers fell to the ground. Others dove for cover behind the trucks. The drivers began firing at them.

The Shadow Patriots came running from the woods and crossed the road shooting at the guards. They split off into smaller groups, each overpowering a target.

Nate ran straight at one of the guards firing his .45 as he chased the man down. Nate dropped him in mid-stride. He then resurveyed the scene, noticed one of the drivers going for the cab of a transport, and took off after him. Nate jumped up on the step and fired point-blank at the driver through the open window.

Another driver knelt underneath the last transport, taking cover while shooting at the unarmed volunteers. Winters still on the ground, fired his pistol at him until he emptied the magazine. None of his rounds hit their target. He grabbed another magazine from his pocket and reloaded. Winters willed himself to slow down and to take better aim. He let off three consecutive rounds, the last one finally hitting him in the throat.

Winters looked around and saw men everywhere crying out for help. Several huddled in groups trying to protect each other, while others died where they lay.

The gunfire started to slow down and then came to a halt when all the guards and drivers were dead. Winters got up off the ground and looked around trying to absorb the battle scene. Bloodied men lay about haphazardly, some dead, others continued to cry for help.

He jerked around when gunfire rang out from inside the building. Seconds later, the door swung open. Winters raised his gun, aimed and waited for someone to exit. Fortunately, Winters recognized Elliott, who sheepishly peered around the door not wanting to be shot at. Winters let out a breath as he realized that in the chaos he'd forgotten all about Elliott.

He jogged over to him. "Just one inside?"

"Yeah. Found the little bastard cowering in a corner waving a gun. Figured we'd be better off not having one of them holed up in there while we were out here."

"Good thinking."

They turned toward the melee when Nate yelled to them. "Captain, Rogers has been shot."

They sprinted to where Rogers lay. His friends knelt on the ground and tried to help the man. Winters got there to find him becoming very pale. His friends held both his hands. He shook and coughed. The men around him tore off his shirt. He'd taken two in the chest. They feverishly tried to stop the bleeding. One of his friends ripped off his jacket and bore down on the wounds with it. Blood soaked through in no time. As it turned out, their efforts were in vain and all they were able to do was try and comfort the man as he slipped away.

CHAPTER 15

No one said a word nor moved for what seemed like an eternity. The survivors from Minnesota then started to come out from their hiding places scared and confused.

Winters stared at the horrific scene as if he were in some kind of slow-motion nightmare. Men moved around in a state-of-confusion. Some yelled for help, others screamed in pain. Blood was everywhere. Winters snapped back to reality when Elliott came to him about getting a first aid kit. They both went inside the building to look for one.

"Bastards," Elliott said rummaging through the kitchen cabinets.

Winters didn't respond as he entered the bathroom by stepping over the body of the man Elliott had killed. Opening a closet door by the shower, Winters found a first aid kit. He reached in and grabbed the large container. He pulled up the lid and found it filled with a variety of bandages.

Winters came back into the hallway. "Found one."

They both hurried back out to the wounded. Winters took it all in and could only think how this was his fault. He should have known the volunteers were to be murdered and just come in and killed the workers.

Elliott took the first aid kit from Winters and walked it over to the Minnesota men who were helping their friends. One of them came up to Winters and confronted him.

"Just what is going on here?"

Winters looked into the face of a man who appeared as though he was ready to beat the hell out of him. "They were going to kill you guys."

"Kill us? Why would they do that, we came here to volunteer."

"I know you did. We're volunteers from Iowa. We found out that's what they were doing there, so we came here to help."

"Help! Some help you've been! You just killed my brother," he said while pushing at Winters.

The man came at him again and drove Winters back. He then followed up with a swing, which connected to Winters' left cheek. The blow knocked him to the pavement, causing his hat to fall off. He then started kicking Winters in the gut but got only two in before Elliott and Nate rushed him. They grabbed the man who struggled to break free all the while cursing at Winters.

Then a couple of Minnesota men came in and grabbed ahold of Elliott and Nate to pull them away from their friend. Elliott twisted away from the hold of his assailant and threw a perfectly placed uppercut. The blow dropped him like a sack of flour. Nate didn't fare as well. His attacker was much bigger and had Nate in a headlock. He received punches to his head when Elliott grabbed the man's collar and pulled it back giving him a clear shot to the face. He swung his left arm, which came straight in and knocked him unconscious.

Before Winters could get up, his attacker jumped on him again and started punching him like a maniac. He received punches to the midsection, knocking his breath out. The man grabbed Winters' throat and started choking him with both hands. Winters swung his right arm around, sweeping both arms off his throat and locking them together. He followed with a strike to the face, which caused his attacker to tumble sideways off him.

Winters then staggered up off the ground, picking up his hat in the process. He stood up and arched his back to work out the kinks. Looking around he saw others getting into shoving matches with his men. He pulled out his gun, pointed it to the sky and fired twice. Everyone stopped.

Winters looked at them for a moment trying to catch his breath. "I'm sorry some of your friends got killed, but had we not come here, you would all be dead."

Elliott rested a hand on Winters' shoulder. "It's true. We're volunteers, like you, from Iowa. We don't know why, but these Patriot Centers are set up to kill us."

"Why didn't you kill them before we got here?" one of them yelled.

"We weren't sure it was going on up here," responded Winters. "We had to make sure what was going on down in Iowa wasn't some isolated thing. Look, we'll tell you everything we know, but first, we need to help the wounded."

Elliott turned his head to Winters. "You okay?"

"Yeah, I'll be alright. Felt like I was back in high school, getting my ass kicked. Don't remember it hurting this bad though."

"What about the Patriot Center?"

Winters knew it would take quite a while to tend the wounded and clean the place up. Not wanting to put any more than necessary at risk, Winters asked Elliott, "How about just you and me go?"

Elliott nodded.

Leaving meant dividing his forces again. It was bad enough not knowing how Scar and Meeks were doing. Not having any means of communications was a significant handicap.

"Who do you want to leave in charge?"

"Leave it to Nate. He'll need something to help get his mind off Rogers. Besides, he seems to like making decisions," said Winters sarcastically.

They walked over to Nate, who stood by the transports. Winters could see the angst on Nate's face, and he had no intention of making it worse for him.

"I'm sorry we lost Rogers," said Winters extending his hand out to

Nate.

"It's my fault."

"The fault is mine. Elliott and I should have known sooner. As a matter of fact, had you not done what you did, more of these men would be dead."

"I feel just awful."

"As do we Nate. Listen, I need to ask you a favor, Elliott and I are going to go back to that Patriot Center. You think you could take over here, get this place cleaned up?"

"Yeah, no problem. What should we do with the dead?"

"Dump the guards in the woods. We should take the dead volunteers to their families. How many do ya think we got?" asked Winters.

Nate looked around and did a quick count. "Fifteen maybe twenty."

Winters shook his head and let out a deep breath as he and Elliott headed to their pickup.

Winters hopped in as Elliott cranked it up and threw it in gear. Winters rolled the window down and sighed with a pang of deep sadness at the bloodbath that lay before him. It reminded him of something you'd see in a war movie, with dead bodies strewn about the living, the injured being helped by the survivors.

"Damn, this was a waste," mumbled Winters.

Elliott gasped. "A waste?" He looked at Winters square in the eye. "What the hell you talking about? We just saved a whole bunch of lives. Yeah, we lost Rogers, a good friend of mine, but look how many we saved. These things are going to happen whether we like it or not. This is just a taste of what we're in for."

Elliott stepped on the accelerator and peeled out onto the road while Winters sat back in his seat digesting what he had said. More will die. Great. Getting men killed was not what he imagined when he reluctantly accepted the leadership position.

After Elliott's reprimand and the loss of his friend, there was a palatable tension between them as they drove to the Patriot Center. Winters tried to make small talk but got only short answers. Elliott didn't want to talk and he understood why. Losing a friend was not an easy thing and Winters understood that heartache.

Winters leaned his forehead on the side window looking out and thinking about what had happened. He started second-guessing himself as to whether or not he could lead these men. The first day on the job and he'd already lost men. Trying to get the thoughts out of his mind, he busied himself by pulling out his Colt .45 and checking the ammo in the magazine plus the spare ones he had in his coat pocket. Satisfied, he put it away and began massaging around the wound on his arm. Doing this brought back memories of yesterday's events and the loss of his friends. Despite getting even, it didn't make things better, though taking them out did give him a small helping of satisfaction. He couldn't help but savor that guilty pleasure.

As they got closer to the town where the Patriot Center was, Winters noticed another vehicle coming their way.

CHAPTER 16

Scar and Meeks drove down the country highway en route to the rendezvous spot that they had agreed upon with Winters. They had made good time with Scar pushing the vehicle over a hundred miles per hour. It was late afternoon as they passed the town where the Minnesota Patriot Center was located and were closing in on the meetup spot.

Scar drove with the window down, enjoying the wind blowing on his face, which felt good after escaping the hot fire.

"The Captain is going to be pretty disappointed when he finds out the army is in on this. I'm so pissed off right now. Hell, it's outrageous what's happening to begin with, but now to see the military being used like this is disgusting."

"I've been thinking about what happened back there," said Meeks.

"And?"

"Well, we don't know for sure how involved they are."

"They just burned down all those houses."

Meeks looked doubtful. "Yes, but they probably had orders."

"They didn't have to follow them."

"I thought you guys always had to follow orders."

"Not if they're unlawful," said Scar.

"Burning down a few houses is an unlawful order?"

Scar glanced over at him. "Yes, especially if it wasn't for any good reason."

Meeks contemplated this. "This will make things a bit tougher than we might have thought. I mean going after a bunch of dumb-asses is one thing, but to take on the Army is quite another."

Scar sighed. "I know. We're gonna be out-manned and out-gunned. Once they find out who we are and what we're up to, they'll come after us with all they got. Then what?"

Meeks grinned looking down at the map. "We'll run and hide. The Highlander way."

Scar switched to his best Scottish accent. "We'll make spears, hundreds of them."

"Braveheart, best movie ever."

"Haven't seen that in ages," said Scar. "Hey, heads up."

"What?"

"Up the road. Grab the binoculars."

"I think it's one of ours," said Meeks putting the glasses to his eyes.

Scar slowed the pickup down and waved. Seconds later the two trucks were side by side.

"Good to see you guys," said Scar. "We got a story to tell you."

"As do we," said Elliott in a serious tone. "We got into a shootout, lot of people got killed, including my friend, Rogers."

"Oh Elliott, I'm sorry to hear that," said Scar. "How'd it happen?"

"It just didn't go right."

Winters detected the anger in Elliott's voice. He moved forward in his seat. "We're headed to the Patriot Center right now, want to join in on a little retribution?"

"That's why we're here. What's the plan?" asked Scar.

Elliott gave him a stern look. "We're just going to walk in and shoot the bastards."

Scar gave him a thumbs up.

Elliott put the truck in gear and took off.

Scar let up on the brake, swung the pickup around and stepped on the gas to catch up to them. He turned to Meeks. "It must have been pretty bad."

CHAPTER 17

BLUE EARTH MINNESOTA

The sun was getting lower in the sky when the two pickups pulled into the Patriot Center. There were several vehicles parked in the lot and more on the side of the street. The building, at one time, had been the home of an American Legion. No one came out to greet them. Scar and Meeks got out of their truck and joined Winters and Elliott, who gave them a nod.

The pain of the day still rested on Winters' mind as he followed Elliott across the parking lot. The last thing he needed was to repeat what happened earlier. He grimaced and furrowed his eyebrows at the thought of not having a plan of attack, but there seemed to be no stopping Elliott who wore a determined look.

Meeks found the door unlocked and opened it for Elliott.

They walked into what looked like a big open dance hall. Chairs were placed around the perimeter, leaving the center of the room empty. A disco ball hung from the ceiling.

To the right was a long bar that stretched to the end of the room. Seated were four men and another one behind the bar, enjoying Happy

Hour. Their drinks sat next to their rifles and all were smoking cigarettes. The smoke hung above them like a storm cloud. They looked over at the Shadow Patriots with little concern. No one even bothered to get up and welcome them.

A slow smile formed on Winters' lips as he realized the five workers were relaxed and were sitting ducks. He slid his hand in his jacket and pulled out the Colt.

The workers kept staring as the strangers approached. Their eyes grew wide when guns appeared. The alcohol they'd been drinking dulled their reflexes, and they were slow to respond.

The four Shadow Patriots opened fire on them. The closest worker got the brunt of the deadly onslaught. The back of his head exploded in a shower of blood and bone fragments. His associate next to him tried to use him as a human shield but the shield toppled to the ground leaving him open to the barrage of bullets. He threw his hands out as if trying to stop them from slamming into his body, which caused him to bounce up before collapsing to the floor.

The man behind the bar ducked and grabbed a shotgun, from underneath the bar. Meeks vaulted over the bar and squeezed off two quick rounds, hitting the bartender just as he raised the twelve-gage.

The remaining two men jumped out of their seats. One made it two steps before Elliott and Scar cut him down. The other threw a table up and hid behind it. He peeked around it and returned fire.

One bullet whizzed by Winters as he emptied his magazine into the table. Elliott moved to the left to flank him and shot at him twice. Both rounds hit him in the rib cage and toppled him over.

The room went quiet.

Winters looked at his companions with a glint in his eye then gave them a knowing grin.

Scar and Meeks scooted across the room and cleared the restrooms. Winters and Elliott headed to the left side of the big hall and reached the first of two doors. He opened it cautiously only to find a storage room. They did the same to the second door and were looking into an empty office.

Scar yelled from the far end of the room. "We're good back here."

He and Meeks hurried back to the bar where Winters and Elliott stood waiting.

"Well that's that," said Meeks.

"A helluva lot easier than the drop-off location," said Elliott looking at Winters.

"So, what happened up there?" asked Meeks.

Elliott gave them an account. He didn't lay blame on Winters but he didn't absolve him either. Winters let him vent his anger, feeling he deserved it anyway.

Afterward, Meeks told the story of their escape from the burning town.

"Ironically, we were all in a firefight today," said Meeks. "You guys in gunfire, and us with actual flames."

Scar angled his head back. "Kind of weird, but yeah."

"Let's clean this place up and get out of here," said Winters.

"We should spend some time going through their papers," suggested Elliott.

"You want to do that while we load the bodies and clean up?" asked Winters.

Elliott walked into the office as the others moved over to the dead. Meeks found some garbage bags and the three of them went to work.

"Thank God these aren't big ole dudes," said Meeks sizing up the five bodies.

Scar contorted his face. "Hells bells, look at this one, he's got his brains all over the bar."

"That was my kill," boasted Meeks.

"Well then, you get to clean it up."

"Hmmm great. Tell me again Captain, why are we cleaning the place?"

"If we can make it appear like these guys changed their minds and quit, it'll create a little doubt for whoever's in charge that we exist. Eventually, they'll find out who we are, but I'm not going to help them do it."

"It damn well better work, cause this is disgusting," said Meeks scooping brains off the bar with a towel and throwing them into a trash bag.

The three of them loaded the bodies into the back of the pickup. Mops and paper towels were put to use as they spent over an hour cleaning up the blood and finding all the spent shell casings.

"So, the military huh," said Winters. "I just can't believe they would do such a thing."

"I'm with you, Captain," said the former Marine, Scar. "It breaks my heart to hear of my brothers in arms killing fellow Americans. I know history is filled with this type of thing but this blows me away."

Meeks chimed in. "The bigger question is who is giving them their orders?"

Scar looked at Winters with a thoughtful expression.

"I think I got something here, Captain," said Elliott coming toward them from the office. "It's called Operation Wildflower."

"What's called Operation Wildflower?" asked Winters.

"This whole Patriot Center thing," said Elliott handing a folder to Winters.

Winters paged through the folder, looking at the documents. "They've got Patriot Centers all around the Midwest. In seven states, they've got nine centers."

Meeks spoke up. "Nine centers, how the hell are we supposed to take out all those centers?"

"One at a time, buddy," said Scar.

"And they're looking to expand the program into other states," said Winters throwing the folder on the bar. He sat wearily on a bar stool. His shoulders drooped as he thought how daunting their task appeared. They had taken out only two centers with the last costing them dearly. "Eventually, the military is going to figure out what's going on. When they do, they'll tighten security and send more men," he finished.

Scar slowly added. "We sure won't be able to just waltz in and kill the staff. We're probably only good for one, maybe two more centers."

"That's when the Army will come after us," said Meeks. "We'll be on the run and that will be the end of it."

"Where to next, Captain?" asked Scar.

"We might as well go to Wisconsin."

CHAPTER 18

ROCK ISLAND ILLINOIS

D espite the early morning darkness, Colonel Nunn could see the condensation of his breath as he approached the small office building. Besides enjoying the crisp air, arriving early and first was a matter of pride for the old man. It told his subordinates that he was still able to outwork them. That immense pride took a hit when his young sergeant greeted him.

Nunn replied with a tepid response before stepping into his office. Sergeant Owens followed him in and placed a cup of coffee on his desk.

"Colonel, I couldn't find last night's fax with the day's tally from Minnesota. Did you take it last night?"

The Colonel looked up. "No, I didn't. Did you call up there?"

"Not yet sir, too early for them to be in."

Colonel Nunn sat down at his desk, picked up his cup and thought about what the sergeant said. He took a sip of the steaming black coffee. In light of what happened in Iowa, Nunn's mind started to race; thinking maybe someone was up to no good in Minnesota. He'd have to be patient and wait until 0800 when the center's personnel would be showing up. Nunn didn't believe in coincidences and thought this was more than just an oddity for another Center to miss a tally.

"You let me know when you get ahold of Minnesota ASAP," he barked out.

After several failed tries to reach the center, Nunn had his sergeant call Major Green into his office.

The major arrived ten minutes later to find Colonel Nunn in a foul mood.

"Colonel, you requested my presence?" he asked.

"Major, I need for you to go up to Minnesota. We haven't been able to reach them, and in light of the train station, we need to check this out. Travel light, I want you to get up there as fast as you can, do you understand?"

"Yes, sir. Have the National Police been contacted?"

Colonel Nunn looked up at his Major with contempt on his face. "This has nothing to do with the National Police. It's none of their business what we're doing, and they have no say or jurisdiction in this operation."

"Yes, sir. I thought they might have men closer and…"

"The last thing we need is help from those incompetent idiots. Get a move on, Major."

"Yes sir," replied Major Green as he turned before being shooed away.

CHAPTER 19

Major John Green grew up in Norfolk Virginia, son of a military family. His father spent thirty years in the Army, retired a Colonel, and then became a lobbyist for a defense contractor in Washington.

Green graduated from West Point in the middle of his class. He was known for his political moves. He earned a reputation as a brown noser and would do whatever it took to get ahead, and at thirty-four, he'd been promoted to the rank of Major. At the start of the war, Green had hoped to be sent out West to fight, but instead got posted to the Midwest in a guard duty role. It disappointed him to be there and to be serving under Colonel Nunn, whom he considered unworthy of his position. His only consolation was having 1st Lieutenant David Crick assigned to him. He was a friend of the family. Their fathers had met in Officers Candidate School and had remained friends throughout their careers. With thick eyebrows, dimples and boyish good looks, Crick could have been a male model and he appeared a lot younger than his twenty-eight years. He had graduated from college and had worked in the corporate world before deciding to join the Army. The younger Lieutenant Crick had always looked up to Green, and since he still considered him as a big brother, was glad to be serving with him.

Green stepped out of Colonel Nunn's office once again feeling slighted. He thought something about the man was screwy. The colonel never asked him a single personal question and didn't update him on anything.

Green proceeded to the mess hall and found Crick eating breakfast.

"Lieutenant, can you take that to go?" asked Green.

"What's up?" Crick asked, setting his bagel down.

"We've got to get up to the Minnesota Patriot Center. We need to travel light and fast, so Humvees only."

"I'll have the men ready in ten," said Crick as he got up from the table, grabbing his bagel and a carton of orange juice.

"Twenty men should do us," said Green.

Fifteen minutes later, five Humvees pulled out and headed north. They would get there by late morning and be back by late afternoon.

Green wondered if they'd have to burn down another town like yesterday. He thought, why do something so severe like that? Seemed a little extreme just because someone walked off the job.

A couple of hours later, Major Green pulled into the parking lot of the Minnesota Patriot Center. Except for some volunteers sitting in a pickup truck, the place looked empty. He got out of the Humvee and was greeted by the volunteers.

Green looked over at them. "You men volunteers?"

"Yes sir, we got here about an hour ago, and knocked on the door but no one answered. So, we've just been sitting and waiting for someone to show up."

"Do we report to you?" asked another.

"No, we're not the ones operating this center. But we'll get this figured out for you."

After banging on the door, Major Green ordered the men to break in. After a few whacks on the door handle, they entered the building throwing caution to the wind. He figured the staff had either had up and quit, or were running very late. They turned the lights on, looked around, and found nothing, but an empty building.

Major Green exited the Center as more volunteers began to arrive. He instructed them to come back tomorrow.

"Lieutenant Crick, take three men, get up to the drop off location, and find out what is going on there," ordered Green.

An hour later, Lieutenant Crick reached Green on the radio and reported that the place was abandoned. Two stations in two days, something was not right. Why would they just up and quit when jobs were so hard to come by these days? Especially a job as easy as this one, drive them from point A to point B. He went back into the building and called Colonel Nunn.

"I'm sorry sir, could you repeat that?" Green asked Nunn.

"I want you to check for any signs of a gun battle, Major. Check the walls and ceilings for any bullet holes. Look for blood stains on the floors."

Major Green knew better than to ask why. He would rip him a new asshole if he asked such a question, but still, he wondered why the old man thought there might have been a gun battle here.

Green got out of the office chair and wandered around the big hall. He didn't notice anything unusual. He proceeded to the bar and leaned over to inspect behind it. His stomach resting on the bar, he looked from one end to the other and saw nothing out of the ordinary. Leaning back, his left hand caught a splinter. After pulling it out, he looked at down at the bar. He ran his fingers across it and found some rough spots along a ten-foot section.

"I did find an area on the bar that looks like it's been chewed up. Could have been gunfire or any number of things. Looks pretty new though," said Green when he called back.

"You and your men wait there to see if any of the staff show up," ordered Nunn.

Nunn adjusted his body in his chair and thought about the situation. Someone is trying to shut down these facilities, either the guys at these two centers are in cahoots with each other or someone has discovered what they're up to. Regardless he needed to get this handled.

He picked up the black phone and punched in the number to the Wisconsin Patriot Center.

"Wisconsin Patriot Center," the man answered.

"Is this Wakefield?" asked Nunn.

"Who's asking?"

"This is Colonel Nunn."

There was silence on the line for a second, and then Wakefield cleared his throat.

"Yes sir, what can I do for you?" he asked nervously gripping the phone tighter.

"Have you talked to the Centers in Minnesota or Iowa lately?"

"No, sir."

"So, you don't know why they're not there?"

"They're supposed to be here?"

"No, not where you are, at their own damn Centers. No one has shown up in Minnesota today and I got a bunch of charred bodies at the Iowa drop off location. Someone torched it. You didn't hear about that?"

"Not at all. We don't know about that, sir. It's all business as usual here, sir."

"Well, keep your men on high alert for anything that might be unusual," commanded Colonel Nunn.

"Yes sir, will do..."

Nunn hung up the phone before he had finished. He didn't have the time or the patience to deal with idiots. They were greedy and lacked any morals, but they did what they were told without asking any questions or giving away secrets. Still, the less he had to deal with them on a one on one basis, the better. He proceeded to call all the remaining centers but found no problems with any of them. He got up from his desk and moved over to the map of the Midwest hanging on the wall. Red pushpins represented each Center. He tapped his left index finger on Iowa and then slid it up to Minnesota. Studying the map, he decided to send Green to Wisconsin the next day.

CHAPTER 20

ON THE ROAD TO WISCONSIN

Winters couldn't get over how horrific yesterday's battle had been. They had lost seventeen volunteers in what looked like a mass murder scene. It reminded him of the massacre of his friends. As gut-wrenching as it was to watch his friends die, this seemed worse. In a twisted way, the responsibility of losing these men ultimately fell on his shoulders. It didn't matter that these men would have all died had they not come to their rescue. The burden weighed on him as if he had pulled the trigger.

During the drive to the American Legion hall which held the Minnesota Patriot Center, Winters had been hesitant to go in with no plan, but once the shooting began, Mister Hyde resurfaced. He didn't want to admit it but that drip of adrenaline racing through his veins was enough to make him want more.

However, it was fleeting because the pain of the day returned once they went back to the drop-off center to help clean the place up. They worked well into the night loading the wounded and the dead volunteers to transport them back to their homes. There wasn't much more they could do, but get them to their families. It was stressful to meet with some of the family members and have to explain what happened. Seeing the pain in their eyes and the crying had been a difficult task.

After dropping off the last of the wounded men, they found an abandoned warehouse, in which they were able to park their vehicles for the night.

The large empty building had trash scattered everywhere as if the occupants had left in a hurry. There was a musky damp smell and it reminded Winters of an unfinished basement. Still, it kept them out of sight and out of the weather.

*　*　*　*　*

It was mid-morning before everyone was awake. They still felt the strain of yesterday's events. There wasn't much chatter amongst the men as they finished breakfast and began to load their gear back on the trucks. An overcast day befitted their overall attitude. Once loaded, the men went to their vehicles and jockeyed for the seats they wanted.

Elliott drove an SUV, Winters sitting next to him, with Meeks and Scar in the back seats.

"How long were you in the Marines, Scar?" asked Winters.

"Four years."

"See any action?"

"I was part of the invasion force in Grenada."

"What was that like?" asked Winters.

"I hadn't been in the Corps very long. It was a lot different than training at Camp Pendleton that's for sure. For us, it only lasted ten days, but we did encounter some pockets of heavy resistance."

Winters was impressed.

"He has a lot more experience drinking and playing poker," laughed Meeks.

"Least I don't lose like you," replied Scar, with a big smile on his face.

Elliott looked in the rearview mirror. "You guys play Texas Hold-em?"

"That would be our game of choice. You play, Elliott?" asked Scar.

"You betcha."

Scar leaned forward. "What about you, Captain, you a poker player?"

"I've played, but not on a regular basis. Blackjack is my poison."

"How often?"

Winters shifted his body in the seat. "My wife and I used to play every once in a while."

"Vegas?" asked Scar.

"Vegas one time, but we'd mostly go to the Quad Cities to the riverboats. Close enough where we could spend the afternoon and be able to drive home. Any of you guys go to the Quad Cities?"

Everyone nodded.

"Those were the good 'ole days. I heard the boats were destroyed by the National Police," said Elliott.

"I heard the same thing," said Scar.

Meeks started to laugh. "So, we're a bunch of degenerate gamblers. That's a good thing, cause something tells me we're going to be doing a whole lot of gambling in the very near future."

Winters gave that some thought. He knew it to be true but had no idea how it would play out. With such a limited number of weapons and no experience, the odds were definitely stacked against them.

As the trip wore on, they came upon a small town with a gas station on the outskirts. Winters had everyone pull over. He didn't want all the trucks to go in at the same time, in case there was a National Police presence. Though there wasn't that big a chance in the smaller towns, especially since most of them were half empty. However, pulling into any town would always attract unwanted attention.

Winters got out of the SUV and approached Nate's truck. "Let's have you follow us in while the rest stay here."

Elliott moved the SUV back on the pavement. Nate followed, leaving the rest behind.

"Doesn't look to me like anyone's here, Captain," said Elliott as he pulled into the parking lot.

"I'll go in," said Meeks, as he climbed out of the truck and heading to the entrance. He reached for the door and yanked it open. He turned, looked at the others, shrugged his shoulders, and entered.

"I better go in with him," said Scar, jumping out and landing with a big thud. "Just in case there's any trouble."

They were in the store for a few minutes before Scar came out and walked over to Winters who still sat in the SUV.

"Captain, man in there says we can have all the gas we need providing we can get it out of the underground tanks cause his pumps aren't working."

"Does he have some kind of manual pump?"

"You bet he does. Meeks is helping him get it."

Winters got out of the truck. Meeks strolled out of the store with another man, who held a pump and a long hose. The man had to be in his eighties. He wore a dirty white t-shirt, which looked as old as the man himself. He glanced at Winters, and ignored him, while he bent down to remove the lid from the storage tank. Meeks signaled to bring the pickups over there. Nate and Elliott both moved the trucks as Scar and Winters joined Meeks.

"I haven't checked the levels in a while so I don't really know how much I got," said the old man. "Could be all of nothing, haven't had my pumps working in months. Not that it matters much, don't have any customers anyway."

"We're grateful for anything you can give us," said Winters.

The old man looked up. "You must be Winters. Your man here told me what you've been up to. Never trusted the government before everything went to hell, and I sure as blazes don't trust them now. Doesn't really surprise me what they're doing. I've seen it happen before in Europe, now the same thing is happening here."

"What do you mean?" Winters asked.

"Russia, Germany, Italy, any number of European countries falling to dictatorships, history just keeps repeating itself time and time again. They killed millions of their own citizens."

"Our Government wouldn't do that."

"Oh really," said the old man. "Don't know your history too well do ya? Stalin and Mao killed tens of millions of people. They made Hitler look like a choirboy.   I'll bet their victims thought they wouldn't do it either. Poor suckers."

"But why?"

The old man looked impatient. "It doesn't matter why. All that matters is; they're doing it. Don't try to come up with a reason why. You'd just be wasting your time trying to figure it out."

The men stood there silently as they watched the old man work the pump, within a minute he had gas coming up out of the ground and spilling on the concrete. Meeks grabbed the hose and shoved it into one of the trucks.

The old man struggled to get his creaky legs moving. Once up, he ordered Scar to take over.

He asked Winters. "So, you ex-military?"

"No sir, I'm not," said Winters who followed him back into the store.

"How is it you're in charge?"

Winters thought for a moment. "I keep asking myself that."

He looked at him in surprise. "What do ya mean? Don't you want to lead?"

"Well, it's just I don't think I'm the one to do it." Winters was glad to be telling someone this. He liked talking to the old man who reminded him of his grandfather.

"What did you do before this?"

"I was a bookkeeper for a manufacturing company."

"So, how'd ya end up in charge?" the old man asked again.

"By jumping out the back of a truck."

He looked confused. "Excuse me?"

"Let's just say I stumbled onto this by accident."

He glared at Winters. "You seem to doubt yourself. What's your first name?"

"Cole."

"Cole, let me tell you something." The old man put his hand on Winters' shoulders. "Those men out there asked you to lead them for a reason. I don't care what you think of yourself, but I don't believe for a second, they would have asked if they didn't see something in you. Maybe you don't see it, but they do, and that's what matters."

The old man disappeared into the back office leaving Winters alone with his thoughts. He began to feel guilty again for resisting his duty. His sense of honor was important to him and as before, he thought he'd failed his friends, who now lay in a mass grave, dumped there like unwanted trash.

He drifted back outside in a mental fog.

"This one's full, Captain," Meeks yelled out to Winters.

Winters didn't respond.

"Captain," repeated Meeks.

The fog faded some. "Nate, why don't you go and get the others," said Winters.

"You got it, Captain."

Nate hopped in the truck, started it, and drove away. Winters kept his eyes on Nate's vehicle as he got back up the road, and thought how much more cooperative he'd become since Rogers's death. He tried to keep him busy with responsibilities, which seemed to help his grief.

Standing in the shade by the store, Winters' mind wandered again to what the old man had said regarding the government being involved in these killings. It seemed logical but still, he couldn't quite believe it or didn't want to believe it. With everything that had happened over the past year, who would want to wake up to that reality? The Government had changed, but had it changed that much?

Some people were even accusing them of setting the dirty bombs that had gone off right before the Chinese attack. Chicago, St Louis and Kansas City had lost tens of thousands of people. The government blamed it on China to shake us up before they attack. Winters shook his head thinking about it. The truth was such a burden. No wonder so many would rather bury their heads in the sand. It was easier.

The old man came back out of the store. "You boys are more than welcome to any supplies you might need."

He came over to Winters. "I hear you're headed over to Wisconsin next."

Winters didn't answer right away. "Huh? Yeah, there's a Patriot Center over there."

"You best stay off the main roads, and don't trust anyone who has anything to do with the government."

Winters was only half paying attention.

"You all right, Cole?" asked the old man.

"Yes, I was just thinking."

"About what?"

Winters took a long moment before answering. "Everything."

They made more small talk while Elliott sat down with Scar and helped him work the pump. Before long, they could hear the rattle of vehicles as they noisily approached the gas station. Meeks moved and guided everyone over to where they should park. After the engines were turned off, there was, for a quick moment, complete silence. It was broken as the men got out and started talking and joking with one another.

"So, these are your men," the old man asked.

Winters nodded.

The old man chuckled. "Little out of shape now, aren't we?"

"Yes, but what we lack in good health, we make up in spirit."

"Well, I hope you guys got a lot of spirits."

Scar interrupted with a big laugh. "What do you think has been keeping us going, old man? You're more than welcome to join us if you think you can keep up."

"Oh, I could handle it," he replied with a smirk on his face.

"I like this guy," Scar said to Winters pointing at the old man.

"You should, he is giving us free stuff."

Scar nodded.

It took over an hour to fill the tanks of all the vehicles, during which time the men found different things to do. They were more than happy to take up the old man's offer to take anything they wanted. Some of the men took advantage of the snack cakes and soda pop, while others lounged around smoking, hard to come by cigarettes.

Winters sat at a table inside the store with Elliott, Nate, Scar, and Meeks, who had quickly become his lieutenants. Scar with his Marine experience would be their primary strategic advisor for combat situations. They looked down at a map and pinpointed where the Patriot Centers were located and mapped out a route they should take.

When it was time to go, the men gave their sincere thanks to the old man for his generosity and climbed aboard the trucks.

"Can't thank you enough for everything," said Winters.

"It's been my pleasure, Cole. Remember what I told ya, okay? You just help as many people as you can, but know this, the longer you're at it, the worse it'll get. They'll throw everything they can at you." He gripped Winters' hand firmly and held on for a few seconds.

"We will, sir. Thank you."

Scar grabbed the man's hand. "You got a hell of a grip there for an old man. You sure you don't want to join us?"

"Wish I could. Boy, I sure do wish I could."

"Starting to think he could show us a thing or two," said Scar with his big smile.

On any other day, this would have been a great day to meet a new friend, but as things stood, they needed to go. It was a sad reminder of their reality. The men got in their trucks and waved to the old man as they pulled out of his parking lot. Knowing, in all likelihood, they would never see him again.

CHAPTER 21

WESTERN SIDE OF WISCONSIN

Winters, feeling a little overwhelmed with everything the old man had told him, leaned his head back on the seat and closed his eyes. The wound in his arm pulsated with every beat of his heart. The area around it had grown stiff and sensitive to the touch. He reached into his jacket, grabbed some aspirin, and swallowed four of them.

He had enough on his mind trying to come up with a plan but after talking to the old man, he wondered if he'd ever be done. Winters thought perhaps the old man had it right about the government. It was a hard pill to swallow because no one wanted to believe their government would do such a thing, but then they did throw out the Constitution. Perhaps they were involved, but to what end? If China has its way, there might not be an America left. What then?

How the government ever got itself in a position to lose a war on its homeland was baffling. The war out West had not been going well. Ten straight years of cuts in the military budget had left a shell of a once great fighting force. They had cut the manpower in half, and many of those remaining were not of the same quality as in the past. Morale had sunk so low that they were forced to reduce the standards to fill the ranks.

During the same period America had been cutting its forces, the Chinese had continued to build theirs. Why would we allow something like that to happen?

Regardless, China saw an opportunity and simultaneously attacked San Diego and Los Angeles. American forces, unprepared, understaffed and ill-armed, collapsed and within a few days, the Chinese took out the Navy on Coronado. Then they bombed both cities for a couple of days before they sent in troops. Tens of thousands of Californians died during the bombing and the ensuing massacre. Within a month, China had conquered Southern California and headed north.

The Shadow Patriots were all alone, fighting a fight no one was even aware of. They could depend on no one but themselves. It was going to be a lonely battle with an unknown enemy.

In the past year, America had fallen down and Winters didn't know if she would ever be able to get back up again. With little to no gasoline and limited electrical power, Americans struggled to survive. Food shortages became the norm, as did medical supplies. Most of the population in the Midwest who had not been killed or contaminated by the dirty bombs had moved south as the war started.

However, conditions were not much better in the South, especially with such a massive influx of people. Thousands died from disease, which ran rampant through the camps. Supplies, already short, ran even lower and had to be rationed. These were truly the times that tried men's souls and America's soul was facing a supreme challenge.

"Captain, we could intercept a truck convoy on the route we're taking," said Scar studying the map.

Winters turned to the back. "Can we get them to stop?"

Scar smirked. "Oh, we can get them to stop alright."

Winters glanced over to Elliott. "What do you think?"

"Be a heck of a lot easier to deal with these guys separately."

Winters nodded in agreement.

Elliott moved his hand from the steering wheel to the console. "You know, I've been thinking about this recruitment program. I remember they were offering this deal to guys our age, only here in the Midwest."

"Surely they're doing it on the East Coast," said Winters

"No, not at all, not for guys our age."

"You sure about that?" asked Winters.

"Yeah, I've got friends back East, and I talked to 'em about it a while back and they were surprised."

"Really?"

"Yeah. When it first started, they only recruited younger guys, and then anyone with military experience."

"But that was happening on the East Coast as well. I remember how people were signing up left and right," said Winters

"Yes, but only the young guys, and once they began to run out is when they upped the age of eligibility, and then to guys our age. Only that phase wasn't put into effect back East."

"When did you hear from them last?"

"Just after summer."

Winters shook his head not knowing what to think about it. Someone must hate Midwesterners that's for sure.

As they traveled further east into Wisconsin, the terrain continued to change with more trees and hills. This would be to their advantage because the steeper inclines will slow down the big transports.

"We're in luck, there's the convoy," said Elliott.

Winters lifted his head and focused his eyes. "I see it." He turned around. "You guys ready back there?"

"Ready to rock and roll, Captain?" said Scar.

The three-truck convoy had just reached the peak of a big hill and would soon be out of sight. Elliott stopped the vehicle before reaching the top. All four of them got out and walked back to Nate's pickup as he pulled up behind them.

"What are we doing, guys?" Nate asked.

"Convoy just up ahead. We're gonna intercept it," said Elliott.

"Yeah baby," responded Nate enthusiastically.

They crouched down when they got to the top, where they could hear the booming engines echoing through the valley before they spied the transports starting slowly up the next hill.

Scar laughed. "They're slower than molasses. Hell, even Meeks could run alongside them and keep up."

Meeks returned the jibe. "Which is funny seeing how I'm always having to wait for you."

Scar held his hands up in mock self-defense.

Winters rolled his eyes. He looked at Scar. "How can we get these guys to stop?"

Scar thought for a second. Why don't we pull up beside them and flag them down; like we need to tell them something."

"Let's do a drive by and shoot the bastards," said Nate.

Winters and Scar exchanged glances.

Scar responded. "No, we don't want them crashing into each other. Think about the volunteers."

"Okay," Winters interrupted. "Meeks, Scar, and I will run up to them. I'll take the last truck, the middle one's yours, Scar, and Meeks, you go for the first one. The rest of you stay put, but as soon as Meeks gets to his, I want everyone to cover the sides."

As he laid out this plan, Winters felt a bit more confident than before. He tried to take the old man's advice to heart.

The men hurried back to their vehicles. They came up over the ridge where Elliott picked up speed and raced down, giving the vehicle a running start up the next steep incline. Reaching the top, they noted the convoy had started its next long climb.

"Alright everybody, keep your guns out of sight," said Winters.

Elliott involuntarily gripped the steering wheel tighter as increased adrenaline coursed through his body. Moments later, he was right behind the transport. He moved into the other lane, got up beside it, and honked the horn. Winters waved his hand up at the driver who returned the wave. Winters motioned him to pull over. The driver let off the gas. The other two slowed down as well.

Elliott pulled back and parked behind them as the convoy came to a stop on the incline of the hill. Winters took a deep breath and reached into his jacket to give his Colt a reassuring touch. He got out and waved to the volunteers in the back. Scar and Meeks joined him as they walked to the first vehicle.

"Stay with me for a second before you go," Winters said calmly.

He hopped up and greeted the driver. "I've been sent by Colonel Nunn to make sure everything is alright with the convoys, and to escort you guys in."

"Is something wrong?" asked the driver who wore a dangling earring.

Winters turned his head and signaled the other two to go. He turned back around, reached into his jacket, pulled out his pistol and told the driver. "Don't make a move, and everything will be alright. Keep your hands on the steering wheel."

The confused driver asked. "Did I do something wrong?"

"No, we just need to make sure you guys are who you say you are, we had that trouble down in Iowa, and so we're just being extra careful now."

The driver relaxed a little and sat in silence, while Scar and Meeks proceeded to the other transports. As soon as Meeks got to his, everyone came rushing out and surrounded the convoy.

"Now listen, my guys are a little jumpy, so I want you to get down nice and slow. Once we're satisfied everything checks out, you can be on your way," said Winters.

The driver, doing what Winters had told him to do, got out and climbed down. They searched the three drivers and moved them together to the center of the road where they asked for their papers. Meeks and Scar made a big deal of trying to sound as legitimate as possible, enjoying the moment.

Winters had the volunteers get out of the transports, and move back to the pickups so he could address them. He explained the whole story to them, and they reacted the same as the others had, surprised, shocked and angry. Two of them more than the others, because they had relatives who had come through the Center recently. Their reaction got Winters' attention. They needed to get up to the drop-off location and he didn't want any trouble from the two angry ones, so he decided to keep all these new volunteers here and out of harm's way.

Winters had just finished briefing the volunteers when Meeks interrupted, "Captain, we need to go. Drivers said they're on a real tight schedule and are expected to be on time."

"Do they still think we're Colonel Nunn's men?" Winters asked.

"Oh yeah, they ain't very bright," said Meeks with a hick accent. "Scar is having way too much fun with them."

"You got their procedures upon entering the drop off point?"

"Sure do," said Meeks.

Winters walked over to Scar, who was enjoying a cigarette one of the drivers had given him. "Thought you said you didn't smoke."

Scar winked at Winters. "I don't normally, but couldn't hardly turn down a nice gesture. Didn't want to be rude, don't cha know."

Winters shook his head. "Well, I'm glad you still have your manners at a time like this."

He turned his attention to the drivers. "Gentlemen, I'm afraid I have some terrible news."

"Is there something wrong? We're who we say we are, I swear," said the driver with the dangling earring.

"No, it's not you, it's us, we're not who we said we are. Colonel Nunn didn't send us, in fact, Colonel Nunn would love to stop us."

The three of them looked dumbfounded as Winters went on.

"We're the ones who burned down the train station in Iowa. Perhaps you heard about that?"

They all nodded.

"Are you going to kill us?" asked one of them.

"No! We're not murderers, unlike you guys," said Winters with contempt in his voice.

They hung their heads low when he said this because no matter how they justified their actions, they knew they were guilty of murder.

Scar turned to Winters. "We should leave them here with these new guys till we get back."

"Yeah, can't say I want a repeat of what happened in Minnesota."

Winters walked back to the group of men who stopped chatting as he approached.

"Listen up guys, we're headed up to the drop-off location. We'll be back as soon as we get done there. Afterward, you guys can either join us or go home, it's up to you."

"Mind if we come with you?" asked someone from the back.

Two people stepped forward. "I'm Burns, and this is Murphy," he said extending his hand.

Winters noticed the firm grip and figured the man worked outside, as his hands were rough and calloused. He had a slender build to him and was nearly Winters' height. His hair was salt and pepper, which matched his facial stubble. He moved with a self-confidence that said he had experienced life on his own terms. Murphy was a bit younger and despite the bags under his eyes, which made him appear older, he had a lot of energy. He had enthusiasm in his blue eyes and came off as a friendly person.

"You guys serve in the military?" Winters asked.

"Ten years in the Army, got out after Desert Storm," said Burns.

"Four years in the Army," said Murphy.

"We could use more guys with experience." He turned back to the volunteers and asked them to guard the drivers while they were gone.

Winters took the two new recruits over to his crew, who were milling around by the big trucks, and introduced them.

"Excellent. Two more with only one name. We're big on that here. I'm Meeks and big foot over there is Scar."

Burns and Murphy went around and shook everybody's hand.

"So, what's the plan?" Burns asked.

Meeks gestured to Scar. "We like to keep things as simple as possible, some of us aren't all that smart."

Burns turned to Murphy. "Looks like we're gonna fit right in then."

"Ha, I like this guy already," Meeks said excitedly.

Winters stood by Elliott, and said in jest, "great, two more comedians."

"At least we'll never have ourselves a dull moment," responded Elliott.

"I like dull sometimes," said Winters.

They found a spot off the road to hide the men and their pickups. Elliott and Winters hopped in the first transport, Scar mounted the second and Nate the third. Everyone else climbed into the back of a truck where they readied their weapons. Engines started and screamed as they inched their way up the big hill.

An hour later, they reached their destination. Elliott rolled up his window, hoping the afternoon sun reflecting off the window would, once again, conceal his identity. Tensions built as they approached the entrance. Elliott would be the first one into the parking lot and the first one out of the cab. He began to sweat and nervously tapped the steering wheel.

Winters took a deep breath. "I'll exit after you get out and sneak around like we did at the first pickup place."

Winters saw that they had a much bigger space to get across than the first time they had done this in Iowa.

Winters spoke in a soothing tone. "You good to go?"

Elliott nodded.

They pulled into the oversized lot and parked where the original drivers had instructed them to go.

Two men exited the small building, each carrying M-16's. They walked forward but stopped halfway across the parking lot when they saw the trucks park in the wrong spots. They raised their weapons.

Winters half-yelled. "Those drivers lied to us."

CHAPTER 22

BUFFALO COUNTY WISCONSIN

Another man came rushing out of the building to join the first two. They waited for the drivers to get out.

Elliott said in surprise. "Whoa, Captain, look, Scar is walking over to 'em."

Winters leaned forward to find Scar walking toward them. "What on earth?"

Scar approach them with a big grin on his face, which seemed to lighten the tense moment.

Winters grabbed the door handle. "Change of plans. You go to the back and pretend to give instructions to the volunteers. I'll help Scar."

Winters tried to be as nonchalant possible but hurried at the same time to get with Scar.

Scar stood in front of the three men who he tried to put at ease with a friendly appearance.

"Yeah, Colonel Nunn is anxious about what happened down in Iowa, somebody somewhere screwed the pooch. Whoever it was, I'm sure wasn't doing their job like you guys here," said Scar to the men who still firmly gripped their weapons.

One of them nodded.

"Any of you guys got a cigarette?" Scar asked them.

A man wearing thick, black-rimmed glasses reached into his pocket. "Right here, man. What did you say your name was again?"

"Scarborough. I'm part of Nunn's private security detail. We're just making sure everything is hunky dory up this way. Where's everyone else?" Scar lit the cigarette taking in a deep drag.

"They're inside, probably wondering who you are," said the man with the glasses.

Winters approached the group.

"Oh, this here is Cole," said Scar. "He's Colonel Nunn's, right-hand man. I was just explaining to these gentlemen who we are and what we're doing here."

"We should probably get to it," said another one of the men.

"Get to it?" asked Winters.

"Yeah, you know get to the volunteers."

"Yes, you do that, we'll go inside, and let 'em know why we're here," said Scar.

Scar and Winters started walking toward the building.

"Nice move," said Winters.

"Thought you might like that."

They reached the door and walked inside. It took a second for their eyes to adjust to the dim light and to the three men pointing .45's right in their faces.

Scar put his hands up. "Hey, hold up there, fellas. Colonel Nunn sent us to make sure everything is going okay up here."

"I wasn't informed of this," said the boss.

Scar squared up to him. "Of course you weren't. This is a surprise security check. You don't give a heads up on surprise inspections. Now get your guns out of my face, and point me to the bathroom."

The boss seemed perplexed but relented. He lowered his weapon and pointed the way to the bathroom. "Down there on the left," he said. "Where are our drivers?"

"Oh, don't worry about them, they'll be along on the next trip," said Scar as he sauntered to the bathroom. "Man, don't you guys ever clean this place. It smells like an outhouse."

Trash littered the hallway and the low light made the green walls look even uglier.

Scar reached the bathroom, turned around, and could see Winters, who made eye contact with him.

Gunfire was heard from outside. The sound made Winters jump. It didn't alarm the boss, figuring his men were doing their job. The shooting came in several short bursts and was sporadic. This got the attention of the boss. He was used to continuous gunfire and some screaming. He started back toward the door to see what was going on but noticed Winters had drawn his weapon. The boss instinctively raised his sidearm. He was too slow, and Winters pulled the trigger. Two rounds found their mark and dropped the man in his tracks. Scar did the same, and immediately took down the remaining two, who yelled out, but for only a moment.

"Well, that's that," said Winters.

"Captain, you're a pretty cool customer, you'd have made a good Marine."

Winters shook his head in a non-committal way, it was nice to hear, but he was too unsure of himself to be a Marine.

Winters tucked his pistol back into his waist. "Let's get outside, and see what happened."

"Be happy to get out of this dump."

They left the building and saw their crew crouched on the ground in a semi-circle and Nate running up to them. "Captain, Meeks got shot."

"How bad?" asked Winters in a concerned tone.

"Not bad, just took a bit off his arm."

Scar shook his head. "Hells bells, we're never going to hear the end of this."

They hustled over to the group where Burns was attending to Meeks.

"What happened?" Winters asked Elliott.

"We had them disarmed, except one of 'em had a pistol hidden in his jacket. He got a shot off before we could gun 'em down."

Scar knelt by his friend. "What happened to your cat-like reflexes?"

"Well, thank Gaawd for those reflexes. Otherwise, I'd be lying dead on the ground, and you'd be looking down at me crying your little eyes out."

"I'd certainly be looking down at you."

Meeks grabbed the corner of Scar's jacket. "Oh, you'd be shedding some tears. Think I should get a purple heart for this?"

Scar shook his head. "Captain, I told ya. We'll never hear the end of this."

"Yeah, I can see that," said Winters who silently thanked God for such a minor wound.

Winters turned to Nate. "Let's dump the bodies somewhere along the way. I want to get back to those volunteers as quickly as we can. Elliott, scavenge the place, and grab anything we might be able to use."

Fifteen minutes later, they pulled out of the parking lot and headed back to pick up the rest of the volunteers. They had found a well-hidden place in the woods to park all the vehicles. This didn't alleviate his concern about leaving those men for such an extended period. If some of them took off in the pickups, there would be nothing they could do. He hoped they didn't go back to the Patriot Center to try and take matters into their own hands. It needed to be done but in the right way.

His thoughts turned to Meeks. He was lucky to be alive. It also made him realize that none of them had any medical experience. He tried to think in favorable terms, but the fact remained; how would they deal with future injuries.

An hour later, Elliott noticed it first. "Geez Louise, Captain, up ahead, is that what I think it is?"

Winters squinted his eyes. "What is it?"

"Looks to me like we got a string of Army Humvees coming our way."

"Oh hell," said Winters in an elevated tone.

CHAPTER 23

BRIGGSVILLE WISCONSIN

Major Green reached the Wisconsin Patriot Center located in Briggsville, just north of Portage, about a hundred miles from the Illinois border. He had never personally visited this Center before and didn't know the man who ran it or any of his employees.

Green pulled into a disorganized parking lot. Vehicles of all types were parked haphazardly, spilling out onto the street. When volunteers came through these centers, they typically left their vehicles. Family members would pick them up later, while others simply abandoned them, figuring they would never be coming back. Most of the centers had places the vehicles could be stored for later pickup.

The limited space forced Green's convoy of Humvees to park on the street. The man who ran the Center came out to greet him.

He walked over to Green. "You must be Major Green."

"I am, and you are?"

"Eddie, Eddie Wakefield," he said sticking his hand out.

Green shook his hand.

"So, what's this all about?" asked Eddie who apparently had never turned down an opportunity to eat or drink beer. His girth appeared to be more than his height. His long, greasy hair matched his unkempt beard.

"Colonel Nunn wants me to visit all the centers personally and make an assessment of their operation. I noticed your parking lot is quite full. Why haven't you moved all these cars off the lot? Don't you have a storage lot?"

"Storage lot? We don't need no storage lot, we've got an 'ole boy that comes around and picks them up. He should be here sometime this week."

Green cocked his head back. "Picks them up? Where does he take them?"

"He takes them down south and sells them."

"Sells them?"

Wakefield saw the innocence in Green's eyes when he asked the question. He realized the major knew nothing about Operation Wildflower. He remembered Colonel Nunn telling him, no one but his employees were to know about their operation. What he didn't know until right now, was that Colonel Nunn had kept that vital information from Major Green.

"Yes, sells them for the volunteers. You know, with fuel shortages and all, anything on four wheels is getting pretty useless, so we sell them and get the money to their families."

"Okay. As far as I know, none of the other centers provide such a service."

Wakefield suppressed a smirk. "We do everything we can to help out."

Green spoke to him pointedly. "We've had some delays at a couple of the other stations. Crews have disappeared. So, we wanted to speak to you personally to determine if there were any problems, which might encourage you to do the same thing?"

"No, can't say we got anything wrong here. We love what we're doing and it feels good to be able to serve our country in its time of need," said Wakefield with a smile that hid his contempt for America.

Wakefield was an avowed Communist and well known around

Wisconsin before the war started. He handpicked his workers from the movement and had no problem finding like-minded people to help in any way they could to bring America to its knees.

Green and his men walked into the center, to inspect the place, it was dirtier than most of the ones he had seen, but he didn't uncover any clues which might suggest something was wrong. Green chatted with Wakefield a bit longer, before he and his men remounted their vehicles to go to inspect the drop-off location.

"That place was disgusting," said Lieutenant Crick, getting into the Humvee.

Green slid into his seat. "Tell me about it."

"They smelled like they've haven't bathed in a month. Are these the best people, the government could come up with? They're about as bad as hippie protesters."

"Our best and brightest are out West," said Green with a reflective tone.

"Doesn't leave much hope for our future if these are the people we're fighting for."

"I'm sure they're a tiny minority."

An hour later, as the Humvees were headed to the drop off location, they spotted transports coming toward them.

"Should I signal them to pull over?" asked Green's driver.

"Absolutely."

As they got closer, they slowed down, flashed their headlights, and came to a complete stop about fifty yards from the incoming transports. Green and Crick got out of the Humvee and waited for them. The transports stopped about twenty yards away from the Humvees. Green nodded to Crick and they walked to the first truck.

CHAPTER 24

E lliott looked over at Winters. His hand shook as he started to fumble around with the gear shift. He downshifted and slowed the transport down.

"What are we going to do?" asked Elliott.

"Don't pull up all the way up to them, let them walk to us."

Elliott shifted his eyes to his side mirror and saw Scar signaling the guys in the back of the truck to stay quiet. Winters grabbed his Colt and watched the two soldiers come closer.

Major Green walked to the side and locked eyes on Elliott.

"I'm Major Green and this is Lieutenant Crick. We're with Colonel Nunn's detachment, and as you may or may not know, he is in charge of the Patriot operation."

Elliott feigned concerned. "Is there something wrong?"

"No, we just wanted to ask a few questions," said Major Green. "Can I assume Wakefield has filled you in on what's been happening at some of the other Patriot Centers?"

Elliott didn't know Wakefield or what to say, so he decided to act ignorant of the subject. "No, can't say I know anything about it. Has something happened?"

"We've had some guys missing at a couple of other Centers in Iowa and Minnesota, and we can't figure out why."

Elliott gripped the steering wheel tighter. "Did something happen to them?"

"We don't know. We think they just up and quit their jobs. Which seems rather strange, especially with jobs so difficult to come by."

"Well yeah, I'm grateful for mine, even if I'm having to do things I normally wouldn't want to do."

"What do you mean by that?"

"By what?"

"Doing things you normally wouldn't want to do?"

Elliott didn't know what to say and was puzzled by this question. Killing people, was not obvious enough? He didn't dare glance over to Winters, nor did he dare break eye contact with the major, who waited for an answer. He had a genuine look of curiosity. This made Elliott wonder what kind of heartless man stood before him, that he thought nothing of killing innocent people. He had to come up with something, which would satisfy the major.

"Work for the government," said Elliott putting a smile on his face. "No offense, but I used to be a farmer. Never thought I'd have to work for the government."

"Yes, well these are trying times. I'm sure you'll get to farm again someday. You know, you're a lot older than most of the drivers I've seen at other centers."

Elliott waved his hand in the direction of the other trucks. "Oh really? Well, we're all about the same age."

"We're inspecting all the centers. Have you had any problems with Wakefield and his operation?"

"No, can't say that I have," Elliott responded.

"How about at the drop-off location?"

"Ah, well no. I mean we just left there. Everything looked normal to me. Is that where you're headed next?" asked Elliott hoping not to sound too anxious.

"Yes. Thanks for your time."

"Anytime, Major."

Green and Crick retreated to their Humvee.

Elliott let out a deep breath. "That was interesting."

The Humvees drove past them.

Winters slouched in his seat. "Yeah, to say the least. What the hell was that all about, asking what wasn't normal in killing people?"

Elliott straightened up. "That's what I was wondering. He must be a cold-hearted bastard."

"No doubt. Oh, and kudos to you. You were pretty quick. Work for the government. That was brilliant."

"Yeah, don't quite know where that one came from."

Ten minutes later, they pulled over to where they left the new volunteers. Everyone got out of the trucks and hurried over to Elliott and Winters.

"What the hell was that all about? I thought for sure we were going to have a shootout," said Meeks.

"You and me both," said Elliott.

Winters spoke up. "That guy was Major Green. He's investigating the missing men for this Colonel Nunn guy, seems our little plan of deception is working."

"There was something not quite right about him," said Elliott.

"Why's that?" asked Meeks.

"We got into this weird conversation about how jobs were hard to come by these days, and I told him how grateful I was to have one, even if I had to do things, that weren't normal. You know implying that killing innocent people wasn't normal. He seemed a bit baffled and asked what I meant by it."

"What did you say?"

"I played it off by saying I had to work for the government."

Meeks slapped Elliott on the back. "Damn, Elliott, you're about as quick as Scar with a good lie."

Scar turned to Winters. "We'd better double-time it, Captain. That major will be pretty pissed off when he finds no one up there."

Winters turned to him. "Where?"

"To the Patriot Center."

"We're not going now."

"Why not?"

"We won't have time," said Winters.

"Sure we will, we don't have as far to go."

"Yeah, but those Humvees are a lot faster than these transports."

"We'll be alright."

Winters raised an eyebrow.

Scar tried again. "If we don't go now, we'll never get another chance."

Winters grudgingly agreed.

They all turned to walk into the woods, and as they came to where they left the volunteers, they spotted bloodied bodies lying motionless on the ground.

CHAPTER 25

BUFFALO COUNTY WISCONSIN

Green and his men pulled into the parking lot of the drop-off location. His driver drove up to the building while the rest of them parked off to the side. Green got out of the vehicle. Both he and Lieutenant Crick walked toward the entrance of the building. Green took in a deep breath and immediately smelled an awful odor. He then glanced at Crick and pointed to a big garbage pile at the edge of the field.

"You'd think they'd take the time and burn their garbage," said Green.

Crick cringed. "Bad enough having to look at it but to have to smell it, is unbearable."

"I thought the Center was disgusting, but I think this place is even worse."

"Well, the caliber of people is not ideal."

"They're representing the government, perhaps we can encourage them to clean up."

"I wouldn't count on it."

"Seems too quiet here, you'd think someone would have come out."

Crick jerked the door open, and both stepped in. They instantly balked at the smell, which was much worse inside. Flies buzzed around in celebration of their surroundings. They both shook their heads in disgust as they entered a long hallway. Green yelled out for anyone. When no one responded, he nodded to his lieutenant and they unholstered their side arms. They crept down the hall and opened the first door only to find an empty storage room. They proceeded to the next door and saw a few sleeping bags sprawled out, and clothes haphazardly lying about. The end of the hall emptied into a much larger room. A makeshift kitchen had dirty dishes on the counter along with opened cereal boxes. In the corner, a garbage pail overflowed with trash. Green walked over to a glassed-in office on the far side of the room and found nothing but a messy desk with piles of paper.

"I'm going to call the Colonel," said Green.

He then moved to the desk, sat down in a tattered swivel chair, which squeaked as he scooted it closer. Picking up the phone, he dialed the number. While waiting for the connection, he thought back to the transports he had pulled over. He suddenly realized they were the only things that appeared out of place.

Nunn's sergeant finally answered.

"Colonel Nunn's office, Sergeant Owens speaking."

"Owens it's me. Is he in?"

"Yes sir, he's in."

"How's his mood?"

"The usual. So, is it good news or bad?"

"Don't know yet. Put him on," said Green.

Green held onto the phone, patiently waiting for Nunn to pick-up. "Major, what do you have for me?"

"Well, we went up to the Wisconsin Patriot Center, and I had a chat with Wakefield and all seemed well. He appeared stable and content with his situation."

"And?" Nunn asked impatiently.

"We've arrived at the drop-off and there's no one here. Which is strange, but even more strange, is on our way here, we happened to meet their convoy heading back to the Patriot Center. They said everything was fine when they left the drop-off."

Nunn kept his silence and continued to listen.

"It's not so much what they said, but how they looked. They were a different breed than people who usually staff these centers."

"In what way, Major?"

"Well sir, they weren't the typical scum, and they were much older than any of the others."

Nunn straightened up in his chair.

A prolonged silence made Green wonder if the connection had been lost. "Colonel, you still there?"

"Major, get back to that Patriot Center as fast as you can. You find those bastards you pulled over. For whatever reason, they're trying to stop our operation by killing our staff."

"Yes sir," said Green.

"I'll call Wakefield and warn him," said Nunn.

CHAPTER 26

ROCK ISLAND ILLINOIS

This news solidified what Colonel Nunn had suspected. These Patriot Center workers weren't running off but were being killed. It had to be the volunteers doing it.

Colonel Nunn hung up the phone after putting Wakefield on high alert. He told him to trust no one until Major Green arrived.

Nunn opened the bottom drawer of the desk and took out his bottle of Scotch. He reached for an empty glass and poured himself a larger amount than usual. The smoky aroma hit his nostrils before he finished the pour. After setting the bottle down reverently, he raised the glass and took a sip. He then leaned back in his chair as he thought about the situation.

Someone must have caught wind of their actual operation, and now was trying to shut it down. This meant they took out three of the nine locations, and more than likely recruited a fair number of men. These volunteers couldn't be too heavily armed. They had been instructed not to bring any personal firearms. They probably have only what they took off the dead.

Some of them might have gone back home and procured weapons they weren't supposed to have after the government's weapons reclamation program. What a disastrous program, trying to encourage citizens to give up their firearms. Nunn chuckled to himself when he remembered they had even resorted to a buyback scheme. Of course, some brought their weapons in for sale, but they were mostly old or broken ones. As a last resort, they had tried to reward folks for ratting out their gun-loving neighbor. The only thing that accomplished was to anger even more people and forced the government to finally back off.

His thoughts turned back to the current situation and how this could be a disaster for him if the volunteers spread the word about what these centers really were. For all practical purposes, they were out of business in those three areas. The best thing he could do was to find these men before they hit the remaining centers. Operation Wildflower; more like Operation Wilting Flower, he snickered to himself. He glanced at his watch and decided to call his boss Director Reed. He finished his drink before picking up the phone and dialing the number.

"Director Reed's office," his assistant answered.

"This is Colonel Nunn, I need to speak with him."

"One moment please," came the response.

A couple of minutes passed before Reed picked up the phone. "Colonel, what's the good word?"

"We've got a problem," he answered.

"What kind of problem, Colonel?"

"The exact problem we wanted to avoid."

"Someone is aware of what we're doing."

"Oh, it's worse. I think we've got ourselves a rebellion. I found out Decker and his men most likely didn't walk off the job. More than likely, they were killed, as well as those in Minnesota. Major Green was at the Wisconsin Center, and they seemed to be experiencing no difficulties. He then proceeded to the drop-off location, which he found abandoned of all personnel. He's heading back to the Patriot Center as we speak."

"You've lost a third of your Patriot Centers?" an astonished Reed asked.

"For all practical purposes, yes."

"Do you have any idea who it is?" asked Reed.

"Maybe. Green encountered our trucks from the drop off point heading back to the Center. He pulled it over to ask them some questions. He said they were older guys, but didn't think anything of it at the time."

"Perhaps it wasn't such a good idea not to tell him about Operation Wildflower."

"Maybe so, but he's not an individual who would have voluntarily been involved in this operation."

"Well, in light of what's happening he'll need to be informed, don't you think?"

"Eventually."

"How do you think he'll respond?"

"I can handle Major Green. It won't matter much because whether he likes it or not, he's participated in these killings. Albeit from the sidelines, but his records will disclose his involvement in Operation Wildflower."

"I knew there was a reason I wanted you on our team. Listen, I'm sending someone out there to give you a hand."

"Who?"

"Commandant Boxer."

Nunn didn't like what he heard.

CHAPTER 27

Winters gave in to Scar's suggestion that they would have time to go and take out the Wisconsin Patriot Center before Green got back. They all headed into the woods to pick up the Wisconsin volunteers and the first thing they noticed were three dead bodies on the ground with the volunteers standing around them.

"What the hell happened?" asked Winters staring at the bloodied dead men.

No one answered.

"Who are those guys? Where are the prisoners?" he continued.

The men stood still. Scar walked over to the dead men and rolled one of them over. The man's skull was caved in and was unrecognizable. Scar squatted down and put his finger on an earring hanging off a piece of flesh.

These are the prisoners, Captain."

Winters yelled out. "Would someone mind telling me how this happened?"

"They killed our friends," a voice finally spoke up.

"Yeah, my cousin came through here last week, they deserved to die," yelled one of the men who Winters had been afraid might be inspired to take matters into his own hands.

"So, you decided to start beating the men?" asked Winters.

"No, we were only asking them questions about what you said, and they wouldn't answer. So, we started roughing them up a little, and things got out of control."

Winters threw up his hands in anger and walked away from them.

Elliott came up alongside him. "Captain, don't go off on them, remember how angry you were when your friends got killed."

"Yes, but prisoners," retorted Winters.

"Cole, I know, and I'm with you, but all of this is new to them. Hell, it's new to all of us."

Winters stopped and took a deep breath. These men didn't know him and more than likely don't care either. Not wanting an argument, he decided to give them a pass.

He returned to the men and explained the plan. "We'll get you guys back to the Patriot Center, and then you can decide what you want to do. You can either join us or go home and spread the word so no one else shows up at this place, which is just as important," said Winters laying the last bit on thick. After the murder of the prisoners, he didn't really want these men to join them.

With everyone loaded in the trucks, they were now heading to the Patriot Center. They would have to hurry if they wanted to get these Wisconsin men on their way before Major Green came back.

Winters stared out the side window thinking about the day. He was impressed with Scar and how bold he had been walking up to those guards. Winters wondered if the man was that confident or did he merely put up a good front.

Winters' own nerves had about done him in as he walked up to Scar and those guards. Meeting your enemy face-to-face had been more nerve-wracking than sneaking up on a sleeping drunk adversary.

He was also impressed with Elliott and how he handled himself when confronted by the major. He had been pretty calm and collected, which was quite a change from when they had pulled into the Iowa Patriot Center where he had been nervous and unsure of himself. He figured they'd all get better as they went along.

Winters began thinking about the dead prisoners, and how they were clearly murdered. Being associated with such an act made him uneasy, but then again, these same prisoners would be dead had the Shadow Patriots attacked them at the drop off location. Winters shifted in his seat at the easy rationalization. Amazing the great lengths, the mind will go through to justify one's actions. First, he justified the killing at the train station because they needed to be stopped. Now he had done some mental gymnastics on murdering prisoners. He adjusted his hat while contemplating how much he was going to change over the coming weeks and what he would morph into. Would he be any different than the workers at the Patriot Centers? A lump formed in his throat at the notion.

He forced his mind off the subject and thought about what the old man had said regarding the government throwing everything at them, which will be the case now that the Army knew they existed. It would get much worse for the Shadow Patriots. They were nothing but a disorganized group of old men who couldn't even stop prisoners from being murdered.

Twenty minutes later, they reached the town where the Patriot Center was located, as planned, all the pickup trucks pulled over, and allowed the transport trucks to continue into town. When the three transports arrived at the Patriot Center, Winters wasn't too surprised that no one was outside to greet them. He figured the major called and told them to get out of here. The men dismounted and maneuvered their way around all the vehicles, which cluttered the parking lot. Winters, Elliott, Scar and Meeks walked toward the entrance of the building as Nate, Murphy and Burns walked around back.

They walked in and found no one inside.

Elliott turned to Winters. "Well, where do you suppose they all went, Captain?"

Meeks' face lit up. "Oh hell, these pansies skipped out of here."

"They probably got a call from that major," said Winters.

"Here come the others," said Elliott seeing the pickups full of the Wisconsin volunteers coming toward them.

"I'm kind of hoping these Wisconsin guys don't stick around. No offense guys," said Winters turning to Burns and Murphy, their newest recruits from Wisconsin.

Burns replied. "None taken. We don't even know them. We're not from here."

"Where you guys from?" asked Scar.

"Chicago," said Murphy. "We left as soon as the first dirty bomb went off. Kind of thought there'd be a lot more of those being deployed."

Burns added. "Yeah, so we came here. Figured it'd be safer."

"Safe in the land of cheese heads," said Murphy.

The vehicles pulled up and parked on the street and immediately the men poured out. Some of them walked straight to their vehicles, got in and took off. Others came up and asked to join the Shadow Patriots, acknowledging they didn't agree with what had happened.

"We're gonna need a couple of those transports, Captain," said Elliott. Winters nodded.

Meeks snapped his fingers. "Captain, I've got a great idea. Now that they know who we are, why don't we leave them a message. Give them a little something to think about. Maybe even change a mind or two."

"Like what?" Winters asked in a skeptical tone.

"Oh, I don't know," he said turning to Scar. "But I'm sure my good friend could come up with a little something."

Scar stood thinking for a few seconds. "What about we write it on the wall outside, so everyone can read it. Meeks, go see if you can find some spray paint."

Scar sat down at the desk and started to write and within a few minutes had the message completed.

"We found some paint," said an excited Meeks coming around from the back. "Got ourselves a can of gloss black, and look what else we found."

"What?" asked Scar.

Meeks held up a couple of grenades.

Scar reached out to grab one. "Oh, hell yeah, look at those babies, I haven't seen one of these since I was in the Corps."

"Did you come up with something to write?" asked Meeks.

"You might say that," he handed the paper to Winters, who read it approvingly. He gave it back to Scar.

Meeks tried to contain himself. "Let me see. It was my idea."

"Hold on a minute," said Scar as he exited the building.

Meeks shook the paint can while he followed him outside. He then handed it to Scar, who went to work.

The job took several minutes to finish as Scar tried to keep the lines straight. Some of the paint ran down onto the next line, which only added character to the message. Once he finished, he stepped back to admire his handiwork, and asked, "What do you guys think?"

TO THOSE OF YOU WHO ARE RESPONSIBLE FOR TAKING PART IN THE MURDER OF INNOCENT AMERICANS, WE WILL HUNT YOU DOWN. FOR THOSE OF YOU WHO ARE FORCED TO PARTICIPATE IN THIS TREACHERY LEAVE YOUR POST NOW. THIS IS YOUR ONLY WARNING, CONTINUE AND YOU WILL FIND NO MERCY FROM US. THE SHADOW PATRIOTS.

Everyone gave Scar a shout out.

Winters interrupted. "Gentlemen, we need to get out of here."

Scar agreed. "Don't want to take on the Army today?"

"Did you see the machine guns on those Humvees?"

Scar laughed. "Those little ole .50 calibers."

Nate spoke up. "Hey, I got an idea, give this warning a bit more gravitas."

They all waited.

"Why don't we booby trap the place with one of them grenades."

Winters raised an eyebrow. "Where?"

"I'd say either the front or back door," said Nate.

"Back door, I don't want to mess up my message," replied Scar.

"Oh, I can help with it," said Meeks.

Winters shrugged his shoulders and nodded.

As the three of them went into the building to set the trap, the rest of the Wisconsin volunteers got to their vehicles and left. Winters took note of how the parking lot suddenly seemed empty. He didn't know if some of them had taken vehicles, which weren't theirs, but he didn't really care. The dead weren't coming back to claim them. After a few minutes, the three saboteurs came out of the building, obviously very proud of themselves.

"It's a thing of beauty, Captain," said Nate.

This made Winters wince. Something, which will end up killing people, is now a thing of beauty. He guessed that maybe it was when you considered their enemy. He gave them a thumbs up and suggested they leave right away. As they turned toward their vehicles, a car sped down the street and screeched to a halt. One of the volunteers, who had left only a few minutes ago, yelled out to tell them he'd spotted Humvees coming from the north.

Winters turned and glared at Scar who assured him they'd have enough time.

Scar put his hands up. "Let's just go, Captain."

CHAPTER 28

BRIGGSVILLE WISCONSIN

The Humvees reached the Patriot Center and parked out on the street. The soldiers got out of their vehicles and immediately took note of the warning on the wall.

"Lieutenant Crick, go find Wakefield," ordered Green. "I want some men around back."

Green watched his men enter the building. He grabbed his camera and took a picture of the painted message. A moment later, a loud explosion erupted from inside the building. Everyone took cover behind the Humvees.

Crick exited the building and ran over to Green. "Major, someone booby-trapped the back door, I've got two KIA and another two casualties."

"What about Wakefield?" Green asked.

"He's not here."

"Son-of-a-bitch."

The officers ran back in to air their soldiers, when they reached the scene, they found men working hard to assist the wounded. The door had blown apart along with most of its frame. Shrapnel spread out damaging the inner wall and up into the ceiling tiles. The two KIA's had taken the brunt force, while the other two, with the non-lethal injuries, had been their back up and almost out of the blast radius. However, they still needed immediate attention.

Green's demeanor turned to anger. "Get these men loaded up, and get them back to the post." He turned to Crick. "You and I are going after those bastards. That paint is still wet, so they can't be too far away."

Crick, Green, and his driver ran out of the building to their Humvee and sped out of town. A few miles later, they got onto the highway, which allowed them to pick up speed.

Lieutenant Crick raised his binoculars and made a visual confirmation. He came out of the turret. "At your ten o'clock, sir. Out in the field."

"Sergeant, take that road up ahead."

"Yes, sir."

He slowed down and took a right, which took them up an incline. He stopped at the top to get his bearings. The road went to the right when they wanted to go left. Green spotted a road bordering a field. They could take it and catch up to their quarry.

"Take us into the field," ordered Green.

After slowing down at the bottom of the hill, the sergeant veered to his left, the vehicle moved down into the ditch, bounced up on the other side, and crashed through the wire fence. The sergeant floored the pedal and headed east along the rough empty field. After bouncing along for a few minutes, they could see the convoy only a few hundred yards away.

"Lieutenant, get back up the turret and man the M2," ordered Green.

"Yes, sir."

"Sergeant, move us right up beside them."

"Yes, sir."

The tires spun up a rooster tail of dirt as the backend swerved before setting itself straight. The sergeant angled the vehicle to gradually overtake the transports and the two pickups leading the way.

They were now close enough that the drivers turned their attention to the lone Humvee running alongside them. Green glared at the men who were responsible for killing his soldiers. He wanted them dead. Green rolled down his window and took hold of his M4 carbine, while Crick stood up in the turret and ratcheted the bolt on the M2.

Green yelled out. "You ready, Crick?"

"Yes sir," he responded as the wind whipped across his face.

They took aim and prepared to fire when the tarp over the back of one of the transports was lowered and every man in the truck pointed rifles and pistols right at Crick and Green.

Green didn't hesitate a second. "Take cover, get us out of Dodge, Sergeant."

The driver turned sharply as a volley of gunfire rained down on their Humvee. They ducked down from the windows as bullets pelted their armored vehicle.

"You okay, Crick?"

"I'm good, Major."

"Let's return the favor, Lieutenant."

Deafening bursts from the heavy machine gun erupted from the Humvee as he fired at the trucks. Their response was in vain, as the rounds missed at that distance.

Green thought for a moment. "Lieutenant, don't we have an AT4 in here?"

Crick came down from his perch and looked in the back.

"Got two of them."

"Well, feel free, Lieutenant."

Crick grabbed the pre-loaded RPG canister. He climbed back in the turret and laid the launcher on his shoulders. The Humvee bounced around making it difficult for him to get a good bead on the convoy. He decided to aim at the lead transport. He pulled the pin and squeezed the trigger. Smoke trailed behind the rocket as it closed in on the truck. The drivers of the transports saw what was coming and slammed on the brakes. The lead driver watched in amazement as the rocket passed right in front of his windshield.

Green's face tightened up. "Damn it. C'mon Lieutenant smoke those bastards."

Crick bent down and grabbed the last one. "It's too friggin bumpy, can't lock in on them. Get out ahead of them and stop, I'll have no problem then."

"Go, Sergeant!"

He floored the pedal, sped up ahead of the fleeing convoy, and stopped. Dust encircled them as Crick turned his body, and took aim at the transports. As he did this, he heard bullets striking the Humvee and caught sight of a pickup approaching their side.

CHAPTER 29

A pickup, driven by Elliott, came up fast on the parked Humvee. Scar and Meeks standing on the bed and leaning on the roll bar for balance, had M-16s pointed at the Humvee. They barreled across the dry, dusty field, out of the setting sun, which hid them from the view of the Humvee.

"Ram it," ordered Winters.

Elliott closed in as Scar and Meeks began to fire in short bursts at the armored vehicle. They concentrated their aim on the soldier perched out of the Humvee turret holding an AT4.

Bullets ricochet off the turret getting the soldier's attention and he dropped down into the Humvee causing him to lose his grip on the launcher. It rolled off the roof and onto the ground as they pulled away.

Scar and Meeks fired again as Elliott kept up the chase. The Humvee swerved and headed out of the field. Elliott followed suit and went after them.

Scar squatted and peered through the rear sliding window. "We won't be able to stop them, it's an armored vehicle."

Winters told Elliott to keep after them to get them away from the transports. For the next mile, they continued the chase, until finally letting them go and coming to a stop.

"Better to let them go, Captain. Wouldn't be too long before they had reinforcements, and then we'd be in a world of hurt," said Scar.

Winters turned to Elliott. "Think we can find that RPG?"

Meeks' eyes lit up. "Oh, hell yeah, be one fine addition to our small armory."

Elliott turned around and went back to the field. A few minutes later, Meeks yelled, "Stop! We just passed it."

Elliott backed up until he saw it in his side mirror. Meeks retrieved the prize and handed it to Scar.

Scar held it like a baby and broke out in a big grin. "Gentleman, this here is an AT4. Lightweight and quite destructive.

"It's not an RPG?" asked Meeks.

"No. Single use only."

"Well, I'm still calling it an RPG," said Meeks.

Scar shrugged his shoulders.

Winters turned to Elliott. "Well, let's go catch up with the others."

Elliott let off the brake and headed eastward to the main highway. Once on the pavement, he picked up speed, and twenty minutes later, they caught up to the transports. Winters wanted to get as far away from their pursuers as possible before they pulled over for the night.

An hour later, they pulled into an empty field and found a secure location far enough off the main road where they felt safe lighting a fire. The trucks parked in a large circle and the men disembarked. Getting out of those rough riding trucks put everyone in a better mood.

Winters' legs cramped up when his feet touched the ground. He tried working out the kinks while looking around at the men. Everyone was still pumped up with the excitement of the chase. Their animated voices reverberated as they chatted about the day's events.

Winters hobbled off to the side still trying to work the cramps out. Elliott walked over to him and handed him a jug of water. Winters grabbed it and drank the cool liquid.

"Thank goodness Scar suggested we split up after we left. No telling what might have happened had we not," said Elliott.

Winters didn't respond.

"Whatcha thinking about, Cole."

Winters took a moment. "I don't think leaving that grenade was such a good idea."

"Why not?"

"I don't know. I just think they might not have come after us had we not left them a booby-trap."

"It must have worked pretty good."

Winters took another sip and handed the jug back to Elliott. "Right, but think about it. They chased after us with only one vehicle, which was pretty stupid. Especially when they didn't know what they were up against, yet they came anyway. Only someone who was very angry would throw caution to the wind and do something like that."

"I'd imagine he was pretty pissed off."

"Exactly. You know up until this point, we've only been taking out their workers."

Elliott didn't respond.

"It's just that I don't believe for a second, all those soldiers agree with what's happening. Hell, we even left them a big ole note to leave their post, but then we turn around and leave a booby-trap."

"Yeah, I get where you're going with that."

Winters' tone changed. "Well, we've made it personal now and believe me I know what it is to want revenge."

CHAPTER 30

MARQUETTE COUNTY WISCONSIN

Winters kept thinking about the booby-trap they had left. It was cold-hearted and had only managed to enrage their enemy who would now have more resolve to find them and return the favor.

He shouldn't have listened to Nate. Seems every time he did, something terrible happened. He almost brought that point up to Elliott but didn't want to risk upsetting him. Since he and Nate were lifelong friends, it also ran the risk of him thinking it was petty. He then might turn around and tell Nate.

Winters let out a heavy sigh. He wondered if he'd put too much consideration into what everybody else thought, especially the other side.

He still couldn't accept that everyone involved was against them. There had to be soldiers who disagreed with this. Americans fighting fellow Americans, how could they want to be part of this? But then how did soldiers in other countries take up arms against their own? They had to be lied to. Are American soldiers different than other soldiers? Winters pondered that for a moment. Hell, yeah. But then why are they doing this? They had to have been lied to.

After taking a couple of deep breaths, Winters turned around and walked toward the men.

He entered the camp, where everyone greeted him, with some shaking his hand. The new recruits from Wisconsin were elated that they chased off the Humvee. Winters wondered how long their enthusiasm would last once some of their friends started dying.

A roaring fire had been started and now its flames danced high into the cold night air, giving off much-needed warmth and comfort to the Shadow Patriots.

Winters began. "Alright, I'm sure we're all thinking the same thing. And that is, we are, without a doubt, up against the damn military. It breaks my heart to no end to know that. If we don't have the support of our armed forces; then we can't count on help from anyone."

He looked at the faces staring at him. Some seemed as disappointed as he was. Others wore serious expressions. A few though still appeared optimistic.

"Hell, I'd like to know why they're doing this. We may or may not find out why." He paused for a moment. "More importantly, what are we going to do? Today we saw a lone Humvee come after us without knowing what they were up against and yet they came anyway. They were brave, arrogant and overconfident."

Someone shouted out. "They must have thought they had us by the balls."

At this, the men laughed and some cheered.

Someone else chipped in. "They don't though, do they?"

Again, laughter moved through the group.

"They thought we were just a bunch of old men," said another.

WARREN RAY

"But we are," someone shouted out in jest.

Winters enjoyed the lightheartedness of the men. "Yes, we are, but we're young at heart. But more importantly is the fact that we love our country, and I would wager to say most of us are willing to die for it."

The men all nodded in agreement.

Winters continued. "We can fight them and we can win. If Washington and his men could survive Valley Forge, then there is no reason why we can't show the same fortitude. We'll take it one day at a time and keep pushing forward till it's done."

Winters wondered where all that came from. Definitely not Mr. Hyde, he mused to himself. The positive response he received from them gave him confidence and made him think back to what the old man said about how they saw something in him.

He walked over to where Scar stood.

Scar patted Winters on the back. "Nice speech."

Winters nodded.

"We headed to Rockford tomorrow, Captain?" asked Scar.

Winters didn't respond.

"It's the nearest one from here."

"I'm pretty sure they'll have remaining Centers guarded by now," said Winters.

"Maybe and maybe not."

Winters quipped with a half smile. "Oh, like we'll have enough time before that major got back to the Patriot Center huh?"

"Well, yeah, but had we not dilly-dallied about we'd have been okay," said Scar.

"Ah huh."

"Let's at least go down and take a look. They may not have been able to round up enough extra guys for a defense yet."

Nate interrupted. "Well, we're not going anywhere till we can get these big trucks fueled."

Winters turned to him. "Are they all low?"

"The ones we just took are pretty much on empty, and with all the new recruits, we need lots of supplies."

Winters hadn't given much thought to re-supplying and arming this growing militia. The bigger they got, the more difficult the logistics would become.

He would also have to figure out what else to do besides shutting down the Patriot Centers. Destroying them all was out of the question, and if they wanted to have any real impact, they would have to go up against the Army or the National Police; quite possibly both. The thought made his heart skip a couple of beats because he knew if they were to engage either of those forces; then a lot of these men would die.

CHAPTER 31

Morning came and Winters woke to the smell of bacon frying. He thought this was the perfect aroma to start the day with. He sat up and saw one of the men with a skillet over a smoldering fire. Winters moved closer and grabbed a slice. His mouth began watering even before he took a bite. The smoky flavor of the bacon made him recall breakfast with his wife. She had always gotten up early and had everything ready for him and their daughter. She had been raised a farm girl and had picked up the habit of cooking mostly bacon and eggs from her mother. This spoiled him and the thought made him smile.

He continued to sit in a blissful state until Elliott walked up.

"Captain, one of the pickups is gone."

"What? Where did it go?"

Elliott shrugged his shoulders.

"Who's missing?"

"Haven't taken a head count yet."

"Damn. You know they could have just told us. We sure as hell can't afford to be losing any vehicles," said Winters shaking his head in disappointment.

Elliott surveyed the barren field. "This empty field reminds me of when I was farming. Right about now, I'd be getting ready to plant my fields. Would hardly have enough time in the day, be so busy."

Winters waited for him to continue.

Elliott took a long pause. "What about you?"

Winters crossed his arms. "I'd be working seventy hours a week trying to get the taxes done for my boss."

"You miss it?"

"You mean sitting at a boring desk job all day, or the stress?"

Elliott gave him a half smile.

Winters took off his hat and rubbed his forehead. "I miss going home at night."

Elliott tilted his head. "Hard to have imagined all of this."

"What about you?"

"With everything in the country going to hell for the past year or so, it feels good to be doing something meaningful, but then I wish we were fighting the Chinese."

Winters nodded.

They stared out over the expanse of the empty fields. There was a certain beauty in being able to see all the way to the horizon with no trees or hills to block the view.

Winters glanced at Elliott who seemed to be really relishing the moment. He wondered if Elliott felt as much anxiety as he did. Probably so, as it wasn't easy for any of them to come to grips with knowing you are fighting your own countrymen.

His thoughts turned back to his wife, how he wished she were here so he could seek her advice. She always knew when something bothered him.

Even in high school, he'd had a secret crush on her but was too shy to ask her out. She'd sensed his fondness and asked him. They dated throughout high school. After graduation, he had decided on community college instead of going away to a university and leaving her behind. Their relationship blossomed into a thirty-year marriage. He was always in a better mood when he was with her. In all their years of marriage, the two were rarely apart but now that he had been plunged into war, she was starting to become only a beautiful dream.

Meeks walked up with Scar. "Morning, Captain."

Winters snapped out of his thoughts and turned to them.

"Morning. Elliott informed me someone took off with one of the trucks."

Scar turned to Meeks. "Quiet little bastards. I didn't hear a damn thing."

"It's not like we're holding a gun to anyone's head," said Winters.

They walked over to the fire, grabbed coffee and food, and bantered amongst themselves. Soon, everyone was awake and moving around the camp; getting themselves ready for the day. Small talk amongst the men focused on those missing, and why they felt like they needed to go off the way they did.

"So, we headed to Rockford?" Scar asked Winters.

"We need to get supplies before we go anywhere."

"Surely, we can spare two or three of us."

Winters set his coffee cup down. "I don't think that would be such a good idea, if something goes wrong, we'll need everyone with us."

"Yes, we might, but then we might not. A few of us could go and just check things out."

Winters didn't answer.

Scar stubbornly tried again. "I know you're hesitant to split up the group, but it'd save time and more lives than if we wait."

Winters picked up his cup and took a sip. Scar's guilt trip started to work on him. He didn't want to endanger his men any more than he had to, but on the other hand, by not leaving right away, it meant a death sentence to the volunteers at the Rockford center.

"Okay fine, we'll go, of course, I'm assuming you want to go?" Winters asked.

"Yeah, I'm really not much of a scavenger."

"Uh hum," said Meeks without opening his mouth.

Scar smiled at him. "Well, you sure you can handle it with that little flesh wound of yours."

"Well, despite the agonizing pain, I can man up."

Winters turned to Elliott. "You up for this?"

He nodded.

"I'll go as well." Winters figured he would rather go with them, than worry all day while they scoured the countryside looking for supplies.

Nate came walking up. "Go? Go where?"

"Rockford," replied Winters.

"What about fuel and supplies? I told you last night we need to re-supply."

"I know, but at the same time, I'd hate to have any more of those Illinois boys get murdered because we needed supplies."

Nate didn't respond.

"Do you think we could siphon off enough gas for two pickups?"

Nate replied with an attitude. "That's not a problem. I take it the four of you are going?"

Winters sensed Nate felt left out. "Yes, and I really need your help rounding up supplies, and most importantly, keeping everyone safe."

Nate glanced over at his friend Elliott. "Fine. I'll get ya a couple of trucks ready."

He walked off.

Elliott got up. "He'll be okay."

Winters felt bad for Nate, but on the other hand, the last thing he needed was someone too gung-ho, who could get them in a bind.

Winters didn't like splitting up his forces. If one group got into trouble, how would the other know? Not having radios or any other kind of communication equipment put them at a disadvantage. A bad feeling swept over him thinking about it, and his stomach began to knot as he prepared to leave most of them behind.

CHAPTER 32

ROCK ISLAND ILLINOIS

Colonel Nunn sat at his desk reading the report from Major Green. He shook his head after finishing it. He was angry because of the situation he was in and wondered what was going to happened once Commandant Boxer arrived. He yelled out to his sergeant. "Have the Major come in."

"Yes sir," responded Sergeant Owens who turned to Green.

Major Green stepped to the room.

"Tell me about yesterday's events, Major."

Major Green stood before Colonel Nunn and gave him a complete rundown of the previous day's events, including the deaths of two of his men and how Lieutenant Crick was wounded.

"How's Crick?" asked Nunn.

"He's fine, the bullet just grazed his arm."

Green waited as Nunn took a deep breath and lowered his head to read the report Green had prepared for him. Green was surprised that Nunn hadn't yet blown a gasket, so he continued and showed him a picture of the message left on the building.

Colonel Nunn took the picture and read the message. "What do you think we're dealing with here, Major?"

"A bunch of old men who are nothing more than murderers," said Green.

Nunn looked up at him. "Well Major, seeing how they killed two of your men, I don't think we should underestimate them."

"Yes, well their action was completely unexpected. We certainly weren't anticipating any kind of resistance."

Nunn changed his tone. "Exactly. You didn't have your men properly prepared, and now we've got a hell of a mess on our hands."

Green continued his defense. "Well sir, I'm a little confused as to how prepared I should have been. Why would I expect someone to be shooting at us? Also, what exactly does this message mean? Are we killing innocent Americans?"

Nunn crossed his arms. "What the hell are you implying, Major?"

"It's a little strange that someone would want to take out these Patriot Centers. What do they know that I don't, Colonel?"

"I don't think I like your tone, Major."

"Quite frankly sir, I don't care. Two of my men are dead and another three injured. I want to know why?"

Nunn got out of his chair. "You are on a need to know basis, Major. Your job is to hunt these men down and I expect you to do your duty. Do I make myself clear?"

Major Green did not respond.

Nunn tried to control his anger. He didn't want Green to leave in too foul a mood. No telling what might happen. Green had a way with his men and they liked him. He could easily persuade them to mutiny. At some point, the major would learn what's really going on. Operation Wildflower was a delicate subject, and Nunn knew it wouldn't sit well with the men. Although the money was good, and he had made a deal to stay out of jail; bottom line, it even left a sour taste in his mouth.

"Major," he paused. "I will overlook your insubordination in light of the loss of your men. I'm not heartless. I know what it's like. However, you need to remember who your enemy is, Major. Despite our personal differences, it is not I. Now you need to get out there and capture the bastards who killed your men."

"Yes sir, I'm sure it'll just be a matter of rounding them up now that they've had their moment of resistance."

"We'd better hope so because I have some explaining to do to the head of the National Police. He's arriving here any minute."

CHAPTER 33

J ames P. Boxer, Commandant of the National Police, arrived thirty minutes late for his meeting with Colonel Nunn. The colonel needed a reminder of the gravity of this operation, and how a rebellion could easily thwart their plans.

Boxer wore glasses on his cherub-cheeked face and tried to part his hair to hide his balding head. He had a Ph.D. in Psychology and had worked in public affairs for the government for the past ten years. He had been instrumental in the ongoing propaganda campaign initiated by the new National Government. His use of political correctness had been most effective in subduing those in power and the population in general. This and his overall brown nosing had secured his current position.

"Commandant Boxer, please come in," said Nunn who towered over his visitor.

"Good morning, Colonel. A pleasure to meet you." Boxer extended his hand to give him a limp-wristed handshake.

"Have a seat."

Boxer sat down. "Colonel Nunn, let's get right down to business, shall we?"

Nunn didn't respond.

"Colonel, we cannot afford to have a rebellion on our hands and we certainly can't have anyone spreading vicious rumors. The media, will, of course, report what we tell them. However, if things continue to escalate, word will eventually leak out to the public, and then chaos will ensue."

Nunn nodded.

"So, in light of this, the National Police will be taking over. I'll need you to give us all the support I require."

Nunn protested. "The Military is not under the authority of the National Police."

Boxer looked confident. "It is now, Colonel. If you had done your job properly, we wouldn't be having this conversation. You think I really want to be stuck out here in Hicksville cleaning up your mess?"

A surge of energy exploded inside of Nunn, who wanted to reach across the desk and wring the arrogant bastard's skinny neck. He restrained himself only because he knew Boxer had powerful connections in Washington. He didn't like this guy, and he sure as hell didn't trust him. If things went south, no doubt the little weasel would put the blame on him. He had to be careful and play his cards right with Boxer, who was intelligent, for sure, but very arrogant.

"Commandant Boxer, I apologize, it just threw me for a second. We'll certainly give you all the assistance you need to crush this rebellion. What can I offer you immediately?"

Colonel Nunn's demeanor pleased Boxer.

"Oh, and one other thing, Director Reed wanted me to tell you he wants a meeting with you in Washington tomorrow. So, I've got my jet waiting."

CHAPTER 34

DAVIS JUNCTION ILLINOIS

The hour and a half drive from Wisconsin down to Illinois had been uneventful. They hadn't seen a single vehicle on the interstate. Besides a dwindling population, the lack of fuel and the increased cost attributed to the absence of traffic. The government controlled the distribution and kept a large portion for their exclusive use. Any fuel available on the market came at such a high price most people couldn't afford it. Routine driving was out of the question and vehicles were used only for emergency purposes.

The two pickups pulled into another little town south of Rockford, Illinois. It was a farming community, and like most others had a small downtown filled with dilapidated brick buildings. The obligatory grain silo stood as a tall sentinel, greeting all those who entered. The houses lined up on the main street needed their lawns mowed but that wouldn't be happening anytime soon.

Winters wondered if the Patriot Centers were all located in small towns to avoid too much attention to their real purpose.

They quickly spotted the Center by the large American flag flying outside. They parked the trucks one street over and walked to the back of an abandoned house to survey the area.

"Heck of a nice flag they got," said Meeks.

"Yes, it is," said Scar.

"Methinks, that flag needs to come with us."

Scar patted Meeks' shoulder. "We could use a nice flag."

"Seems pretty quiet, Captain," said Elliott.

"Sure does."

The four of them continued to watch the building for another thirty minutes. During which time, a couple of the workers came out to smoke, but there was no other movement.

Scar suggested he and Meeks go ahead and sign up. They debated whether the four of them should storm the place or just send in two volunteers. After some back and forth, Scar persuaded Winters to let Meeks and him go in alone.

"Okay, Scar, but I don't want you guys to take any chances, if you get nervous, get back outside and we'll cover your escape."

"No problem, Captain. We got this," said Scar.

They each stuffed a pistol in their waistband behind their Carhartt jackets and headed back to their beat-up truck.

Winters and Elliott watched from across the street as they pulled up to the Center.

As soon as Scar and Meeks got out of their truck, two guards, carrying shotguns, approached them.

They put their hands up and Scar asked. "Hey, what's with the shotguns, is this how you greet volunteers?"

"Never know what kind of trouble you get out this way," said one of the workers, who had a lazy right eye.

Scar smiled at the two. "Well, we're no trouble. We just want to sign up is all."

"Go on in, they'll get you taken care of."

Meeks held the door. Scar walked in and headed toward the man sitting behind a desk. The man was young and bald-headed with multiple tattoos running down his neck.

The tattooed man put down his coffee cup. "You guys are pretty early."

Scar came toward him. "We got done with all our errands and had nothing else left to do."

"Well, it's going to be a while. Our first run doesn't leave till the afternoon. You guys can take a seat and fill out this paperwork while you're waiting."

Scar leaned across the counter to pick up the questionnaires and pens and sat at the table sitting to the right of the entrance. As they both filled out their paperwork, a short man with a red beard, which matched his curly red hair, walked in from the back. He had an AR-15 hanging from a sling around his chest. He made eye contact with Scar and Meeks but didn't acknowledge them. He looked at his tattooed friend behind the desk who shrugged his shoulders.

Meeks curled his mouth into a half smile and raised an eyebrow at Scar miming, "What a strange man."

They finished filling out the one-sheet questionnaire with contrived answers.

Red Beard stared at Meeks and finally asked him. "Don't I know you from somewhere?"

Meeks replied. "I don't think so."

"No, I'm sure I do."

"Don't you hate it when that happens."

"Are you from around here?"

"No, live south of here."

"I'll remember, I never forget a face."

This made Scar and Meeks uneasy. With two guards outside holding shotguns and Red Beard with a semi-automatic rifle, their situation quickly became more tenuous than they had anticipated. They would need everyone to relax before they tried to draw on them. Plus, they didn't know if there was anyone else in the back. Scar motioned his head in the direction of the door and Meeks winked in agreement. They both got up and started to head out. Before they reached the exit, Red Beard spoke at them again.

"Did you play college ball?"

The question surprised Meeks. He initially thought about lying and debated it for a second, but decided to go ahead. "Yeah, I played."

"I thought so, you were a running back weren't ya?"

"Right again. You a big football fan?" asked a surprised Meeks.

"Die-hard Illini fan. You played for Iowa, didn't you?"

"You got me again."

"Now don't tell me, let me think," he said snapping his fingers. "Meeks, you're Meeks."

"Wow! I'm impressed with your memory, cause that was a long time ago."

"Ya, I was just a little kid, but I never forget a star player in the Big Ten, especially one who embarrassed us a time or two."

"Those were fun times."

"So, if you played for Iowa, what are you doing over here in Illinois?"

Meeks didn't expect this kind of questioning and wasn't prepared. He stood thinking of something to say, and finally said, "What do you mean?"

"Well, if you're from Iowa, why would you be over here?" asked Red Beard in an elevated tone.

"I have family in the area," replied Meeks hoping this would satisfy him.

"Family huh." He kept staring at Meeks while he continued to talk. "I ask only because of some trouble over in Iowa at another Patriot Center. So, we're just a little skittish here."

"Can't say as I blame ya."

The man kept his attention on Meeks and Scar, and the next few moments passed in an awkward silence. "Aren't you gonna to ask me what kind of trouble it was? Hell, if someone told me that, I'd be a bit curious about it."

At this point, Scar knew they were in trouble. He started to think about the pistol tucked in his waistband, but when he began to move his arm, Red Beard lifted his AR-15 and aimed it right at his face.

"Move back to the table," he yelled.

They both backed up until they hit the wall.

He grabbed their paperwork. "Well, look who we got here, Steven Cuyler and Thomas Barnes. That's really interesting cause I could have sworn I was just talking with a guy named Meeks. So, what's the deal here?"

CHAPTER 35

ROCK ISLAND ILLINOIS

Major Green sat at his desk, studying the map of the Midwest, trying to come up with a strategy to catch the rebels, when his sergeant came to the open door.

"Major, we got a report on some pickup trucks trying to get fuel from a closed down gas station over in Wisconsin."

"How long ago? Who reported it?"

"Ten minutes ago. Wakefield called it in."

"Wakefield? I thought he got killed."

"Apparently not, sir. He's pretty sure these are the guys we're looking for. He said he'd follow them and call us back."

"Sergeant, find Lieutenant Crick and tell him we need to be combat ready."

"Yes, sir."

While Green hurried to his quarters to grab his gear, he thought about the men he'd lost yesterday. This time, he'd take no chances when confronting the bastards.

After gathering his gear, he headed to the office. He made the first step of the stairs when the door opened up. A short bald headed man dressed in a suit and tie walked out and passed by without acknowledging him. Must be from the National Police, Green thought as he entered through the glass doorway, he took a right and headed for Colonel Nunn's office. Nunn stood at the entrance to his office staring out through the hallway window.

"Colonel Nunn."

"Major?"

"Wakefield just called, said he spotted some pickup trucks in Wisconsin. He thinks it's them. I'm headed up there now," said Green.

"You better hurry, because as of today we're going to be answering to the National Police."

"What do you mean?"

"The little weasel who just left my office is none other than Commandant Boxer and he informed me, he's been appointed to take over this operation."

"They can't do that, can they?"

"They can, and they have. Get these rebels rounded up today, Major, and we might get him off our backs," said Nunn sitting down in his chair.

"I will, sir."

"Oh, and I'm leaving for Washington for some meetings, so I'll be gone for a few days."

"Yes sir," responded Green as he turned around and left Nunn at his desk.

Major Green walked up the hall and stepped outside where Lieutenant Crick and the rest of his men waited. Clouds had moved in mid-morning and changed a promising beautiful day into a cloudy overcast one.

Green walked to Crick. "How's the arm?"

"Burns a little is all."

"We good to go?"

"All set, Major. This is going to be a hell of a day for us, sir."

"Let's hope so, Lieutenant."

Green slid into the Hummer.

During the two-hour ride, Green thought about the situation. He reached into his jacket and took out the picture of the message he'd found written on the wall of the Wisconsin Patriot Center.

TO THOSE OF YOU WHO ARE RESPONSIBLE FOR TAKING PART IN THE MURDER OF INNOCENT AMERICANS…

Green studied the picture. He wondered, who was being killed and who were the killers? Did it refer to Americans in the war out West? Or that the government shouldn't be fighting the war? Who were these people? Were they really volunteers or anarchists? Did something happen that he wasn't aware of?

The way Nunn had kept him out of the loop, he wouldn't be surprised if there was a lot he wasn't aware of. Nunn never gave a reason for anything; like, why burn down a bunch of houses. It was the strangest order he'd ever been told to carry out. Nunn definitely hadn't filled him in on everything.

Green held the note up again and reread it: FOR THOSE OF YOU WHO ARE FORCED TO PARTICIPATE…

He thought about this a few times. Who would be forced? Not the Center's paid workers. Of course, it couldn't be the volunteers because they had come to volunteer. The only thing he could come up with was the military, but surely, he would know about it. Regardless of the reasons, these Shadow Patriots killed two of his soldiers.

"Up ahead, Major," said his driver.

They pulled into the abandoned gas station, which sat just off the interstate. The place looked like it had been closed for a while. Trash was everywhere and grass grew out of the cracks in the concrete. Faded plywood covered the windows and the nozzles were missing from the pumps. As they pulled in, Wakefield got out of his car. He waved at Major Green and walked to the parked Humvees.

"Major Green," said Wakefield putting his hand out.

"Wakefield, could have sworn you'd gotten yourself killed yesterday," said Green, not returning the man's handshake offer.

"Yeah, that was a bad deal. After Colonel Nunn called, I didn't want to stick around. Wasn't sure when you'd get back. Real sorry to hear about your men getting blown up."

"Now, what can you tell me about these men you saw?"

"I was up there on the interstate," he said pointing across the field. "When I saw these three trucks parked over there, I thought it a little suspicious, so I slowed down to take a gander."

"What were they doing?"

"Wasn't sure at first, so I pulled over to the other side and snuck back across the road. They parked right over there, where they put the fuel in the tanks. They were siphoning gas into cans."

"Did you recognize any of these men?"

"No, and that's when I realized, maybe these were the guys you're looking for."

"Which way did they go?"

Wakefield pointed. "Over in that direction, they're only about fifteen minutes from here."

"You know where they're located?" asked Green.

"From way up there," he said pointing up to the overpass. "When they left, I was able to watch them for a couple of minutes, so I took off after them. They turned off into a field, don't know how far back they went but I figure until they couldn't be seen from the road and then they set up a camp."

"How can we find where that is?"

"In about five miles, just look for tire tracks to your right, heading into the field."

"Wakefield, you've been most helpful, I'll be sure to tell the Colonel what you've done here."

"Do you want me to come with you?"

"No, we can handle it from here. Good day."

Major Green got into the vehicle and they took off in the direction Wakefield had pointed.

He radioed Crick who was bringing up the rear of their convoy.

"You got your maps of the area, Lieutenant?"

"I'm looking at them now. It's all open fields out here but in about five clicks, there's a wooded area on the east side. It would be a perfect hiding spot."

CHAPTER 36

MARQUETTE COUNTY WISCONSIN

G reen spotted the tire tracks in the dirt. They indicated someone had been moving in and out of here recently. The field, like most others in the Midwest, was overgrown with weeds due to the lack of cultivating.

Green split his convoy of six Humvees into three groups of two. He would drive straight at them while the other two would come at them from the north and south, cutting off any possibility of escape. After giving the flanking groups a five-minute head start, he moved into the field at a fast pace.

Josh Bassett was Green's young corporal and he was up in the turret manning the M2.

"See anything, Corporal?" asked Green.

Basset focused his binoculars. "We got that tree line about a half mile up ahead."

"If they're still there, that's where they'll be," said Green who then got on the radio and ordered the other two groups to head to the tree line.

"Major, I see some vehicles up ahead, and our two transports."

"Are they moving?"

"Not yet."

As Green moved toward them, the rebels finally recognized them for who they were and scrambled to their vehicles.

Green yelled out. "Light them up, Corporal."

Bassett aimed at a vehicle backing up and sent off a burst of lethal projectiles into the front of the truck. The bullets rattled through the cab, killing both men inside. The dead driver collapsed with his foot on the gas pedal. The truck slammed into one of the transports, catching both vehicles on fire.

Bassett sprayed another volley of into a fleeing pickup. The men in the back screamed as bullets ripped through them. The truck continued to race forward. So, Bassett targeted the wheels with another barrage shredding both tires. The driver, his shirt soaked with blood, fell out of the cab to the ground.

Green and his companion Humvee came to a stop too far away for the camp's small arms to adequately respond. He had his soldiers continue to shoot at the fleeing men.

The two flanking groups executed the classic Hammer & Anvil attack firing as they approached. They had their enemy pinned down. Some of the pickups and the transports caught on fire as tracer bullets tore through the gas tanks. The spreading smoke gagged the men who tried in vain to put up a fight. Within a few minutes, one of the volunteers waved a white flag.

Green hopped out of his truck and glanced up at Bassett, not bothering to contain his pleasure.

"These old men aren't so tough now, are they?"

Bassett studied the men for a moment. "No sir, they're not, I'd say they're rather pitiful."

"Yes, they are," said Green.

Green watched from the side of his vehicle as his men moved in and took control of the situation. He had hoped for a bit more resistance so he could extract more vengeance, for killing his two soldiers, but they had given up, so he'd have to take them prisoner and transport them back to base. He immediately recognized this was going to be a problem because there were a lot more men than he had anticipated.

Bassett still stood in the turret. "Hell Major, look at them all."

"Didn't figure they'd be so many of them," replied Green.

He directed his men to give medical attention to the wounded, then walked over to his prisoners sitting on the ground. Green noticed that despite the loss of their friends, these prisoners didn't seem dejected. Perhaps it was an age thing, probably glad to be still alive after being shot at.

Green spoke up. "Who's in charge here?"

No one responded.

Green showed little patience and reached for his sidearm. Pulling the Beretta M9 out, he walked up to one of the men and knelt to his level. Resting the gun on his right knee, he repeated the question. "Who's in charge?"

"No one's in charge," the man answered defiantly. "We're all free men, we come and go as we please."

"What's your name, old man?"

The man raised an eyebrow. "Old man?"

Green leaned closer. "Well, you're older than me, so yes, it's old man till I get a name."

"It's Bill Taylor."

"Mr. Taylor, my name is Major Green, and you guys killed two of my soldiers yesterday."

Taylor gave him a dismissive look. "Don't know what you're talking about, Major."

Green snapped. "You don't? You didn't have anything to do with the attack on the Wisconsin Patriot Center yesterday?"

"My friends and I are just out here camping trying to have a good time. That is till you came in shooting up the place."

"Camping huh? Why did some of your friends try to leave when we came?" demanded Green.

"Wouldn't you, if you had the damn Army shooting at ya?"

His fellow prisoners chuckled.

"You have two of my transports here."

"We found 'em here. You should be more careful where you leave 'em.''

More chuckles.

Green stood up. "Mr. Taylor, I do believe you're trying to put one over on me. Tell me, why are you armed? You're not supposed to have any firearms."

"Can't be too careful these days, I heard there's a gang of killers on the loose."

The men continued to snicker.

"And it's our second amendment right to bear arms."

"It was your second amendment right, Mr. Taylor, you and I know full well that's no longer the case. No one is allowed to have guns."

Taylor turned his head. "I didn't vote for that. Did any of you guys vote for that?"

No's, could be heard from the prisoners.

"It wasn't up for a vote. All of you are in violation of the Government's ban on possessing firearms, and from what I can see, you're the killers we've been hunting."

Taylor spat on the ground. "So, you gonna execute us now?"

"I beg your pardon?"

"You gonna kill us?"

"Of course not. Why would we do that?"

Taylor glared at him. "Well, it's what you do, isn't it?"

Green looked perplexed. "We're going to take you in, and you'll stand trial for your crimes."

"Well, you got yourself a bit of a problem then, cuz you just shot up most of our vehicles, and we ain't all gonna fit into those Humvees."

"We'll find some transportation."

Green walked back to his Humvee and got on the radio. He was unable to report to Colonel Nunn because he had left for the meetings in Washington. So, he ordered some transport trucks to come out and pick up his prisoners.

CHAPTER 37

DAVIS JUNCTION ILLINOIS

A gun-wielding man was confronting Scar and Meeks, and their hearts pounded in fear. Scar knew it was going to be up to him to get them out of this precarious predicament. As he studied Red Beard, he thought about his options. They could wait for the right moment, pull their pistols and shoot their way out, or just wait for Winters, who by now, was probably wondering what was taking them so long. He remained calm and decided to try and talk his way out. He was getting ready to speak when the door opened and in walked the two guards from outside. Scar's heart sank when he realized his task had just gotten twice as difficult.

These guys reminded Scar of Decker. They were the same type of low life losers who thought of nothing but themselves. They would do anything for a buck, even if it meant killing people.

"What's going on here?" asked Lazy Eye.

"Well, we've got ourselves a couple of liars," said Red Beard. "This one is Steven Meeks, he was a star running back for Iowa back in the day, but he's calling himself Steven Cuyler, and the other one says his name is Thomas Barnes."

"I am Thomas Barnes," Scar said defensively. "Meeks changed his name because of his notoriety, he didn't want any special treatment. Hell, you even recognized his face, most people only remember him by his unusual name before they start treating him differently. I understand why you guys are jumpy. We heard what happened in Iowa, heard the news on the radio, that's why we didn't ask. Plus, I'm kind of intimidated by a guy holding a gun on me, so would you mind pointing that thing somewhere else?"

Scar hoped that by doubling down with a demand, he could confuse these guys, who seemed dimwitted.

"Yeah, put it down man," said the tattooed man behind the desk. "This is going to get handled anyway."

Scar and Meeks both knew what the comment meant.

"Don't worry yourself about these two guys," said Lazy Eye.

"Yeah, you're right," said Red Beard with a sneer.

"Sorry about the confusion guys," said Meeks reaching forward to the man and shaking his hand. "Had I known this would have caused so much trouble, I wouldn't have bothered. You cool?"

"Yeah, it's all good."

Scar wanted an excuse to get outside to talk to Meeks. "Okay, I need a smoke now," said Scar. "Anybody have a cigarette?"

The tattooed man got up from his desk and handed him one. He and Meeks walked out into the chilly air.

Meeks let out a deep breath. "That damn little leprechaun pointed his AR at my face."

"Leprechaun?"

"Little short red-haired guy, all he needs is a green jumpsuit, he'd be a dead ringer."

"Don't forget the pot of gold.

Meeks let out a laugh.

Scar shook his head. "I can't believe he remembered you."

"No kidding, of all the time and places to get recognized, just as I'm putting down bullshit answers. Friggin amazing."

Scar put the cigarette in his mouth, took out his lighter and lit it up. He inhaled the smoke, sucking it deep into his lungs.

"I'm thinking there's five of these guys here," said Scar.

"You'd think they'd have extra guys on guard duty or something."

"Right, especially with the way we've been hitting these places up."

"Unless there's more people in the back. Although, I'd think with all the yelling, they would have come to see what's going on."

"Kind of what I was thinking."

"Well, what do you want to do?"

"We can't leave now," Scar responded as he took another pull off the cigarette. The smoke raced into his lungs as smooth as it did ten years ago, before giving up his lifelong addiction.

Scar casually turned his body in the direction of Winters and Elliott, trying to locate them. A second later, the door opened and out walked one of the guards.

CHAPTER 38

Winters and Elliott lay on the ground next to an abandoned house. They continued to wait but were beginning to wonder what was taking Scar and Meeks so long. They were relieved their two friends stepped outside but then saw a guard walk out and join them.

Winters tried to ascertain what was happening by their interaction with the guard. He kept watching as Scar tossed his cigarette butt on the ground and snuff it out with his toes. They must have decided to do something else inside because Scar opened the door and held it for the guard and then Meeks. Scar put his hand on Meeks' shoulder and said something to him as they walked in.

As soon as the door closed, gunfire erupted.

Winters and Elliott both jumped up, pulled out their weapons, and ran across the street. As they reached the building, the door flew open. Both men stopped and pointed their pistols.

Scar timidly peeked around the door.

"Figured you'd come a running," said Scar.

Winters tried to catch his breath. "What happened?"

"Oh, nothing much, except this one guy, recognized Meeks from his college football days."

The three of them walked inside, stepping over the dead.

"Isn't that right Meeks?"

Meeks turned. "What?"

"You being famous and all."

Meeks hit his forehead with his hand. "Oh yeah, can you believe it, and I had just finished filling out the check-in form using a fake name."

Scar laughed.

"But leave it to ole Scar here to come up with a whopper. You should have seen him in action even strongly suggesting to them to get their guns out of his face. If I hadn't been so nervous, I would have peed my pants from laughing so hard."

Scar grinned.

"How'd you take them out?" asked Elliott.

"As we walked in, I had Meeks turn and face me, I looked behind him and saw everyone facing away from us, so we pulled out our guns and boom, they're done for."

"Yeah, that son-of-a-bitch went down first," said Meeks, pointing to Red Beard.

"What now, Captain?" asked Elliott.

"No point in hiding the dead anymore is there, Captain?" asked Meeks.

"No, can't say there is, let's get out of here," said Winters.

"Only after we grab that beautiful American flag out front," said Scar.

As the four of them walked back outside, they heard a vehicle come screaming down the street toward them.

CHAPTER 39

Winters with the other three, stood behind a truck bed holding their weapons as they watched the Ford F-150 skid into the parking lot. The truck stopped and out jumped Nate.

"What's happened? What are you doing here?"

"To tell you the damn friggin army came in and shot up our camp. They've got everyone prisoner."

"What? When did this happen?"

"Just over an hour ago."

"Anyone get killed?"

"Some did, not sure how many though."

Winters took off his hat and scratched his head. "They have everybody?"

"No, Burns, Murphy and I were still out getting supplies when they attacked. We were coming back when they moved across the field to the camp."

"They didn't execute them?"

"No! I mean, we thought for sure they were goners, especially the way the soldiers came in shooting the damn place up. Hell, they took out most of the vehicles. Our guys weren't able to put up much of a fight, after a minute or so they waved a white flag."

Elliott turned to Scar. "People actually do that? I thought that was just something from the movies."

"Hell, with those M2's blasting away," said Scar. "I'd probably wave one too."

Elliott turned back to Nate. "How long did you stay? I mean are you sure they're still prisoners?"

"I don't know, and I'm not sure how they're gonna to move them all, cuz they showed up in Humvees."

Winters asked. "Where's Burns and Murphy now?"

"They're keeping an eye on things."

Meeks broke in. "What are we going to do, Captain?"

Without hesitation, he answered. "We're going to go get our men back."

They turned to each other and nodded in agreement.

"That's what I like about you, Captain," said Meeks. "No fear and you got our backs."

Winters grunted to himself and then swallowed hard. Little did they know how scared he was, and worried about how to get them back, or if they would even succeed. All he knew for sure was he had to try to rescue his men.

They all headed for their vehicles.

Scar stopped. "Hold on a minute."

He hustled back to the building, reached up and grabbed the big flag hanging by the door. "Now we can go."

An hour later, the three vehicles were still speeding up the interstate. Nate took the lead, then Elliott and Winters with Scar and Meeks bringing up the rear. Winters sat in the passenger seat and thought the only good thing about the lack of fuel and an ever-dwindling population was; no traffic.

He tipped his head back and look up at the roof tapping his fingers on the seat. As fast as they were traveling, it wasn't fast enough. His thoughts raced from scenario to scenario that could be happening to his men right now. They had to get them back, even if it meant dying. If he didn't, he'd never be able to live with himself.

Nate slowed down to exit the interstate. He didn't bother obeying the stop sign and swung a hard right continuing north on a county highway. A few miles up, he turned into a field, which led them to the wooded area where Burns and Murphy were keeping an eye on the situation. After they parked their vehicles, Burns came out to meet them.

"Captain, am I ever glad Nate found you."

Winters extended his hand to him. "So are we. What's been happening?"

Burns gripped Winters' hand tightly. "They've just been waiting around. They shot up the transports, so we figure they had to send for some more."

"How many killed?"

"Can't say for sure but quite a few, they've been burying them right there."

They all walked further into the woods and found Murphy peering through a pair of binoculars. "Guys, you're a sight for sore eyes," he said, letting his binoculars fall to his chest. "Transport trucks just pulled in and they're loading up our guys."

"Which way did they come from?" asked Winters.

Burns pointed. "From the south."

They kept hidden from view as they watched what was going on.

"What's our play, Captain?" asked Meeks.

Winters considered their predicament for a few moments. "Do we have that RPG with us?"

"The AT4 is in the back of my truck," said Scar.

Meeks chuckled. "Never leave home without it."

"Hell no."

CHAPTER 40

MARQUETTE COUNTY WISCONSIN

To be able to take his men away back from the Army with only seven men, Winters' options were limited. So, he decided to, once again, rely on a tactical ambush. They determined their best plan would be to try to intercept them before they got onto the interstate. They mounted up and took off to be in place before the military could get ahead of them. The five pickups reached the end of the field, took a left, and headed toward the interstate. Having faster vehicles gave them plenty of time to set up.

A huge warehouse sat next to the entrance ramp of I-39. Elliott crashed through the gate of the chain-link fence that surrounded the empty building. The parking lot wrapped around to the back of the building where they parked, grabbed their weapons, and after climbing the fence, walked through a narrow, wooded area onto the entrance ramp.

Scar scanned the ramp. "This will do, Captain."

They split into two groups: Burns, Murphy, Elliott and Nate would take the tail end of the convoy, while Scar, Meeks and Winters took the lead. They all hid behind trees and waited.

The wait seemed endless to Meeks. "They are taking forever," he complained.

"We're not waiting for sports cars," replied Scar.

"Yeah, but still."

It wasn't long before they all heard the bellow of the engines in the distance. The transports downshifted to slow down, and one by one, they took the turn onto the ramp. In the lead, as expected, was a Humvee followed by another, behind them were five transports. Still turning onto the ramp and bringing up the rear were the remaining Humvees.

The lead Humvee started to pick up speed when Scar carrying the AT4, ran onto the road about thirty yards in front of it.

It came to an abrupt halt. Winters and Meeks both ran up to the lead Humvees sticking their rifles into the rolled down windows.

Winters pointed his weapon right at Major Green's face. "Don't make a friggin move. My boy up there is itching to try out the RPG, you so graciously left on the field for us."

Green smirked. "RPG huh? You sure he knows how to use that thing?"

"My, aren't we pompous," commented Winters.

Green grunted.

"I want you to get out of the vehicle slowly. Major Green, is it?"

Green did as he was told. "So, you can read name tags. Funny, I don't see one on you. Who do I have the pleasure of speaking to?"

"That's not important right now. The important thing is, you've got my men and I want them back."

"You mean all those old men I had no trouble rounding up?" Green retorted.

"Yeah, well you forgot a few of us, and it would seem we now have the upper hand."

"At the moment, old man."

"Tell your men not to make any threatening moves. If they do, I can assure you, you'll be the first one I take down."

Green slowly picked up the radio mic and reluctantly, once again, did what he was told.

Meeks ran to the back of each transport and was greeted with cheers as the Shadow Patriots jumped out of the vehicles. They ran to the side of the road and grabbed all the Colt M4's away from the soldiers. They then ordered them out and onto the ground.

Green gave him a scornful look. "Now what, old man, are you going to murder us like you've been doing?"

With a calm and steady voice, Winters responded. "I'm no murderer, Major."

"No? What about that grenade you left behind? You killed two of my men."

"Two of your men? Is that all? Your damn Patriot Centers have been murdering us by the hundreds."

"I have no idea what you're talking about."

Winters considered his response for a moment and then realized the reason for Green's line of questioning when he had pulled them over. "You really don't know, do you?"

Green didn't respond.

"What's been happening at these Patriot Centers," continued Winters.

Green responded disdainfully. "What I do know is you guys have been killing innocent workers at these centers."

"We're fighting because they've been killing us, Major. That's what these centers are all about."

Green shook his head. "I don't believe you. Why would they be doing such a thing, and if that's the case, why don't I know about it?"

Winters stared at him ignoring the question. "What I'm telling you is the truth. If you don't believe me, then go to each of the drop-off locations and walk around them. You'll find each one has a mass grave site filled with the dead. Perhaps your Colonel has been keeping things from you, Major."

Meeks walked up. "Captain, everyone is secure."

"Captain is it? You're in charge of these men?"

Winters didn't respond.

"What you're saying is the truth?" asked Green in a quieter voice.

"My friends, people I grew up with, are laying in one of those pits, I watched them being gunned down, Major."

"If what you're telling me is the truth, I can assure you, I wasn't aware of it," said Green earnestly.

"Had you known, would you have stopped it?"

"I have orders to follow."

Scar had walked up and looked at Green harshly. "You're not obligated to follow unlawful orders."

"Ex-military?"

"Marine."

Green straightened up. "Well, this isn't the same country you served, we have new laws and new directives. If someone is considered an enemy of the state, they will be arrested."

"Including a bunch of old guys," said Winters. "Welcome to the new National Government where all the old rules are out the door. Funny, you don't hear anything about these murders in the media. They must want to keep them a secret."

"Sounds to me like they're afraid of an uprising," said Scar.

"Well, they're getting one and it started with the Iowa Center," said Winters.

"You won't win, Captain," said Green mockingly.

"Why the hell not?"

"Because this operation must..."

Winters interrupted. "Operation Wildflower?"

Green gave him a quizzical look.

"I believe that's what it's called."

"Well, Operation Wildflower must be damn important to them. Because of your activities, Washington has directed the National Police to take over and put a stop to your little rebellion."

"The National Police?"

"Yes, they've even sent the Commandant from Washington out here to take over."

"Commandant?" asked Winters.

"He's in charge of the National Police."

"The government sent their top guy?" Winters paused wondering the significance of the National Police taking over.

"What are you going to do with us?"

Winters gave Scar a nod to follow him off to the side.

"Cocky son-of-a-bitch, isn't he?"

Scar agreed.

Nate walked up. "We should kill these bastards."

Winters shook his head. "They're prisoners, Nate."

"Yeah, so what? If you saw the way they came in with guns blazing, you might think differently."

Winters glared at Nate.

"Hey, they killed some of my friends."

Winters tried to keep his voice under control. "I understand, but we don't kill prisoners. Nor do they. As you can see the rest of our guys are alive and they even treated out wounded."

Nate stomped off.

Winters understood Nate's frustration, seeing friends killed was not an easy thing.

He turned back to Scar. "Let's take everything we can use from these guys, smash their radios and flatten their tires."

"Can't flatten Humvee tires," said Scar.

"You can't?"

"Nope."

"I did not know that. So, what do we do then?"

"Ask Nate."

"Ask me what?" he responded hearing his name.

"We need to disable the Humvees," said Winters.

"No problem, we'll just cut the battery cables."

Winters turned back to Scar. "We'll take the transports to get everyone out of here. We should tie the soldiers up too. Let them work up a sweat."

The Shadow Patriots moved down the column of trucks, taking whatever they needed. They also informed the soldiers, why they had taken up arms. Some of them became angry when they learned the truth. Others didn't believe them or didn't care.

Winters walked over to Scar who was tying Major Green's hands.

"Despite what you think Major, we don't murder people, even when we don't have the capability of taking prisoners. So, this is your lucky day."

Undeterred Green replied. "It is my lucky day. I now know what I'm up against and it isn't much. I can promise you, Captain, we will meet again."

"Major, I have no doubt I'll have the pleasure of tying you up, again." Winters turned to Scar and winked.

Scar looked down at Green. "Or perhaps, you could get yourself a conscience or a set of balls and come join us, we could always use a good soldier."

"That'll be the day," Green responded quickly.

Scar laughed. "A set balls or a conscience?"

Green didn't bother to respond as Scar and Winters walked away from him chuckling to themselves. The Shadow Patriots climbed aboard their rides and left, leaving the soldiers to squirm on the ground as they tried to loosen their bonds.

Winters fell into his seat with a straighter back and let out a sigh of relief. Getting his men back without firing a shot was a job well done. He took a moment to soak it all in before getting back to the problem at hand. He glanced over at Elliott who, since he was driving with just one hand appeared relieved.

"The head honcho of the National Police is here," said Winters.

"Can only mean one thing, Cole," said Elliott. "It's like the old man said, the whole stinking government is behind this."

"Indeed they are." He paused for a moment. "I don't know how or where this will end. I'm not sure how we're supposed to win or what winning even looks like now. We're barely hanging on as it is, Elliott."

"We just keep going, kill as many of them as we can."

"It's not good enough. They'll just keep sending more men, till they get what they want. They'll never stop."

The ominous statement hung out there like a cold, damp cloud putting a chill over their successful rescue operation.

CHAPTER 41

A cargo ship pulled into Port Duluth-Superior soon after midnight. The dock was empty of workers. Inside the ship, there was close to five hundred men from the Middle East. They had been quartered at the decommissioned Fort Drum Army Post in NY. Their training, which had just begun, had been interrupted by unforeseen events.

Their timetable had been moved up and now their voyage through the Great Lakes via the St Lawrence Seaway ended. It was the beginning of a long-awaited Jihad for these men. They had come to America, the Great Satan, to destroy her.

* * * * *

WASHINGTON D.C.

"You think Boxer can round up these rebels?" asked the billionaire George Perozzi, who was in his seventies. Although he was failing miserably, he made a desperate attempt to hang on to whatever youth he imagined was left, by spending a lot of time working out. He sat at a booth with Lawrence Reed in a District restaurant having a late night drink. Reed was a man who loved a good steak and it showed. His waist was bigger than his chest. He wore wire-rimmed glasses that sat too low on his nose. He and Perozzi were enjoying a Double Corona cigar.

"Commandant Boxer is quite capable. He'll have these rebels rounded up in no time," said Reed.

Perozzi paused and took a pull on his cigar. "Regardless, I've decided to make some changes in our plans."

"Oh, how so?"

"That little something we were saving for later."

"The terrorist cell you've been funding?"

Perozzi nodded and let out a cloud of smoke.

"How many men?"

"All of them."

Reed snickered. "All five hundred? That's a small army you've let loose."

Perozzi took another drag and blew a smoke ring. "Think of Sherman's march to the sea."

"Total destruction," said Reed, picking his Scotch up and taking a swig.

"Exactly. The citizenry will be begging for protection and will leave the area in droves."

"When and where?"

"They're to arrive in Duluth tonight."

"Tonight? When did you decide to do this?"

"As soon as I heard about the rebellion."

"Don't have much faith in Colonel Nunn, do you?"

"I'm not taking a chance with Nunn or Boxer. I want assurances that nothing goes wrong."

"Is Boxer aware of this?"

"He is. It's the main reason he's in the Midwest, I need him to be my eyes and ears."

"What about Colonel Nunn?"

"That's why I have him coming to Washington. I want to make sure he's on board when I inform him of our next step in this operation. As far as I'm concerned, Operation Wildflower is finished. We now move on to the next phase, Operation Sweep."

"Should I close the remaining centers?"

"No. We still need them to lure in our little band of rebels. Worst-case scenario, it will keep them busy while our Islamist friends get up and running."

"And Colonel Nunn?"

Perozzi straightened up. "I want Nunn to have limited contact with our new friends, perhaps an occasional show of force for appearances. I'm having Boxer keep him on a short leash. I don't want Nunn to be too successful if you know what I mean."

Reed laughed. "Yes, I do. I wouldn't worry too much about it, especially with that Major Green working for him. The boy is not the sharpest knife in the drawer."

"No, he's not. It wasn't too smart to let those rebels go when he had them right in the palm of his hand. He actually had them pulled over for questioning. What a dumb-ass."

Reed shook his head. "Can't argue with you on that one. But he's loyal enough and wants to be promoted, so he'll do what he's told in the end."

"I think he's a little too concerned with getting promoted," said Perozzi signaling the waitress for another round of drinks. He admired her backside when she turned to walk away. He wondered if she was wearing a thong or nothing at all underneath the short black skirt.

"So, we've got five hundred offloading in Minnesota, how many more men can we get?" asked Reed.

"As many as we need, but I need to strike a deal with them," said Perozzi taking the last sip of his Glen Velvet.

"Where will this bunch go first?"

"They're heading down through Minnesota, then they'll make their way south into Wisconsin," said Perozzi smiling and nodding to the waitress as she returned with the drinks. He decided she wasn't wearing anything underneath, a much more satisfying notion. She just started working there, so he'd leave her a big tip, perhaps she would show her appreciation on his next visit.

"Is Boxer still to report to me?"

Perozzi shivered. "Yes, I don't need to talk to him. I swear he'd talk the ear off a manikin."

"He is a bit long-winded, isn't he?" chuckled Reed picking up his Scotch. "He's a smart one though."

"Yes, he is and he knows it, which is his damn problem. You'd think a guy with a Ph.D. in Psychology would realize a little humility goes a long way."

Reed sighed. "Some people want everyone to know they're the smartest person in the room."

Perozzi grumbled, "Insecure people if you ask me. Does he ever get laid?"

"I've seen him with some ladies."

Perozzi gave him a sideways glance. "I don't mean hookers."

"Oh, well, then I don't know."

"No matter. Just give me the abbreviated version of his reports."

"Not a problem."

"These next few months will be crucial to the overall plan. We can't afford any more screw-ups," said Perozzi.

CHAPTER 42

MILLE LACS COUNTY MINNESOTA

As the afternoon wore on, the air got chillier by the minute. Several days had passed since the rescue, and the Shadow Patriots were using the downtime to rest and get organized. They set up a new camp back in Minnesota, outside of Little Falls, deep in the woods.

With no means of taking care of his wounded, Winters had them transported to various places for medical treatment. Most of the severely wounded had already died. The Shadow Patriots had sixteen killed and another ten injured.

Hospitals were quite limited, with many having closed over the past few years. As the economy collapsed, the closures accelerated. Once the war began, the government had drafted many doctors and sent them to California. Any hospitals left were in the larger cities. They were understaffed, and more than likely being monitored.

The Shadow Patriots had grown to just over a hundred. Some had trickled in as they made their way back to Minnesota. The members had also recruited others while out scavenging for supplies. Feeding these men had become a nightmare, which reminded Winters of one of Napoleon's more famous observations, "An army moves on its stomach."

The last couple of days hadn't been easy for Winters. The guilt he felt for his men being killed still haunted his dreams, which made sleep difficult. Why hadn't he been among the dead? Death would be preferable to this nightmare. Now every time he talked to any of the men, he wondered if he was talking to the next man to die. He shook his head, disgusted at how morbid his thinking had become.

He did take satisfaction in how they had reclaimed their men. The seven of them had come together to work as a team and overpower an entire squad of soldiers.

He walked over to where Burns, a former soldier, was showing the men how to disassemble, clean, and fire, the M16 and M4 carbines. Like most people, they'd only seen them in the movies. He wanted all the men to be proficient with every weapon they possessed even though not everyone had one. This was his second biggest concern, how to acquire more weapons.

Elliott came up to Winters. "Captain, ya got a minute?"

Winters nodded.

They moved away from the weapons instruction and walked over to a pickup.

"Captain, Murphy came back with some guy who's from up north of here," said Elliott. "I don't know if he's just scared or a bit on the crazy side."

"What's his story?"

"He said he saw a large group of Middle-Easterners walking west along the highway."

Winters raised an eyebrow. "Like American Muslims or something?"

"Nope. He said these guys were carrying rifles and backpacks."

"What? Where is this guy?"

"He's with Murphy getting something to eat."

They walked the fifty yards to a campfire where fresh game was being roasted.

"Captain," greeted Murphy.

"Murphy, I understand your new friend has an interesting story."

"It's not a story," interrupted the man.

"I'd like to hear it, I'm Cole Winters," he said putting out his hand.

The man finished shoving a hunk of venison into his mouth and wiped his hand on his red and black checkered flannel shirt before he took Winters' hand. He introduced himself as Eddie Perlee. He shook hands longer than necessary, then he finally let go and picked up another piece of meat.

"So, they tell me you saw some Muslims walking along a highway," said Winters.

"I guess they were Muslim, they definitely were not from around here."

"How many did you see?"

"Can't say for sure, I was driving along pretty fast and they were sitting off to the side of the road under some trees. There were fifty, seventy-five, maybe a hundred or so. I went by them real fast. Wasn't expecting to see something like that. What did strike me as really odd was, they were all carrying weapons."

Winters gave Elliott a concerned look.

"What kind of weapons?"

"Rifles, long guns, that sort of thing," he said talking and chewing at the same time.

Winters tone changed. "Which highway were they on?"

"Out on 210. I can't say for sure when, but they'll be passing through Brainerd," he said, filling his mouth with more venison.

"You sure they're not from around here?" asked Winters in a skeptical tone.

"I'm sure. These guys weren't dressed for no Minnesota weather and they had this hard look about 'em," reflected Eddie.

Winters turned to Elliott. "We need to check this out. Are Scar and Meeks back yet?"

"Not yet. It's getting kinda late, though. So, I'm sure they'll be back shortly."

"Okay, as soon as they are, let's get together and figure out what we're going to do here." Winters turned back to Eddie. "I really appreciate you coming down with Murphy and telling us about this. Feel free to stay with us as long as you like."

Eddie stopped eating. "Stay with you? Hell if everything Murphy's been telling me is true, I'll fight with you."

"Thanks, we can always use another hand." Winters walked off leaving the three of them to their meal.

Winters' mind couldn't get a handle on why a large group of Middle-Easterners would be running around in Minnesota. Could there be an enclave he didn't know about; like there was in Dearborn, Michigan? Maybe they were out in search of supplies or something of that nature. He wondered if the Government had anything to do with this but quickly discounted the thought as something way too far-fetched. Surely, no one could be crazy enough to arm a bunch of people who absolutely hated America.

What would they do if, on top of everything else, they had to deal with a bunch of Al Qaeda-ISIS types? The thought tied his stomach up in knots.

An hour later, Elliott found Winters sitting on the ground, staring into one of the campfires.

"Scar and Meeks are back."

"Oh good, where are they?"

"Getting something to eat."

"Have you talked to them?"

"No."

Winters had sat in the same position too long and his body had become stiff. He had to shift a couple of times before he was able to push himself up. He labored to straighten his aching back and gimped a few strides before stretching his legs loosened up.

Upon reaching the food table, he sat down with Scar and Meeks and proceeded to tell them about Eddie Perlee.

Meeks put down his fork. "Sounds pretty strange, what the hell could they be up to?"

Scar took a drink of water. "Oh, they're up to no good, that's for sure."

"Out looting, maybe," Meeks suggested.

"Could be, but why don't they have any transportation?"

Meeks shrugged and shoveled more food into his mouth."

"We need to go check it out first thing in the morning," said Winters.

"It's weird we're finding out about this," said Scar.

"Why's that?" asked Winters.

"Meeks and I ventured out to St. Cloud, which was like a ghost town, really eerie with so few people around. What we did notice was an unusual amount of National Police."

"What's an unusual amount?" asked Winters.

"Lots, several hundred or so."

"I suppose they're looking for us."

Meeks got serious. "So, we've got Al Qaeda to our north and National Police to our south. That's not a real good thing, Captain."

Winters shook his head. "No, it's not. Gentlemen, something tells me tomorrow is going to be a very bad day for someone."

Meeks eyed both of them. "Yeah, but for who?"

CHAPTER 43

LUCAS COUNTY IOWA

S ince being ambushed by the Shadow Patriots, Major Green's attitude was not good. He'd been stewing ever since he got back. They had managed to break their bonds and find a working telephone nearby. Then it had taken most of the night for help to arrive and get the Humvees running.

He obsessed with the thought that he might be involved in the murder of innocent Americans, which did not sit well with him and had given him a restless night. So, the next day, he and Lieutenant Crick took a ride up to the train station, to verify what he had been told.

Only Crick accompanied him to the station. Green thought that if he was able to confirm this information, he didn't want his men to know yet, and trusted Crick not to say anything.

Ever since Crick was little, Green could always count on him to keep quiet if either of them got into some kind of trouble. Like the time Crick had spied Green sneaking out of the house late one night, and living next door, tried to join his older friend. Crick had gotten caught but never told his dad why he wanted to leave the house, even after a severe whipping.

They arrived in the early afternoon during the start of a sprinkling rain. The charred remains of the burned station had weeds growing all around and in the cracks of the parking lot.

Green pointed. "Pull into the field over there."

"Check out all the birds."

"Drive toward them."

As they pulled up, some of the birds flew off. When they got closer, they saw the large burial pit. As soon as they stepped out of the vehicle, the smell of the rotting corpses assaulted their senses.

Crick winced and covered his nose with his gloved hand. "Oh my God, it's awful."

"We need to see it for ourselves, Lieutenant, so suck it up."

When they reached the edge of the pit, they both stood in silence, trying to absorb what they were looking at. There were hundreds of bodies strewn everywhere, and the birds were happily feasting on the remains.

"I've seen enough," Green said quietly.

They walked back to the Humvee.

Crick slid in and asked. "What are you going to do?"

Green considered the question for a moment. "I don't know, but I'm going to get some answers from Nunn."

"Think he'll tell you?"

"Oh, he'll tell me something, whether it's the truth or not, is another question."

"What about the men sir, are you going to tell them?"

"No, not right now. No reason to get them riled up," said Green, not pleased with his own answer. He knew this didn't satisfy Crick either, but until he confronted Nunn, he didn't know what else to say.

Colonel Nunn had gone to Washington for meetings, which Green thought was out of the ordinary. However, since Commandant Boxer was still here, he felt confident that both Boxer and Nunn knew all about these murders.

It made no sense to him. Why would they be killing the volunteers? Even more sickening was the top levels of the Government had apparently given its blessing. Or, perhaps it came from a rogue group not officially sanctioned by the Government. Was Colonel Nunn genuinely involved with this? If so, Green thought, then the U.S. military had also been complicit. The thought sent shivers down his spine.

Green had witnessed how the military had transformed in the past few years. The changes had been happening slowly for the last couple of decades. Men and women, with different attitudes and values, had infiltrated their ranks. They didn't have the same dedication to duty, and sense of honor that had once been the hallmark of a U.S. serviceman. For a lot of them, it was just a job and a paycheck in a lousy economy. He also noticed men with an attitude of entitlement and sensed the "We're in charge and can do whatever we want" mentality. It had started in the officer corps and filtered down through the ranks. All of this was leaving a bad taste in the mouths of the men and women who had signed up to actually serve their country.

During that time, Green had been flexible with those changes. However, the killing of innocent American citizens crossed a sacred line for him. The fact that they had hired such losers to do their bidding seemed proof enough, they were keeping this from the general population.

CHAPTER 44

BRAINERD MINNESOTA

Winters didn't get much sleep as he lay awake thinking about their situation. Having met Major Green and discovering his ignorance of the Patriot Centers, he wondered if maybe the Army wasn't that involved after all. Regardless, the head of the National Police now being in charge of capturing them confirmed the notion someone in the Government was giving the orders. Someone very high up.

Even more puzzling, if terrorists were in the area, how did they get here and what did they want? This was, of course, a rhetorical question. They want to kill infidels. American infidels.

The day had started early for the Shadow Patriots. The men ate, broke camp and packed everything into their vehicles. Winters and Nate established a rendezvous location where he, Elliott, Scar and Meeks would meet the body of their force after trying to find the armed Middle-

Easterners.

Elliott pulled out of the camp driving a Ford Crown Victoria.

"This is the first time we've all driven in a car," said Meeks from the backseat.

Scar turned to him. "Well, if you don't behave it might be the last time."

Meeks cracked a slight grin. "Behave. Define behave."

Scar smacked him playfully. "Not being a pest for one."

"I'm not being a pest."

"The day is young," said Scar. "See that sign, Baxter, ten miles, think you can handle it, little buddy?"

"I can do ten miles in the back seat of any car."

When they approached Baxter, a small town just west of Brainerd, they observed several cars heading toward them.

Elliott tightened his grip on the steering wheel. "Who in the heck is coming at us?"

"Whoever they are, they're sure in a hurry," said Winters.

"Should we pull over or something?"

"Slow it down."

Elliott slowed to a stop.

"Flag them down," said Winters.

Scar stuck his arm out the side window and waved as Elliott flashed the headlights. The lead car, along with all the others, came to a stop. Inside were two older ladies and a young mother with two children in the back.

"What's going on up there, what's on fire?" asked Elliott.

The driver frantically shouted. "You best not be going up there."

"Why, what's happening?"

Tears started streaming down her face. "They're shooting up the town, killing everyone and setting everything on fire."

"Who is?"

She tried speaking without choking on her words. "Al Qaeda, ISIS, whoever the hell they are, they're killing everyone."

She stepped on the gas and sped off. The two vehicles followed her with one of the drivers yelling out to not go any further.

Elliott and Winters exchanged glances.

"Step on it," roared Winters.

"Looks like we found out what they're up to," exclaimed Elliott.

Winters didn't respond.

Elliott got the speed up to nearly ninety miles per hour and blew right through the small town of Baxter. Crossing the Mississippi into Brainerd, they spotted a few teenaged girls running through a parking lot and heading north on Chippewa Street. Behind them was a group of men dressed in Middle-Eastern garb.

"Elliott," Winters barked.

"I got it, Captain," he said interrupting Winters, knowing what he wanted him to do.

Winters turned to the back. "Get ready."

The tires squealed as Elliott took a hard left. The five terrorists were oblivious to the approaching car. They were too preoccupied with hunting their prey.

Winters screamed out. "Run the bastards over."

Elliott came up fast behind the men. He had a clear shot. He punched the pedal to the floor. The engine roared alerting two of the slower ones, and both jerked their heads around. Their eyes got big as the car came screaming at them. The first one fell face forward as both left wheels ran him over. The second man flew straight up, bounced off the hood and landed on the pavement. The other three heard the screams and took off running in different directions.

Scar and Meeks leaned out the windows, with their weapons aimed at the fleeing men. They squeezed the triggers and cut them down.

The three girls stopped to watch as Scar and Meeks got out of the car, walked over to the terrorists to give them each a double tap to the head. The girls then turned back around and continued running up the street toward the woods.

Meeks and Scar jumped back into the car, and Elliott smoked the tires as he spun it around. At the end of the block, he took a left and headed down Washington Street. A few blocks later, he pulled into a parking lot behind a building. All four got out, to the sound of gunfire and screams.

They rounded the corner of the building to find people fleeing in all different directions. Scar pointed over to several men dragging a screaming woman away by her arms.

Scar and Meeks both took aim and fired at them. One fell. The rest ran for cover. The woman got up and ran away.

They now all fired at the fleeing terrorists.

Scar glanced around and saw more coming. He got Winters' attention and pointed. "Captain, we've got a hell of lot more than we can handle."

Winters looked around and saw a small army swarming in.

CHAPTER 45

A large group of terrorists came running up the street, shooting wildly at them. Scar and Meeks laid down cover fire as they all ran back to the car.

Out of breath, they all scrambled in. Elliott cranked up the engine and threw the car into reverse all while bullets flew past them. He spun the tires as he pulled out of the parking lot.

Winters turned to the back. "Sure as hell more than a hundred."

"At least twice that," said Scar.

Between breaths, Meeks leaned forward. "Remember that one who was thrown from the hood of the car? Damn, Elliott. Helluva a job."

Elliott drummed his fingers on the steering wheel.

The car flew back across the river and through Baxter.

"We're going back aren't we?" asked Elliott.

"Hell, yeah, we are," growled Winters.

"Bunch of pansy Jijis," replied Scar.

Meeks looked at him askew. "Jijis?"

"Yeah, you know short for Jihadis," said Scar.

"Jijis. Sounds feminine."

"Damn right brother, it's just what they are, little girly men."

Winters and Meeks nodded in agreement.

The drive to the rendezvous took about twenty minutes. After the initial excitement, they drove the rest of the way, in silence, each in their own deep thoughts.

Meeks was shocked at what he had witnessed. He'd felt as if he was inserted into a war movie about the Middle Ages, with the other side on an unstoppable rampage and winning. He wondered how something like that could be happening in America.

Scar sat in his seat disgusted. He wanted nothing more than to get back there and annihilate them. He didn't serve in the Corps to back out of a fight, especially when it could stop the slaughter of innocent Americans.

Elliott kept thinking about running the terrorists down with his car. The way he had slammed into them and the sound of their screams. A wave of exhilaration came over him as he thought about how he had reacted to the situation by sheer instinct. He had just stepped on the gas, locked his elbows and tightened his grip around the steering wheel. He'd never forget the frightened eyes of his victims as he plowed through them. They had the looks of certainty that they were about to die. Elliott curled his lip at the thought.

Winters again wondered the reason behind this and still couldn't wrap his mind around it. Who were these terrorists and how did they get here? He shook his head to get it out of his mind because he had a more vital question to be answered. How would the Shadow Patriots perform? Taking out Patriot Centers had been relatively easy because they'd had the element of surprise. However, taking on an army of terrorists was going to be a much more daunting task.

There was only one thing he knew for sure. By the end of the day, he was going to find out just how good their aging group of patriots were.

Elliott pulled into the new makeshift camp and everyone stopped what they were doing to wait for the news.

Winters got out and yelled to Nate. "Get everyone armed and ready."

Burns stood up. "What do we got, Captain?"

"Friggin terrorists, shooting up a town."

Burns wrapped his arm around Murphy. "Let's give them a proper welcome."

"Let Allah do that. We'll just facilitate the meeting," said Murphy.

"Make sure everyone has plenty of ammo, we're in for a long afternoon," ordered Winters. "Scar, can you map out our line of attack?"

"No problem, Captain," said Scar who turned to his fellow ex-servicemen Burns and Murphy. He pulled out a map and the three of them went to work.

Winters yelled to Meeks. "Now would be a good time for that RPG."

"I'm on it, Captain."

The men all gathered whatever was available, checked their weapons, loaded the vehicles, and headed back to Brainerd.

"We'll keep it simple, Captain," said Scar, once again in the back seat of an SUV with Meeks. "We'll park the vehicles just south of downtown. Go in, do a quick recon and find out exactly what we're up against."

As they got closer to Brainerd, smoke continued to climb high in the sky as the fires consumed the town. As soon as they crossed the river, they headed south and parked all the vehicles behind the high school.

The men exited their vehicles and formed a circle around Winters anticipating his orders.

Winters inspected them and saw some exhibited considerable anxiety, while others appeared impatient and ready to go. "I need Scar, Meeks, Burns and Murphy to recon. Everyone else stays here, till we find out where the largest body of them is concentrated right now."

The five of them took off running across a field and came up behind the public library. They ran across parking lots and crossed two more streets. They stopped when they came upon two bodies lying in the street. It was a mother with her arms around her child. Blood soaked through her dress making it difficult to see where the terrorists had shot her. Her little girl's eyes were open and listless.

Scar muttered under his breath. "Bastards."

As they moved further up the street, it was obvious the mother and child were not alone. The dead were scattered everywhere.

Thick gray smoke drifted overhead adding to the horrific scene and obscuring their view of the town. Gunfire rang out all around.

They kept pushing forward through the disturbing sight, finally reaching the downtown business section. They entered a three-story building, through the back door. A staircase led to the top floor. So, they climbed to the roof where there was an unobstructed view of the town.

All five of them crouched down and made their way to the edge.

Looking through his binoculars, Scar immediately sighted a disturbing scene.

"Got some Jijis over there. They're holding a small group of young girls, Captain," said Scar pointing.

"Seems they can't wait for their seventy-two virgins," quipped Meeks.

Scar spoke sternly. "Their wait is about over."

"They're mostly scattered all over the north part of town now," said Burns. "Over to the east, it appears more fires are being set."

Scar put down his binoculars and turned to Winters. "They've got their force pretty well split up, Captain. I think we should bring our guys up the same way we just came in."

"Murphy and I can handle the sniper duties from up here, Captain," said Burns.

"Okay, Meeks, go back and get everyone moving, and go get those girls," ordered Winters.

Ten minutes later, Meeks came back with everyone else and then headed off with five of them to rescue the girls. The rest split into two groups with Nate and Elliott each leading one. They spread out over a couple of blocks and took up firing positions.

Winters and Scar moved down one floor so they could shoot through the windows unobserved. Five terrorists came out of a storefront onto the street, yelling at each other in incomprehensible gibberish.

Scar raised his rifle and squeezed off a few rounds. Two of the Jijis were hit dead center and tumbled to the ground. The sound blended in with all the other gunfire and the crackling of the fires, raging through the town. The other three spent the remainder of their lives in a state of confusion. Winters joined Scar to clean things up and shot them dead. This attracted the attention of more terrorists, who began pouring out of the woodwork.

Ten, twenty, then thirty of the Jijis came running to where their five companions lay dead. They fired wildly, aiming at nothing, but hoping to hit whomever just killed their friends.

Burns and Murphy watched them run to the bodies of their friends. They patiently waited for more to enter into the kill zone. They turned to the right and noticed the men who had been holding the girls had left just one of their number to guard them.

Meeks and company had watched them leave. He snuck around from behind and crept up on the man, who was paying more attention to what was going on than to the girls. However, he still had his rifle pointed at his cache of virgins.

Meeks inched closer and put his finger to his lips to silence the girls. Pulling his knife from his belt, he got in behind the Jiji, put his arm around the victim's head, covered his mouth, and shoved the sharp blade into the man's throat.

"Let's get out of here girls," said Meeks dropping the dead man to the ground.

They didn't hesitate for a second and obediently followed Meeks.

"Do you have somewhere we can take you?" asked Meeks.

"Yes," said a cute blond girl of about twelve. "We're supposed to get across the river."

"Is there someone waiting?"

"Our Pastor will be there. When the shooting started, we got, like, separated from our youth group in the park."

Meeks instructed two of his men to make sure they were reunited with their Pastor before coming back. The girls took off, some giving Meeks a hug and thanking him as tears ran down their faces.

"Okay guys, let's get into this thing and kill these bastards," ordered Meeks getting up.

* * * * *

Winters and Scar were taking too much fire to their position. They exited the building from the back and ran to the end of the block. As they turned the corner, Jijis fired at them from across the street. A window shattered and out came an AK-47 drawing a bead on them. Scar raised his M-16, but before he could fire, the man fell out of the window courtesy of Burns who had been watching from his sniper perch. He and Murphy had been waiting and covering Meeks as he got the girls out of harm's way. Now they began to make use of their vantage point.

Another contingent of Jijis poured in from the east side of town, taking up positions against Nate and Elliott's men. Meeks brought his squad in behind the terrorists to effectively boxed them in.

The Shadow Patriots proceeded to rain hell down on the Jijis who screamed at each other as they tried to get organized. They broke out storefront windows in an attempt to gain a covered position. Their wounded yelled in agony as they tried to crawl to safety.

The Shadow Patriots engaged the enemy for the next twenty minutes. They had taken them off guard and were inflicting heavy causalities. Up on the roof, Murphy noticed the enemy's numbers below were dwindling. He stopped firing and looked up the street. He saw that the enemy was coming at them in such numbers that they looked like a massive swarm of hornets. Then, from the corner of his eye, he spied a rocket racing in on his position.

CHAPTER 46

The grenade smashed into the left side of the building, and the ensuing explosion threw broken bricks in every direction causing a part of the roof to collapse. Murphy had managed to throw himself onto Burns before the impact. Both men were stunned and neither of them could hear anything. Murphy pointed to the door and shoved Burns to get him moving. They crawled across the rooftop on their hands and knees and tumbled through the door and down the stairs as another RPG ripped through the area they had just vacated.

Elliott and Nate ran over and helped them out of the building. Both were still dazed but managed to tell the others about the arriving reinforcements.

"Let's get these guys back to the trucks," shouted Elliott to his men. "Nate, go and tell the Captain what's coming."

Nate quickly found Winters and Scar, "Captain, those RPG's hit where Burns and Murphy were at. They told us there's hundreds more of the Jijis coming at us."

Winters looked mortified. "Are they okay?"

"Yeah, Elliott's got them, and they're headed back to our rides."

"Good, run over and tell Meeks to fall back. Fight another day?" said Winters looking at Scar.

Scar nodded.

"Sure as hell a lot more than two hundred men."

"Probably a small battalion."

Winters tilted his head in confusion.

Scar recognized the look. "A good five hundred men."

Winters and Scar kept firing, covering the men who were falling back. Finally, a couple of blocks up, Nate, Meeks, and his squad were also retreating. They reached the corner of a building but the heavy fire kept them pinned down.

One of the guys handed Meeks the AT4. Holding it in one hand, he peeked around the corner for a quick look. A group of twelve Jijis huddled together between two buildings using the alley as cover. He signaled his men to initiate cover fire. They laid down an impenetrable barrage. Meeks shouldered the launcher and took a quick breath before flipping around the corner. He zeroed in on the target and squeezed the trigger. The rocket bolted across the street and detonated in a blinding explosion. It was a direct hit. Pieces of brick and mortar blew out onto the road. A blanket of thick, black smoke spread over the dead and out into the street.

Wasting no time, Meeks yelled for everyone to get moving. They had one more block to go before they would be able to safely escape. They were crossing the street when the enemy returned with their own RPG, which exploded into the side of the building where the last of Meeks' men were waiting.

The concussion knocked him and Nate to the ground.

Winters' eyes grew wide at the carnage and ran toward them with Scar behind him.

Scar helped them up. "You guys alright?"

Winters ran to check on the other men. The thick smoke spread throughout the block, giving them needed cover. He dragged one man to safety and ran back to see the others. They were still on the ground, and upon arrival, he discovered all were dead.

Winters was shocked at the horrific scene. He had witnessed the death of his friends back at the train station, but this was altogether different. These men were missing limbs and their burnt skin left them unrecognizable. The unsettling scene forced a gag reflex. He turned away and clenched his jaw to suppress throwing up.

The smoke began to clear making him a perfect target as Scar ran to him. "Captain, we need to leave now, there's nothing we can do for them, boys."

Winters, snapped out of it when he realized bullets were zipping past him. He ran back to the one he had dragged to safety. As he helped him up, more lead came flying down around them.

Scar laid down cover fire as they barreled across the street to the next block. Elliott and a couple of his men were on the opposite side of the street. They brazenly exposed themselves and started firing at the Jijis, giving their friends the cover they needed. They maintained the rear guard until everyone was a safe distance away, and then turned and ran back to the high school.

The Shadow Patriots loaded up, tore through the parking lot, up the street and finally crossed the Mississippi. Elliott and Winters brought up the rear of the escaping convoy.

They all took a right on Highway 371 and headed north. Just as Elliott had finally made the turn, Scar caught a glimpse of other vehicles coming from the west.

"Who in the hell is that?" he asked from the back seat of the SUV.

Winters reached for a pair of binoculars and tossed them to Scar. He grabbed them and turned around in his seat. "I'll be damned."

"Who is it?" snapped Meeks.

Scar put the glasses down. "It's the friggin National Police and they're coming straight for us."

They all looked at one another in disbelief.

"And here they come," grunted Scar.

Four black SUV's, with police lights flashing and sirens screaming, raced up on their tail end. Moments later a voice came booming through a PA system ordering them to pull over.

Winters shook his head at the confirmation that the cops were also involved. Major Green had not lied to them. He balled his hand into a fist and slammed it against the door. He turned in his seat and motioned to the back. "They're all yours."

"We're on it," said Scar smacking Meeks on the chest as he squeezed between the seats to get to the back of the big Ford Excursion.

Meeks handed him their weapons then joined him.

"Let's do a little show and tell." Scar turned his head. "Elliott, get this glass down."

Elliott fumbled with the buttons and at last found the one that controlled the back window. Wind blew through the SUV, as the glass came down.

Scar and Meeks leaned out the open window with M-16's. As soon as they did, the lead police car immediately slammed on the brakes. They heard the sound of crumpling steel as the cops all rammed into the back of one another. Meeks and Scar broke out in laughter, as they watched a live showing of the Keystone Cops. This gave them some much-needed relief after losing some of their men.

"What a bunch of dumb-asses," said Meeks trying to catch his breath.

Elliott kept the Excursion close behind the rest of the Shadow Patriots, as they drove away from the devastation that had befallen the small town of Brainerd.

Winters leaned back in his seat, slumped his shoulders, and stared out the window. His mind raced, thinking about what the old man had told him—not to trust anyone involved with the government. The old man had been right. They would not be able to count on anyone for help. They were all alone.

Before now, he had found it difficult to see everyone as the enemy. He had been sure there were some that didn't agree with the Patriot Centers, and that there was a line never to be crossed. He felt that line surely prohibited terrorists killing innocent women and children. His faith in mankind sank to a new low.

His mood then turned to anger as he thought about the men they lost today. They fought bravely and never questioned their task. Their sacrifice saved many innocent lives. He hoped his men wouldn't let their anger over losing their friends cause them to lose their focus because the National Police would now know their approximate location.

CHAPTER 47

ROCK ISLAND ILLINOIS

Commandant Boxer sat in an office he had commandeered and was fit to be tied when Lieutenant Stiver called in to report what happened when he ran into the rebels.

He screamed into the phone. "What do you mean you let them go? You're in a high-speed pursuit of the rebels and you let them go? Explain to me why you would do such a thing."

"They surprised us," defended Stiver.

"Surprised you how?"

"We were trying to get them to pull over and all of a sudden they stuck automatic rifles out of the back window of their SUV."

"Why didn't you return fire?" Boxer asked, still yelling.

Stiver hesitated. "Well, they didn't actually fire their weapons."

Boxer sounded bewildered. "What?"

"They didn't fire at us, not that it mattered because I reacted pretty quickly. I think they were just trying to scare us is all."

"Well, it worked now, didn't it?"

"Yeah, I guess so."

Boxer raised his voice. "You guess so? You slammed on the brakes causing a four-car collision, I would say they scared the crap out of you."

There was silence on the line.

"I don't know what else to say to you," said Boxer shaking his head.

"We were kind of lucky though. I mean if they had wanted to, they could have taken us out, but they didn't, so that was good."

Boxer ignored this. "What about our friends? Did these rebels engage them?" asked Boxer.

"Yes, and they took out a bunch of them."

Boxer quickly replied. "How many is a bunch?"

"Around seventy-five to a hundred. Some of their men got killed as well."

Boxer sat silently thinking on the other end of the line. These rebels knew about their friends from the Middle East. Not only do they know about them, but they killed a significant number as well. Reed was not going to be pleased.

"Sir, what do you want us to do?"

"Which way did you say they were headed?"

"North."

"I want you to get everyone up there, right now. Get those roads closed. We'll surround them and cut off any chance of escape. Do you understand?"

"Yes, sir."

Boxer threw the receiver down onto the phone's cradle, making it fly off his desk and crash to the floor. He tapped his fingers, wondering how to explain the information he had just received to his superiors. There was no point in trying to keep the news from them, as they'd find out soon enough. It'd be better for him to report accurately now than to get a call later and have to explain himself.

He rose out of his chair, picked the phone up off the floor, and set it back on the desk. He lifted the receiver and dialed his boss, Lawrence Reed.

Reed's secretary answered. "Director Reed's office."

"This is Commandant Boxer, is the Director in?"

"One moment," she said.

He used the wait time to compose himself.

"Commandant, how's it going out there in the Midwest?"

"You mean besides missing a good bourbon and a steak dinner," he tried to sound upbeat.

"You just left here, didn't you have some steaks shipped out there?"

"I did, but it's not the same out here in no man's land. I'd much rather be sitting at the Four Seasons enjoying a fine martini served by an even finer waitress."

"I'll give you that. You deserve combat pay for just for being stuck out there. So, what can I do for you?" Reed asked, not wanting to chat with Boxer all night about his woes. He, in fact, had a dinner appointment and did not want to be late.

"Our little band of rebels is still active."

"Go on."

"We made contact with them up in Minnesota. My men unexpectedly encountered them, but they escaped."

"Where exactly did they run into them?" snapped Reed.

Boxer knew this would anger him. "Up in Brainerd."

Reed didn't respond right away.

"So, they've seen our friends from the Middle East?"

"Yes. They engaged them as well," said Boxer in a lowered voice.

Reed shouted. "They engaged them? What the hell, did they kill any of them?"

"Don't have an accurate count, but we're probably talking close to a hundred. Some of the rebels were killed as well."

Reed drew a long breath. "What are you going to do, Boxer?"

"Well, that's the good news. They headed north, which means they've boxed themselves into a corner. Lake Superior is to the east. They can't drive into Canada without passing our border guards. I've got my men up there sealing off all the roads. They won't be able to get far. We'll soon be rid of them once and for all," he finished, feeling more confident than when he first got on the phone.

"You damn well better. We can't afford for them to know your men are in the same dammed area as our friends, and not doing anything about it."

Boxer didn't answer.

Reeds voice turned scratchy. "And we sure as hell can't have these sons-of-bitches shooting at them again."

"I understand."

"You need Colonel Nunn's men to get involved?"

"No, I've got enough in the area, with more coming in."

CHAPTER 48

CASS COUNTY MINNESOTA

Winters woke up to a cold, dew-covered morning. The moisture from the surrounding lakes in the Chippewa National Forest had created a fog so thick it made it difficult to see anything ahead. However, the fog enabled him to send out teams of scouts to recon the roads in relative safety.

The Shadow Patriots had arrived in their new camp last night in a bittersweet mood. On the one hand, they were glad to have killed a lot of the enemy, but on the other, they had lost ten of their friends.

The makeup of this force is comprised of several different clusters of men, each one coming from a common area. The people in each individual group had known each other for most of their lives. So, when there was a loss it was difficult for the group as a whole, but especially within the small groups. Yesterday's deaths had been spread out over several groups. Consequently, it affected the whole force.

All that morning, Winters could see that last night's low morale hadn't improved much. Not only the battle losses but also the idea of terrorists killing innocent women and children in their own country shocked one's senses. To top it all off, coming face to face with an enemy you only heard about in the news or had seen on TV had been a surreal experience. It remained their topic of conversation all night.

After yesterday's fiasco, Winters had noticed a little paranoia seeping into his thoughts. He looked around to observe his men, wondering if anyone was conspiring against him. As their ranks had grown, more than two-thirds had never had a say in who should lead them. Even though he had loathed the position, and hadn't thought he was up to the job initially, he now felt responsible for the group and wanted to see it through.

Hearing the bullets whiz by his head had made him wonder when he'd be the one they mourned. He let out a sigh thinking it'd be a lot easier dying than watching his men die or having to watch his country fall further into despair. He took a deep breath thinking about just how far America had fallen, with no end in sight. It was like living in a horrible nightmare, still hoping to wake up and find it nothing but a bad dream.

Elliott approached Winters, who was sitting on the tailgate of a truck. "Captain, Scar and the boys are back."

Winters turned away from him and wiped his eyes. "How are the roads?"

Elliott sat down next to him. "Not good, looks like they've got 'em all blocked."

Scar, Meeks, and Nate, holding coffee and power bars in their hands, walked over to complete the tactical leadership.

Winters nodded as they approached. "I take it we're surrounded."

Scar set his coffee on the truck bed. "They must have been moving in all last night."

"We shouldn't have stopped last night," said Winters.

"Wouldn't have mattered much," said Nate. "Most of the trucks are low on fuel. We wouldn't have gotten much further anyway."

"Now what?" asked Meeks.

"Don't seem like we have a lot of options," said Elliott.

Meeks choked on his coffee. "We have options?"

With a harsh voice, Nate said. "Oh, we got choices all right. We either give up like a bunch of pussies or kill as many of those sons-of-bitches as we can. Quite frankly, I think it's pretty obvious what we should do."

"I'm with Nate on this one," said Meeks. "I'm not giving up."

Elliott got off the tailgate. "It won't take them long before they get us all, Nate."

"Yeah, well I'd rather go down fighting."

Meeks patted Nate on the shoulder and looked at Scar.

Scar shrugged half agreeing.

Nate turned to Winters. "Well, Captain, I think it's settled. Question is where do we want to fight them, north or south?"

Winters stared into the distance looking for an answer. He agreed with Nate to kill as many as they could, but then he knew Elliott was right. The cops had them surrounded, and would eventually kill them. There had to be a better way out of this. He remembered how they had come together, calling themselves the Shadow Patriots because they kept to the shadows while chasing the enemy, coming and going as they pleased, making the bad guys question their existence.

What was so different about this situation? Nothing. Nothing at all. Winters kept searching for a solution. Then his face got flush as an idea struck him, instantly lifting the weight off his shoulders.

"Guys, I've got an idea."

Everyone turned to him.

"Remember when we first formed together as a group. We kept our existence a secret for as long as we could. You know, cleaning up our messes and making it seem like we were never there."

They all looked at each other and nodded.

"It's our namesake and it worked like a charm," continued Winters.

Meeks gave Scar a resounding pat on the back.

Winters turned to Nate. "Nate, I know you want to take them head on and I'm with ya, but we're at such a disadvantage."

Nate shrugged.

"More than likely, we've got most of the National Police force surrounding us. Right now, we're just not ready to go head-to-head against something like that. So far, we've been the ones picking the time and place."

Nate spoke first. "What are we going to do then?"

Winters took a second before he answered. "Guys...we're going to walk out of here. This fog will give us enough cover to get away."

They all stared at Winters in disbelief.

"What about the trucks and all our stuff?" asked Elliott.

"Take what we can carry and dump everything else in the lakes, should buy us some time."

"It'll be tough for some of the guys," said Elliot.

"Some of the guys," snickered Meeks. "More like most of us, we're no spring chickens."

Winters held up his hands. "I don't see any other choice. At some point, they'll start closing in on us."

Scar threw the rest of his coffee on the ground. "Well, let's get to it."

The men broke off and started to prepare.

An hour later, the Shadow Patriots were good to go. Every man had taken what they thought they'd be able to manage and left the rest inside the vehicles, which they sunk in a nearby lake the local Minnesota guys knew about.

"Captain?"

"Yes, Burns?"

"I was talking with Bill Taylor and he knows a place we can go."

"Oh?"

"Yeah, he says he's got an old friend up north of here who has a farm on the outskirts of Big Falls."

"How far is that from here?"

Burns pulled out a map and gave him an approximation of their location in the Chippewa National Forest. "It's at least forty miles."

"The wooded countryside won't make this any easier," said Winters, shaking his head.

CHAPTER 49

ST PAUL MINNESOTA

Commandant Boxer sat in the plush surroundings of his temporary home located in the suburbs of St. Paul. The house used to belong to a wealthy lawyer, and like the majority of the population, he had moved to the warmer climate of the South. By the indication of the man's wealth, Boxer assumed he hadn't ended up in the camps, like the common people. He was probably with his family sipping margaritas in Florida or somewhere in the Caribbean. The well to do in America were able to set their families up somewhere nice during the transition of the government, mostly facilitated by bribery of government officials.

He thought about how lucky he had been to live in D.C. at the time, and to have a government job. His input to the propaganda program was a stroke of genius and had facilitated his rise to power. The new bosses certainly were gracious to those who enabled them to control the masses.

The position of Commandant had its benefits, but only if you were in Washington. Here in the Midwest, there was no nightlife or decent food. As soon as he caught the rebels, he'd head back home. He would use his aptitude for lying to convince Perozzi, that Colonel Nunn could keep an eye on their Islamic friends.

The loud ring of the phone snapped him out of his daydream.

He paused before picking up the receiver. "This is Boxer."

"Sir, it's Lieutenant Stivers."

"Where are we, Stivers?"

"Sir, we've not been able to find them as of yet. All the roads have been blocked since last night, but so far, nothing."

Boxer not satisfied. "What about the woods?"

"We're searching them now. I've got a couple of our search and rescue dogs helping out as well."

"Good thinking Stiver. I'm sending you a helicopter, should be coming in this afternoon."

"That'll be a big help."

"Keep me posted Stivers."

Boxer hung up the phone and reclined back in his chair. He felt confident he'd have them today.

*   *   *   *   *

James D. Stiver Jr. was young to be a lieutenant in the National Police, but his father; James Sr. was a thirty-year veteran of the Sheriff's Department in Virginia. The last fifteen of those as the elected Sheriff of Loudoun County, and as such, he had many connections. These allowed the younger Stiver, known as Junior, to work his way up rapidly, despite his poor performance.

When the Government nationalized all the city and state police departments in the country, Junior, with the help of his father, was able to secure a position in the newly formed National Police. They sent him to St. Paul as the station commander. Not the greatest location, but a prime position, one that he couldn't resist.

He was out of shape which made his figure look odd in the black assault uniform. It also didn't help his appearance any to never wear a hat on his shiny bald head.

He turned to Sergeant Durbin. "You got Jake and Elwood out searching yet?" He was referring to the department's German Shepherds.

"Got 'em both out in the Chippewa. Hell, if they're in there, those dogs will find 'em," said Durbin.

Durbin was, yet another, political appointee. His family were friends with the Stiver's and he had come with Junior to the National Police. He'd only been a Sheriff's deputy for two years.

"Should we bet on which dog will find them first?" asked Stiver.

"I said, if they're in there."

"Oh, they're in there alright. Ain't no way they got past our roadblocks."

"Well, Junior, it seems to me, we got two bets then," said Durbin.

"Are ya saying you'll bet me a bottle of Jack on it?" asked Stiver

"That's what I am saying. Jack it is."

"Alright, now which dog you want to go with?"

"I'll take the younger Jake, he's a bit more anxious to please than ole Elwood."

"Another bottle?"

"Yer on," said Durbin putting his hand out to Junior.

CHAPTER 50

The Shadow Patriots had been hiking through the thick forest for two grueling days to escape the National Police. At first, the men moved swiftly, but after a day of rough terrain, they were tired. Some of them had stumbled and twisted their ankles, while others got leg cramps and various other injuries. All of which slowed them down. They had plenty of water from the endless lakes they had to walk around but were running low on food.

The demanding march took their minds off the loss of their friends back in Brainerd and also helped them bond, as any such activity tended to do. With so many new recruits, it was needed.

They were about to cross an open field when they heard a helicopter. They had been hearing the chopper off in the distance for the last couple of days. Winters tried to remember the last time he'd seen one. In the past year, other than an occasional military jet high in the sky, no one had seen any air traffic. All the airlines were out of business, anyone traveling by air was a government official, on government-owned jets.

He stood in silence and looked up into the gray sky. He noticed rain clouds were moving in, which would make it even cooler. The clap of the helicopter's rotors grew louder as it blew past the trees where they hid. Crossing the field, it flew low, circling the area, and then back in the direction it came from.

"Should we make a run across the field, Captain?" asked Elliott.

"Let's wait a bit, hate to see them come back this way. How much farther you figure?"

Elliott pulled out a map. "Not much. We're about right here, and we need to get there. Maybe only another five miles."

"We should send someone ahead and see if we can make contact with this guy."

"Meeks and I'll go," volunteered Scar.

"Okay," said Winters, "but you'll need Taylor to go with ya. Where's he at?"

Taylor lifted his canteen. "I'm right here."

"Can you go with these guys to make contact with your friend?"

"I won't have to walk my ass back here, will I?" he asked impatiently.

"No, we can have somebody else do that," Winters responded looking at Scar who cracked a smile.

Once Winters had learned how Bill Taylor had sassed Major Green when they were attacked, telling Green they were just camping, he had instantly liked the man. He'd admire anyone who was facing a situation like that and could still put up a fight.

"What your friends name?"

"Peterson."

Taylor started walking away. "Well, let's go, boys, we ain't getting any younger."

Rain began to fall as the men hurried across the open field. Once they reached the protection of the woods, the advance team left the rest of the group behind.

*　*　*　*　*

Word came to Stiver late on the first day that Jake had picked up the scent. He led them to what looked like a makeshift camp. Elwood ended up getting the fix on the Shadow Patriots northern escape route.

"Jake might have found the camp, but Elwood got 'em hot on the trail," argued Stiver.

"Had Jake not found their camp, we'd still be holding our dicks," retorted Durbin not wanting to lose on their bet.

"Yeah, but we'd still be at the camp were it not for Elwood. Instead, we've already gone fifteen miles. Hell, we'll have those old geezers this afternoon. I mean, come on, how fast can they walk? Hell, I'm surprised we haven't found any of them lying on the ground, dead from a heart attack."

"You wanna double down on that, Junior?" offered Durbin.

"What? Find a dead one?"

"No, not a dead one. When. When will we find them? Today or tomorrow."

"Please, with Jake and Elwood on the trail, we'll have them by this evening," said Stiver.

"I'm going to say late tomorrow afternoon, that'll be three days. I think these geezers are a bit more motivated."

"Okay. You're on. We'll call the last bet a draw, even though I think Elwood won. Still, they were in the forest, so you owe me a bottle for that one."

Durbin gave him a dubious look.

*   *   *   *   *

Later that night, a soaking wet Winters greeted Mr. Peterson. "It's a pleasure to meet you, sir," he said extending his hand. Winters noticed for an old man, he moved around like a youngster. His full head of hair was white as snow and his skin was dark, giving him a striking appearance. His excellent posture made him seem taller than his five-eight frame.

"Taylor filled me in on all you've done, sure do wish I was a bit younger and could join you," said Peterson.

"You look like you can handle yourself."

"I try to stay in shape."

"You'd be doing us a big favor if you could let us stay here for a few days. We've been hiking, and as you can see, we're pretty beat."

Peterson looked at the weary men.

Winters walked with him. "Also, we need to restock our supplies."

"You boys have come to the right place. Between the house and the barn, I've got plenty of room. I can help you with the supplies too. I used to own a sporting goods store. Got some inventory left over. Once the economy collapsed, I was put out of business early on. Nobody had any money, plus I couldn't get anything new shipped in. Whatever you want, you boys are more than welcome to it."

They moved to the back of the house and out to the barn. As they entered, Peterson threw a tarp to the side to reveal boxes of tents and sleeping bags.

Winters looked in awe. "This is great sir."

"You're welcome to all of it. Got a few compound bows and some arrows in there as well."

Winters nodded in satisfaction.

The men settled in for the night, with most dozing off as soon as they got food in their stomachs.

Winters stayed up and chatted with Mr. Peterson. He discovered he had things in common with the man. Ten years back, his wife had also died of cancer, and his kids were scattered across the country. Neither of them had any close relatives in the area. He had done three tours in Vietnam and earned a silver star and two purple hearts.

After some good conversation, Winters climbed the stairs to a guest room, to sleep in a bed for the first time in what seemed like an eternity. He lay down on the soft bed and thought he had gone to heaven. He instantly drifted off to sleep.

*   *   *   *   *

Jake and Elwood had sniffed twenty-five miles of dirt before they lost the trail in the late afternoon of the second day. A thunderstorm moved in, bringing heavy rain, and by morning had washed away any remaining scent.

Stiver pulled out a map of Minnesota and zeroed in on the route they had been on and noted the next town was Big Falls. He reported to Boxer.

CHAPTER 51

BIG FALLS MINNESOTA

The next morning, Winters got up and took a well-needed shower, his first in some time. The hot water cascaded down his back, soothing his aching muscles. The steady flow had such a hypnotic effect that he had to force himself to turn off the water. He was surprised the area had power and wondered where it came from. He gently cleaned the scab on his wound, which was still tender to the touch. It would leave a nasty looking scar but otherwise was well on the way to healing.

The shower put him in a good mood, which improved, even more, when he thought about how lucky they were to have made their escape yesterday. He felt even luckier to have a safe place where they could relax and recuperate from their long march. Since the farmhouse was out away from town, he figured they would have a few days to rest.

He dressed and went downstairs to the kitchen.

Mr. Peterson looked up from the stove. "Morning Cole, a couple of your boys went out on an early morning hunt and got themselves a buck with one of my bows. Got it cooking over a fire."

"Really, that's great. Who was it?"

He shook his head. "Don't remember their names, big fella, kind of funny, him and his friend. They're the ones who came in first with Bill."

"That would be Scar and Meeks."

"Yeah, that's them."

Winters moved to the stove. "What are we cooking here?"

"Oatmeal, I got quite a bit of this stuff left over from my store."

"Wow, I can't thank you enough, sir."

Mr. Peterson stopped stirring and looked at Winters with a thoughtful expression. "There's no need to thank me. What you guys have done and are doing…can never be repaid, by anyone."

Scar walked in from outside. "Morning, Captain."

Mr. Peterson glanced over. "There he is."

"What did I do?" Scar asked putting his hands up.

Winters smiled. "Morning, Scar, heard you and Meeks took down a buck."

Scar laughed. "Yeah, I've got to give credit to Meeks on that one. Even with his little flesh wound, he's a hell of a shot with a bow."

They all walked outside. Scar carried the large pot of oatmeal, while Winters brought out sleeves of plastic cups and spoons.

Most of the men had gathered around the fire, where the deer was cooking on a spit. Winters noticed the men looked to be in better spirits than when they arrived. Amazing what a good night's sleep could do for a person. They chatted aloud, some offering culinary advice, while others talked of their own past hunting trips. It would appear they had put Brainerd behind them.

Meeks, who was supervising the cooking of his prized buck, looked up and waved to Winters, as he approached.

He greeted the men at the fire and acknowledged the others, who stood around in groups. He participated in the friendly banter and listened, for probably the hundredth time, Meeks relating the details of his early morning hunt with Scar.

The Shadow Patriots gladly took advantage of the hospitality Mr. Peterson offered. They took hot showers, washed their clothes, listened to music, read books, and rested their weary bodies. Some sat by themselves, or in small cliques, while others enjoyed the camaraderie of the larger group.

Winters could not be any more pleased with their stay at the farm. It felt like they were on vacation. He just hoped staying here wouldn't put them, and Mr. Peterson, at risk.

CHAPTER 52

ST PAUL MINNESOTA

Boxer paced the floor of his office attempting to compose the verbiage he would use when reporting the loss of the rebel's trail to Reed. He knew Reed would kick the info up to Perozzi. He would have to word it carefully; otherwise, he'd risk losing his position and fall from their grace. If this happened, it would never be the same when he got back to Washington, if he got back. Knowing Reed, he'd leave him out here in the wilderness.

The ring from his phone snapped him back. He reached for the phone and answered it.

"Yes."

"Commandant, we just got a report from our station up Big Falls," said his assistant.

"Go on."

"We did as you asked and checked the power usage in the area. We found an immediate and considerable increase on a farm north of town."

The years before the collapse of the economy, the government had taken control of the utilities and regulated all power usage. The power companies did this by installing smart meters in every home and business. This also turned out to be a great way to monitor any unusual activity in a particular house.

"How unusual?" asked Boxer.

"More than double the normal use," he replied.

"Now that is interesting. Get me Stiver."

Five minutes later, the phone rang in his office. He grabbed the receiver and answered. "Boxer."

"You wanted to talk to me?" asked Stiver.

"I just received a report from the NP station in Big Falls, seems there's a significant increase in power usage out on a farm. I want you to go check it out immediately."

Lieutenant Stiver arrived at the farm late in the afternoon with twenty of his men and had more coming in. They parked their cars down the road and crept into the woods that ran parallel to the long driveway.

He had them spread out southeast of the property line. This gave them a clear view of the house and the barn behind it.

Stiver surveyed the farmhouse through a pair of binoculars. He spied men walking around the grounds, going in and out of the barn and a small group sitting by a fire. With a satisfactory look on his face, he gave the signal.

They opened fire.

CHAPTER 53

BIG FALLS MINNESOTA

The Shadow Patriots were enjoying their day of relaxation at the Peterson farm. The day had turned out to be a beautiful spring day, with not a cloud in the sky. The rain had stopped early in the night and now a cool breeze blew across the farm. Some of the men were taking naps in the barn to avoid the chill.

Winters stood in the kitchen with Nate and Mr. Peterson, heating water for soup, when the gunfire started. Everyone stopped what they were doing and looked at each other's alarmed expression. They dashed into the living room, which faced the driveway, peeked out a window, and saw the cops hiding in the woods.

Pandemonium set in as gunfire rained down on the Shadow Patriots. Everyone took off in different directions taking cover. Some ran inside the house, most others to the barn. It took only a moment before everyone had grabbed his weapon and started returning fire.

Winters took hold of Nate's arm. "Go find out where everyone is and get back here."

"You got it, Captain."

He turned to Mr. Peterson. "Go to the back entrance and wait for me."

Winters ran upstairs to the second floor to get a better view and looked out a window to get a better view. He saw how their situation would continue to deteriorate if they didn't leave right away. Besides the cops firing at them from the woods, he noticed more cars coming up the country highway.

He ran back downstairs and found Scar and Meeks firing from the back entryway. "We need to get everyone out of here. More cops are coming in."

Scar stopped firing. "We need to get to the barn and into the woods behind it."

Winters nodded in agreement.

Nate came running back in.

"Captain, everyone's in the barn except Elliott and four or five others. They're pinned down out by the fire pit."

Winters looked at Scar.

Scar grimaced. "That's a good thirty yards for them to run to the barn."

Winters thought for a moment. "We still got that last grenade?"

Meeks turned his head. "In my backpack snuggled up next to our flag."

Winters motioned him to get it.

Meeks returned holding his backpack.

Scar turned to Winters. "Meeks, Nate and I can handle the cover fire."

"I'll get Mr. Peterson into the barn," said Winters.

They all hurried to the side door.

"Mr. Peterson, I'm afraid I've gotten you in a bit of a bind."

Without hesitation, he responded. "I may be older than you, Cole Winters, but I wouldn't have missed this for the world."

Winters raised his eyebrow, impressed with his attitude.

Scar instructed Meeks on the grenade, and then he and Nate bolted out and laid down a barrage of cover fire. They kept it up until Meeks came out, pulled the pin on the grenade, poised his arm back, and threw it like a football into the midst of the entrenched National Police. They ducked down and took cover. Seconds later it blew.

The grenade exploded in spectacular fashion taking out two cops and wounding several more. The blast effectively stopped them from firing while they took cover and tended their wounded.

Winters and Peterson ran to the barn, while Scar, Meeks and Nate kept up the cover fire.

Elliott and two of the others got up and ran, leaving two of their friends by the fire, dead.

Winters and Peterson reached the entrance to the barn, where they were met by Burns and Murphy, who continued firing at the cops.

"We need everyone out the back and into the woods," he yelled.

Everyone grabbed whatever they could and moved out the back door. Winters hustled back to the front and met Elliott as he reached the doorway.

"You okay?"

"Yeah, got two dead though."

Winters gave him a reassuring nod.

He turned to Scar. "Think you guys can cover our exit? Give us some breathing room."

Scar nodded.

"Where we headed?" asked Elliott.

"We can only go north," Winters responded.

"Canada?"

"How far is it Mr. Peterson?"

"Twenty miles with some open terrain."

CHAPTER 54

The U.S. military dared not enter Canada. The British, at Canada's request, had sent troops to help them protect their border, and neither side wanted a confrontation.

U.S. and British relations had been strained over the past decade and had totally dissolved once the American government nationalized. The Brits had dealt with their own problem of attempted government takeovers by foreign nationals. They forced mass deportations on those who had participated. The process had been painful with uprisings all around the country, but in the end, Great Britain had regained her sovereignty.

With the Chinese Army fighting the Americans on the West Coast, the Canadians took no chances with their security. With its common border, many Americans had fled to Canada seeking refugee status. This became a logistics nightmare. Canada had no quarrel with the American people and helped them in any way they could.

Winters ran into the woods thankful to have escaped the farmhouse. Had the cops been better organized and more patient, they would have had the whole place surrounded. Of course, if he had been smarter, he would have had his men guarding the perimeter, and this would never have happened. Winters had felt safe and hadn't even considered having guards on duty. He wondered how the National Police were able to locate them. The house was out in the country with no close neighbors. They hadn't been firing any weapons, which could have attracted attention.

"Another mystery," thought Winters.

Scar had his men set up just inside the woods, to see if any cops would give chase. More cars came barreling up the driveway, while the original force was still firing on the house and barn.

Scar chuckled to himself. They had no idea the place was empty.

They kept this up for another five minutes before they finally stopped. Immediately, the cops spread out all over the property. Four of them came out of the back door of the barn and headed into the woods where the Shadow Patriots had made their escape.

Scar looked over at his men.

Nate loaded an arrow onto his new compound bow, began to pull the string back a bit and fluttered his eyebrows at Scar.

Scar signaled him to wait.

The four cops moved into the woods with trepidation. Thirty yards in, they stopped and looked around. They stopped talking and strained their ears listening for any unusual sounds. After a few moments, they continued their advance.

Scar, Meeks and Nate followed the four National Policemen leaving Burns and Murphy to continue monitoring the entrance to the woods.

They moved from tree to tree while keeping an eye on their pursuers. The four cops split up into two groups.

Nate whispered to Scar and Meeks. "I'm about done with these guys."

Scar agreed and handed Meeks his bow. "Here, you're better at this than I am."

Meeks and Nate each strung an arrow, moved out from their cover, and came up behind the two closest cops. They both took aim. A whoosh broke the silence, as they launched their arrows at the same time. The two cops fell to the ground with a thud. One cried out in agony sending out an alert.

The remaining two turned and ran toward the cries. They came over a small ridge with drawn pistols leading the way and saw their friends on the ground. They darted their heads looking for the enemy as they rushed to their fallen comrades. As soon as they reached them, Meeks and Nate slipped around their cover and let loose a second pair of arrows.

One of the cops fell dead to the ground when the arrow passed through his body. The other one dropped his gun in shock looking at the metal shaft halfway through his stomach. His hands trembled attempting to grab it in hopes of pulling it out. This only increased the pain, and he dropped to his knees, moaning in agony.

Nate sprinted toward the cop and kicked the arrow shaft so that it completely penetrated the man's body. He yelled out a torturous cry before taking his last breath.

"Bastard," said Nate.

Meeks turned to Scar with a surprised look.

Scar shrugged.

Before they started to head for Burns and Murphy, they grabbed the gun belts off the four bodies. Suddenly, gunfire interrupted the silence of the forest. It had come from the direction of the farmhouse, and they immediately ran toward the noise.

Moments later, Burns and Murphy came running toward them, with cops not too far behind. They took up positions and waited for Burns and Murphy, whose faces lit up when they saw them. Then they opened fire on the pursuing National Police.

CHAPTER 55

ST PAUL MINNESOTA

Boxer sat impatiently in an office he commandeered at Police headquarters in downtown St. Paul. He was waiting for news from Stiver, about the farmhouse when the phone finally rang. "This is Boxer," he answered.

"Commandant, it's them all right. They just took out six of my men, but I've got another twenty on their tail as we speak. I'll have all my men in the area within hours, sir."

"Best news I've heard all day," said Boxer gleefully, not caring in the slightest about the six dead men.

"They're trying to make a run to the border."

"How far is it?"

"Depends on which way they go, it's at least twenty miles or more. The good news is, they're on foot."

Boxer started laughing. "They're on foot? This is going to be a piece of cake. Let's get out ahead of them. We'll shut off their escape."

Boxer depressed the cutoff switch on the phone, then dialed Reed's office. He couldn't wait to tell him. He worried the longer it took for good news, the more likely he'd lose his standing in the district. This was not something to leave to chance. Rumors flew around Washington like a tornado—fast, uncontrollable, and devastating.

"What's your status?" asked Reed.

Boxer tried to contain himself as he spoke. "Sir, we've got those old bastards trapped in between Big Falls and the Canadian border, which is twenty miles away. The best news is that they're on foot. So, we'll have them in no time. I've got men coming up from the rear and more being transported north of their position."

"Excellent news, Boxer."

CHAPTER 56

KOOCHICHING COUNTY MINNESOTA

Winters led the escaping Shadow Patriots away from the farmhouse at a quick pace. He had no doubt they would invariably be pursued, and he wanted as much space between them and the cops as possible.

The sounds of a gun battle began to erupt from the direction of the farmhouse. The inevitable wasn't long in coming; Scar and his men were being engaged by the cops. He ordered everyone to pick up the pace while he and Elliott rushed back to their aid.

Winters stopped when he saw them approaching. "Everything good?"

"We're good. Took out a bunch," said Scar.

"Yeah, they'll tread lightly but they'll still keep coming after us," declared Burns.

Winters nodded. "I need scouts on either side of us and behind us."

Scar turned to Burns and Murphy. "Meeks and I will cover our six if you two will guard the flanks."

Burns and Murphy readily agreed.

Winters jogged back to the front completely lost in thought. The Shadow Patriots started out as the hunters but were now the hunted. Again, not what he had envisioned at the beginning when they "volunteered" him to be the leader. Having cops on their tail meant a loss of control, which went against the bookkeeper in him. Every number had a place and he had known where to put it. Now, they didn't stand a chance and he was unsure of what to do. They were on the run pretending to be able to escape to Canada. He would keep up this charade up for as long as it gave the men hope, but in all likelihood, their journey would end either tonight or in the morning.

Winters turned to Elliott. "What would you do if you were them?"

Elliott thought for a moment. "I'd be getting a whole bunch of guys up in front of us."

Winters took a deep breath. "Yeah, that's what I'd do too. So, we're pretty much walking right into their hands."

"Yep."

"I'm going to have to make up something to tell the men, cuz by morning we're done for."

Elliott didn't respond.

They stopped talking as they continued to walk both lost in their own thoughts and wondering the same thing—when would the cops capture them?

Winters looked back and saw Mr. Peterson. He wondered if he would be able to hack it. The man had been so gracious with his hospitality, and now was being punished for his good deed. As the saying goes, no good deed goes unpunished. No truer words were ever spoken.

Winters slowed down and to walk beside him. "How are you holding up Mr. Peterson?"

Peterson cocked his head smiling. "Are you kidding? I'm thinking I could still kick your ass."

Winters grinned in agreement.

Peterson spoke in a more serious tone. "Cole, this is the gutsiest thing I've done in a long time."

"And what would be the gutsiest thing you ever did?"

"Vietnam. This one time, our platoon was out on patrol, my squad got separated, and before you know it, we were ass deep in Charlie, got ourselves completely surrounded."

Winters' interest increased. "What did you do?"

"Waited till nightfall. Night can be your best friend or your worst enemy. We made it our friend. We created a diversion and found a weak link in their force. Once we had the diversion up and running, they let their guard down and we slipped right on by them."

Winters' eyes grew big and a shiver ripped through his body.

"Mr. Peterson, I could kiss you."

Peterson wrinkled his forehead.

With an excitement written all over his face, Winters ran back up to Elliott and grabbed him by the shoulders.

"What's with you?"

"I've got an idea. We need to get everyone together before sundown. Where's Nate?"

Elliott started to answer but Winters had already taken off to find him.

He raced past the men who were still moving forward. Most greeted him while others simply nodded as he hurried by. He found Nate and told him to go find Scar and Meeks and get them up here on the double. He also sent another volunteer to go get Burns and Murphy.

Twenty minutes later, away from the others, they all waited for Winters. He joined them and asked for their individual reports on the movement of the National Police.

Scar spoke first. "Well Captain, Meeks and I have noticed as the day wore on, the slower the cops moved. They've fallen further back than I would if I was them."

"We scouted our flanks, Captain," said Burns. "They have more men to the west of us than the east."

Winters nodded. "And we can assume they've got plenty of men waiting at the border. So, they've got us surrounded. They're doing exactly what we would do if we were chasing them. Now if they have more men to the west, they must be thinking we'll likely be heading that way."

"A lot more trees over that way," said Burns.

Scar added. "Don't forget we're between two rivers."

"And just before the border, it's big open ground," said Burns.

"The border agents will have no problem picking us off," said Scar, snapping his fingers.

Nate bristled at this and offered. "We should keep to the trees and have ourselves another old fashion shootout."

Meeks looked at Nate. "I'm with you again brother. Let's go down fighting, rather than be captured."

"Yeah, you can count me in too," Scar said raising his weapon.

Winters waited patiently for them to finish. "Guys, I've got an idea how we can get out of this."

Nate gave a half smile. "Here we go again."

Winters raised both of his index fingers at Nate. "Yeah, I know, but hear me out. Burns, you say they have more men to the west. So, it would make sense for us to go and try to break through their lines on the east, correct?"

"Yes," said Burns while the others looked at each other in agreement.

"Well, instead of us trying to break east, we go west. They'd certainly never expect it."

Burns gestured with his hands. "But how?"

"We don't fight them, we slip by them like we did the other day. We create some kind of a diversion to the east, which will make them think that's where we're trying to break out. Their guys to the west will either let their guard down, or get all excited, and head east to try to help. In doing so, they'll pass right by us."

Scar was the first to see the simplicity of the plan. "It's brilliant, Captain. We just need something convincing that they'll fall for, hook, line and sinker."

Nate rolled his eyes. "I don't know how you keep coming up with these ideas of yours."

Winters laughed. "It's just half an idea though. We still need to come up with the diversion half."

Nate replied. "Believe it or not, I think I got the other half. And no, it doesn't involve attacking them head-on. Well, it kind of does, but not really."

"I'm all ears," Winters said.

CHAPTER 57

Elliott walked across a small field and found Winters sitting down, still removing bullets from their casings and emptying the gunpowder. A light wind made the work tedious. The sun had set, and it would be completely dark in thirty minutes.

Winters heard Elliott approach and asked. "Everyone in place?"

"You betcha, Captain, found a bunch of thick trees, that'll keep them hidden. What about the others?"

Winters stood up. "We're almost done."

"Think this will work?" asked Elliott.

Winters shrugged his shoulders in a non-committal way.

"Got to hand it to my buddy, Nate," smiled Elliott. "His gung-ho attitude finally came in handy."

Winters let out a breath and nodded in agreement.

The two of them sat down and finished filling the last sack of gunpowder. Burns and Murphy had returned and were ready to pick it up.

"This wind is blowing from the west," said Winters.

"Couldn't have asked for better weather, no rain and windy," said Burns.

With little sunlight left, they plodded through the woods to the field where Scar, Meeks and Nate were finishing the set.

Upon arriving, Winters spoke quietly. "Are we ready gentlemen?"

"We're good to go, Captain," said Scar.

They all walked to the center of the open field, which was approximately fifty yards long and a hundred yards wide.

Scar began the instructions. "We got ten separate stockpiles of various weapons, five on each side of the field. As you can see, we put strips of white cloth on some branches, so we'd have an easier time finding them on the run. Once we begin, we'll give it ten minutes or so before Burns and Murphy start the fires. After that, everyone run back here. Any questions?"

They all looked at one another and shook their heads. Elliott and Nate then hiked across the field to the west side, while the others advanced to the opposite end.

The plan was a simple one. They hoped to draw the National Police in by setting up a fake gun battle. Each man would run back and forth to each of the stockpiles of weapons and fire them. This should create confusion in the ranks of the cops as they listened to the different types of guns that were engaging in the deceptive faux battle. Winters was relying on the fact that the police would think their fellow officers were involved. They would want to help them and be eager to finish off the old men at the same time.

The cops on the west side of the river would want to get in on the battle. The location of the fight wasn't going to be too far from a county road that had a bridge crossing the river. This was where the rest of the Shadow Patriots would wait for the cops to abandon their positions. They would then have the safe passage they needed to get to the border.

Burns and Murphy, using gunpowder, would set a fire along the edge of the field, and with the slight breeze from the west, would carry it into the woods. This would add to the confusion by igniting two piles of ammunition they had left behind. The additional gunfire would continue while the seven of them would head back across the field to meet up with everyone else.

Meeks was the first to fire his weapon. He pointed it toward the sky and let off a couple of spurts. This was followed by Winters and Scar. Finally, Elliott and Nate got in on the ruse. They all ran up and down the field, spreading the gunfire around as much as they could, trying to convince the cops there were more than a few men involved. The gunfire echoed high in the sky. There was no doubt the other side was listening intently and wondering what was going on.

CHAPTER 58

Lieutenant Stiver sat down to get something to eat, which he desperately needed. There had been little time since they'd been on the hunt for the old men. He felt confident they would soon capture these so-called Shadow Patriots. He had them boxed between two rivers with cops on either side. He also had plenty of men ahead of, and behind them. They had no chance of escaping.

The sounds of battle rudely interrupted Stiver's meal. He immediately got up and joined his men to try to determine where the shooting had come from. Everyone had a different opinion about what types of weapons they utilized.

Stiver grabbed his radio from his side pocket and pushed the button down. "Durbin, what's going on over there?"

"I don't know," he replied.

"What do you mean, you don't know?"

"My men are spread out over a lot of ground. I don't know where they're all at."

"Same here," came Hoyer on the radio. "I can't say for sure where everyone is either. We've been behind them all day, so there's no way they've backtracked on us."

Stiver spoke earnestly. "Well, it sounds like someone got a little too close."

The radio squawked. "What do you want us to do, Junior?"

"I'm thinking," said Lieutenant Stiver pacing back and forth among his men who stood and waited for an order.

The gunfire continued to rage on.

"Give me a map," said Stiver.

He unfolded the map while someone beamed a flashlight on it. Stiver got back on the radio. "Durbin, there's a road up ahead. It'll get you across the river. Get over here ASAP. Everybody move in, I repeat move in."

Stiver spun the rifle off his back and ordered an all-out attack.

They spread out and hurried through the woods. The blackness of the night and the wooded terrain made maneuvering extremely difficult. Low branches hit the men in the face while others were tripping over brush lying on the ground.

Stiver smelled smoke, which he thought at first, to be cordite, but quickly realized there was a fire was burning in front of them. Through the trees, the orange fire glowed brighter as it advanced relentlessly.

The gunfire grew rapid and wild as the piles of ammo cooked off in the fire. Bullets flew in every direction including straight at them.

Stiver heard a bullet whiz by and threw himself to the ground. In all his time as a cop, he'd never been shot at before. The experience was so terrifying that he began to panic.

More bullets flew overhead and Stiver tried to will himself into the ground.

"Junior," screamed a man. "I've been hit."

Stiver didn't move to help him.

The gunfire continued as the brush fire increased in size. The smoke became dense, making breathing difficult. The bright flames threw light and shadows against the trees.

231

Stiver heard his men yelling at each other. One of them came up to him. "Junior, Gibson's been hit pretty bad. This wind is blowing that fire right as us. We need to turn back."

A nervous Stiver ordered everyone to fall back.

The heat from the fire intensified as it quickly burned the dry brush and consumed everything in its path. The smoke now engulfed them. The out of shape Stiver, ran out of breath trying to make his way through the woods. He stumbled face first into a tree. Someone grabbed him and pushed him forward. Moments later, they tumbled into the open field where they had left their gear.

Stiver dropped to his knees, coughing and gagging for air. Sweat ran from every pore and steamed from the top of his bald head. He reached for a canteen and splashed water on his face and head.

His breathing finally began to slow, and he picked up his radio. "Has anybody found them yet?"

No one answered right away. He tried again.

The radio finally came alive. "Durbin here, we've moved in, the fire is moving your way, Junior."

Stiver sounded frustrated. "No shit. We barely got out of there."

He took a deep breath. "Hoyer, come in. Hoyer."

No response.

Stiver shook his head wishing he had sent for Jake and Elwood. He rolled over to his right, bent his legs and struggled to get up off the ground.

Two cops brought Gibson out and carried him away from the fire before setting him down to dress his wound.

Stiver hobbled over to him, knelt down, and noted the bullet had entered the right side of his upper chest. They applied pressure in an attempt to stop the bleeding. Stiver needed to get him out of there before he died. With the fire, still raging, they gathered up their gear, took hold of Gibson and headed south.

He tried once again to get Hoyer on the radio but to no avail.

After the fire had burned out, Stiver came back to the smoldering field and found Durbin.

"Anyone heard from Hoyer?" asked Stiver.

"No," said Durbin. "Maybe his radio is busted."

"What about the old geezers?"

"We haven't seen any of 'em," said Durbin.

"Well, spread out. The bastards can't be too far away."

Over the next several hours and leading into the morning, the National Police poked through the darkness, carefully walking the fields and the surrounding woods looking for the rebels. When the sun rose, they finally found Hoyer and his men, dead. One of the cops checked their rifles and found not one of them had been fired.

Stiver swallowed hard as he realized the rebels had played them for fools.

CHAPTER 59

ONTARIO CANADA

Soaking wet, the last of the Shadow Patriots made their way across the Rainy River, which separated Canada and the United States. They dragged their weary bodies onto dry land exhausted from running all night to reach the border.

After the fake gun battle and the setting of the fire, Winters and the others had bolted to join the rest of their force. As they were fleeing, Elliott and Nate were the first to reach the end of the field. While they were waiting for the other five to catch up, they heard cops coming out of the trees. Then Elliott and Nate had killed them, at last ensuring a safe escape.

In Canada, after Winters helped the last man out of the river, they celebrated, yelling into the chilly morning air and shaking each other's hands. However, their exuberance didn't last long. Their wet clothes made them realize just how cold and hungry they were, plus they were not sure what to do next.

Winters placed his hand on Nate's shoulder. "Brilliant plan Nate, nice job."

Nate smiled, appreciative of the recognition.

"We need to get a fire going," suggested Elliott.

"I'm with you on that," said Winters. "Some food would be nice too."

A few minutes later, as they started walking east, they heard the roar of engines in the distance. With the rising sun shining in their eyes, they couldn't tell who it was. With nowhere to run or hide, they simply stopped and waited.

Winters pulled his hat down to block the sun and caught a glimpse of large dark vehicles approaching. When they got closer, they spread out across the road and surrounded the Shadow Patriots.

A bullhorn cracked, "Drop your weapons. Get on the ground and keep your arms spread out."

Everyone did as they were told, as a cadre of men emptied out of the trucks, their guns aimed at the Shadow Patriots. They moved in and removed all the weapons.

"Who's in charge here?" asked the man with a distinct British accent.

Winters raised his hand. "That would be me, my name is Cole Winters and we are asking for political asylum."

The man approached him. "You that group, the Yanks, have been chasing around all night?"

Winters looked discombobulated. "How do you know that?"

"We've been monitoring their communications. They say you're a bunch of murdering bastards."

"Yes, they would say that now wouldn't they."

The man knelt down and gave Winters a stern glare. "Well, are you?"

"I guess it depends on your perspective."

"From my perspective, seeing how I'm quite aware of what's been happening at those Patriot Centers, then I'd say, they definitely had it coming."

Winters furrowed his brow.

The man rose up and stuck out his hand. "I'm Captain Spooner of the British Tenth Regiment. Welcome to Canada."

Winters got up and shook his hand. "Like I said, I'm Cole Winters, and these are my men."

"Glad to meet you, Mr. Winters."

Winters motioned his men to get up off the ground and proceeded to give a brief description of their journey to the British Captain. He didn't seem surprised making Winters wonder how much they already knew.

Captain Spooner took them to his base of operations and offered hot food, hot showers, and good camaraderie. The Canadians and Brits were most gracious hosts and eager to help. They were chomping at the bit to get into the fight.

Later in the afternoon, they all hopped into trucks and headed to Winnipeg to meet Captain Spooner's commanding officer Colonel Brocket. His headquarters were situated at the James Armstrong Richardson International Airport. In light of the war in the US, the base had been expanded and was now a multi-functional training facility, housing both British and Canadian air and ground forces.

Captain Spooner and Winters walked into his commander's office.

"Colonel, this is the American, Captain Winters."

Winters took off his hat and extended his hand. "Colonel Brocket, it's a pleasure to meet you, sir,"

Brocket was a little younger than Winters. He wore battle fatigues on his lean, tall, muscular build, and his crew cut was silver on the sides giving him a look any wannabe general in Hollywood would give his right arm for. His piercing blue eyes only enhanced his rugged appearance, and his handshake matched his confident motion.

"The pleasure is all mine," he responded with a sharp English accent. "Anyone who can give America's National Police the trouble you've been giving them is an honor to meet."

"Well, thank you, sir, and thank you for taking us in."

"This is my counterpart here, General Standish of the Royal Canadian Air Force. This is his base."

"It's good to meet you, Captain Winters," said Standish, a tall man who had broad shoulders and a barrel chest. He had prominent facial features, including his nose and wide-set eyes, which were dark brown, and seem to match his deep baritone voice. When he spoke, his rich voice grabbed your attention so much that you hung on to every word.

Brocket motioned to the table. "Have a seat, Captain. You must still be exhausted from your harrowing journey. May I offer you a cup of tea?"

Winters sat down. "Yes, thank you. That would be nice."

Brocket looked at Spooner, who walked out of the office to request the tea. The three of them sat down at a conference table that took up a good portion of the room. The blue chairs Winters recognized to be the same as the ones in his old office, where he had sat in a cubicle all day keeping the books. Despite all he'd done, Winters felt intimidated by these men. They were accomplished military men.

"Are you former military?" Brocket asked.

"No, sir."

"Your title of Captain then...?"

"The men just started calling me that," Winters responded, embarrassed by an unearned title. As he began to tell them all that had happened, he was interrupted when tea was brought in by a female corporal. She walked in, placing a sterling silver tea set on the table, and proceeded to pour each man a cup of tea. After serving, she turned and exited the room.

Winters waited for the other two men to reach for their tea before picking up his cup. He sipped on the hot liquid, enjoying the warm sensation in his throat. He then continued. Both Brocket and Standish looked at each other approvingly throughout the story.

When Winters finished, Brocket placed his right hand to his heart. "Yours is an astonishing journey, Captain."

Standish leaned forward. "The title of Captain is certainly deserving and you wear it well, sir."

Winters didn't know exactly what to say, so he politely thanked him.

"What are your plans?" Standish asked, setting his teacup down on the saucer. "What are you looking to do now?"

"Not sure," said Winters hoping they'd offer to let him stay right where he was.

"I would imagine you'd want to get back since you've got Al Qaeda on the loose."

Winters stopped moving the teacup to his mouth. "Al Qaeda? Are you sure?"

"An offshoot of sorts. We have spies in Washington, and I'm quite confident Commandant Boxer won't be doing anything about that situation."

"Who's Commandant Boxer?"

Brocket took another sip of tea. "He's the head of the National Police, more of a figurehead in my opinion."

"So, he is here in the Midwest," stated Winters remembering Green telling him this.

"That would be correct, and be assured, he has no interest in catching those bloody bastards."

"Why do you say that?"

"Because we know who sponsors them."

"Sponsors them?"

"Yes. They didn't get here on their own, someone had to smuggle them in and supply them."

"Who would do such a thing?"

"Your government," answered Standish.

Winters straightened up. "You must be mistaken, they wouldn't do something like that."

"No? Why would they be secretly killing off American citizens such as yourself, Captain?"

"I don't know, I just thought maybe Colonel Nunn went rogue or something."

Brocket snickered. "Ah, Colonel Nunn. Ole "second to none" himself. He's quite a character."

"You know him?"

"Oh yes, I'm familiar with the colonel and his dealings."

"Dealings?"

"Black market arms, he sold stolen military weapons and equipment to some very wicked people. He got himself caught and court marshaled, but then your government fell and the war began. Some of his old friends are now in high places in the new government and they saved him from jail."

"I don't understand why they would be doing these things."

Standish glanced at Brocket. "We haven't pieced together the grand plan, but at the moment it doesn't matter. Right now, you've got Al Qaeda running around killing your fellow countrymen."

"What can we do?" Winters asked looking down at the table.

Standish stared at Winters. "What do you mean what can you do?"

Winters didn't respond.

"Who else will protect the innocent? There is no one else but you."

Winters sounded dejected. "But there's so many of them."

"Yes, you're outnumbered, but what of it? Captain, you've been given the chance of a lifetime."

Winters looked at Standish sitting across from him wondering just what he had meant.

Standish continued. "A man never truly knows what he is made of until he's been put in the direst of circumstances. Will he run or will he fight? Everyone wants to believe that he will stand and fight, but so few do. Very few will dig into their soul and rise up. Even fewer will voluntarily go back into the fire. You've been given a rare opportunity to find out who you really are."

Winters stiffened in his chair trying to absorb all of what Standish had just laid on him. He didn't want to know who he really was. He'd seen enough to change him. He started this journey being reluctant. Sure, his Mr. Hyde had surfaced back at the train station enabling him to kill, but that had been out of sheer revenge and it was a side of him he didn't like. The attack on the first Patriot Center was in self-interest, he had merely wanted to remove his name from any records. He had not intended to stick around. He'd continued mostly out of guilt, even then, he was reluctant, and always unsure of himself. Now, he wasn't sure if he could go back and fight.

"Do you believe in fate, Captain?" asked Standish, seeing the hesitation in Winters' eyes.

"Maybe...I guess so."

"You should. Think about what initially happened to you. You jumped out of a moving truck, which saved your life. You've dodged bullets, eluded the Army, the police and here you are with us. That is fate."

"We've just been lucky."

Standish stood up and in his low baritone voice, spoke to Winters in a slow, serious tone. "You're alive and here for a reason, Captain. Don't... take...that...lightly."

Winters leaned forward in his chair resting his arms on the table, with his eyes fixated upon the tea set. It reminded him of a time he and his wife had visited a small bed and breakfast to celebrate their ten-year anniversary. They got up in the morning and were served with a similar tea set. It had been a lovely morning so long ago. His wife had planned the whole trip, just as she had arranged everything else in their lives. Now, here he sat with the fate of his men in his hands. After learning about the involvement of the government, he realized he had no choice, but to return to the fray.

CHAPTER 60

ROCK ISLAND ILLINOIS

Major Green got up early and grabbed some raw eggs, milk, and sugar, and threw it all into a blender. After drinking the mixture, he headed to the gym. He needed to get on the treadmill and lose himself in thought. Green had not slept well since coming back from the train station with Lieutenant Crick. The sight of those bodies had haunted his dreams, especially since the responsibility for the killings was also his to bear.

Colonel Nunn had returned from Washington, so he would confront him today and get some answers. He let out a scoff thinking of what lies the old man might come up with.

Green walked into the gym and, as expected, found the place empty. He had gotten there early because he preferred to work out alone. He didn't like anyone bothering him, requesting this or that. Putting on his earbuds, he dialed in some classic rock, got on the treadmill and began to jog.

After the run, Green worked his upper body with free weights. His chest muscles were tight and his arms were like lead weights. Perfect. It was just what he had needed. He grabbed his bag and walked out of the gym just as some of the men were filing in. As he stepped outside, raindrops began to fall. By the time he'd reached his quarters, it had started to pour.

After showering, Green, holding an umbrella ran over to the main office for his 0900 meeting with Colonel Nunn. He arrived early and greeted Sergeant Owens, Nunn's assistant. Green set his umbrella in the corner and sat down. A few minutes later, the phone rang and Sergeant Owens told him Nunn would see him now.

Colonel Nunn sat at his desk reading a report. He didn't bother to look up when he told Green to come in and take a seat.

Green sat directly in front of him. "How was your trip to Washington, sir?"

Nunn kept reading. "Very productive, had a lot of meetings."

Green interpreted that to mean he drank most of the week and spent the majority of his time with hookers. "Glad to hear it, sir."

"I'm just finishing your report, Major, and the finer details of your detainment by the so-called Shadow Patriots seem a little sparse. Care to enlighten me?"

"Yes, sir. There's not much more to say other than they surprised us, and took us, hostage."

"You stormed their camp, killed sixteen of them then took the rest prisoner and yet you somehow end up as their prisoner?" asked Nunn.

"Yes, sir."

"I'm amazed they didn't kill you."

"As was I."

"You met their leader? What kind of a man is he?"

"Polite and unassuming. Just an average guy, definitely not a military man."

"Polite, unassuming and not a military man, but yet he takes you, hostage."

Green got defensive. "Yes, well, some of his men were former military. One's a Marine for sure, quite confident and a bit arrogant."

"You didn't put anything in your report about your conversations. I'm assuming he must have said something to you."

"Yes. He told me why they were attacking the Centers."

Nunn lifted his head. "And just what did the man say?"

"He told me we've been killing all the volunteers."

"Did you believe him?"

"No, sir." Green paused for a moment. "Not at first."

Nunn put the report down and looked directly into Green's eyes, waiting for him to finish his thoughts.

"I called him a liar and a murderer. He told me if I didn't believe him, then I should go back to the train station, and check out the field where there's an open burial pit full of dead bodies."

"Did you go to the train station?"

Green nodded.

"And?"

Green replied with intensity, "Just like he said. It's filled with hundreds of dead bodies. Birds were feeding off the remains of citizens we've been killing and I want to know why?"

"I don't think I like your tone of voice, Major."

Green snapped back. "Quite frankly, Colonel, I don't care. Please, enlighten me as to why we are killing those people?"

"Certain facts were withheld on a need to know basis," retaliated Nunn.

"So, you're not even going to try and deny it?"

"I won't insult your intelligence, Major. Of course, I know what's going on, I'm in charge of this whole region. I know about everything."

"What about Commandant Boxer?"

"He knows. Hell, it was his idea. He's the one who took the idea to his superiors and they latched onto it."

"Why?" Green asked frustrated.

"I don't know why, Major."

Green knew this had to be a lie. Nunn was a shrewd man, and wouldn't do anything if he didn't know every detail of the operation. "I don't believe you."

Nunn's eyes got wide. "You listen here, Major. I'm following orders, just like you, and they come from the highest level of government."

"It's an unlawful order."

Nunn snorted. "Unlawful. What does that even mean anymore?

These days all the lines have been blurred." He started gesturing with his hands. "The volunteers are being killed for a reason. They're considered enemies of the state. This is our new reality and if you're not careful, you too could end up in one of those pits."

Green reared back. "Are you threatening me, Colonel?"

Nunn lowered his voice. "No Major, I'm not threatening you." He paused and sighed. "I'm telling you to be careful. If you don't follow the rules, you might find yourself in trouble. Not by me, but the National Police. I have no sway with them, and they have spies everywhere. You'd do well to remember that."

Green tried to grasp what Nunn had told him and thought about the concern in his voice as if he really was trying to look out for him. Learning the truth was reprehensible. Perhaps Nunn felt the same way, and didn't agree with his assignment but had no choice in the matter. It could be the reason why the man was always in a foul mood.

"So, we're to do nothing?" Green asked.

"That's right. Besides, I received a report just before you came in. We have some Al Qaeda like terrorists running around killing people in Minnesota. I need for you to check it out."

Green looked surprised. "Al Qaeda, here? How many?"

"I was told there was a small group that caused some trouble in Brainerd, Minnesota."

"How are we supposed to find them?" Green asked eagerly.

"I'm trying to check in with the police, but they're a little busy chasing your guys up on the Canadian border. I should have more intel later this afternoon on their whereabouts. So, by tomorrow you can go and do what we've been trained for. Listen, Major, I know what's been happening is wrong, and extremely distasteful, but like I said, we live in a different time now. The best thing you can do right now is your job. So, I need you to focus. If we got some rag-heads stirring up trouble, I need your head back in the game."

Green walked out of Nunn's office, satisfied he had a real assignment.

CHAPTER 61

WINNIPEG MANITOBA CANADA

Since arriving in Winnipeg, the Shadow Patriots were able to get some well-needed rest and relaxation. Many took advantage of the medical facilities to have their aches and pains massaged and anointed soothing liniments.

Winters wasn't fortunate enough to receive a soothing treatment for the wound in his arm. The gouge from Johnny-boy's bullet had scabbed over and turned dark red surround by a yellowish tinge. The doctor examined it and told him it was healing about as well as could be expected without stitches and that the area would be tender to the touch for some time.

Winters shrugged his shoulders at that news.

The Canadian military offered some basic tactical training, which included some top-notch instruction on the firing range.

The men had a productive three days, and they would have liked to stay longer to hone their new skills. However, with an enemy running amok and wantonly killing Americans, they needed to get back.

Winters tossed and turned in bed trying to fall to sleep. He looked up at the clock. The blue digital numbers read 4:30 am. He lay there and tried to remember if he had fallen asleep or just had some bad dreams about not falling asleep. He decided to get up and check on the equipment the Canadians had been so generous to give them. It included vehicles, food, weapons, ammo and two-way radios. None of which had any kind of Canadian or British markings.

Taking refugees was one thing, but arming a force to fight against the American government was quite another. The two governments weren't enemies, but then they weren't exactly allies either.

"Politics. Gets you in and out of trouble all at the same time," thought Winters, as he got out of bed.

He grabbed his freshly washed clothes, put them up to his nose, and inhaled deeply. They reminded him of home where there were always clean clothes. Winters walked out of his room and into the long narrow hallway, passing the closed doors of bedrooms, where his men were still sleeping. He reached the end of the hall and opened the door. The night was clear and chilly enough to vaporize your breath. He zipped up his jacket and walked over to the vehicles.

"Can't sleep either?" asked Elliott in a low voice, trying not to startle Winters.

"Elliott, didn't expect to see you here."

"Get any sleep?"

Winters thought for a second. "I'm not sure if I did or not. You?"

"Couple of hours maybe. Couldn't stop thinking about everything. Just can't believe our own government would bring jihadis here."

Winters shook his head. "Too painful to think about, which is why most people probably wouldn't even believe us. Easier to assume we're liars instead of having to face the truth."

Elliott relaxed his stance. "Well, if they hadn't been trying to kill us, I can't say I'd believe it either."

"Question is—can we stop them."

They milled around the trucks and checked the gear and the condition of the vehicles. They then walked over to the mess hall and found they were not the only ones up early. The big cafeteria was bustling with people, some just getting off work and others going on. They grabbed a tray and took ample helpings of what would be their last hot breakfast for a while.

As the two of them walked in, Winters had noticed some of the military personnel looked up from their plates to watch him and Elliott get in line at the cafeteria. Since arriving at the base, the Shadow Patriots had garnered a lot of attention and gossip. Everyone had been generous in welcoming and assisting them. Winters turned his head to the left and received nods from a table of British Special Forces. Winters wondered if they were just now getting up to train or had already finished.

As daybreak broke, all the Shadow Patriots were up preparing for the day. They would re-enter America as they left, through Minnesota. Late last night, the Brits intercepted a National Police radio transmission confirming that Al Qaeda had been located on Hwy 10 and were headed toward Detroit Lakes, Minnesota.

Winters finished his breakfast and decided to grab a shower before they left. He had no idea when he'd have the opportunity to take another one.

Once again, he had to force himself to shut off the water off. An endless supply of hot water was an open invitation to lose one's sense of time.

After getting dressed, he packed his gear and went back to the mess hall.

He walked up to where Scar and Meeks were sitting. "Eat up guys, got a big day ahead of us."

Meeks looked up. "How far is it?"

Winters sat down. "About 250 miles, give or take. We're not exactly taking the most direct route."

"Got to avoid them National Pooolice," Meeks said snickering. "I can't imagine they'd want to miss us yet again."

Scar laughed. "Well, if they only knew what we're packing now, they might think differently."

"You got a point, Mr. Scarborough," said Meeks. "Why, I'll bet we could just blast our way through the border crossing."

Nate yelled out in agreement. "Hell yeah, we could."

All the men sitting at the table started laughing at Meeks as he described, animatedly, how the cops would react once they saw him coming at them.

Winters noticed Mr. Peterson at another table, so he got up and walked over.

"Mr. Peterson, I sure am going to miss having you around."

He scooted over for Winters. "Well Cole, it's been a grand adventure being with you and the boys. Getting chased into the unknown has made me feel alive again. Makes you appreciate life. Someday, when this is all over, you'll look back with pride on what you've done. You'll especially miss the guys."

"I'm not so sure you're right about it being over someday."

"All wars end at some point," reassured Mr. Peterson.

After a few minutes of conversation, they both stood up and firmly gripped each other's hands. Winters was glad to have met Mr. Peterson, he was wise and had a good attitude about life. He was sure to run into him again since Colonel Brocket had invited him to stay in Canada. He would help with any other refugees Winters was able to send their way. They would give them some training and get them ready if they wanted to go back and help.

An hour later, Winters, Scar and Meeks, were once again, passengers in another SUV driven by Elliott. A convoy of twenty vehicles consisting of trucks and cars followed. They had crossed the border about ten miles west of Noyes, Minnesota cutting across farmland. They headed east, toward Detroit Lakes. Cars, which were all over the place in Canada, disappeared once they got back into the States.

Winters looked around. "Kind of strange to see it so desolate."

Elliott tapped the dash with his right hand. "I can't believe I'm gonna say this, but I kinda miss being in traffic."

Winters turned to the back. "When was the last time any of us sat in a traffic jam?"

"It's been a while," said Scar.

Meeks smacked the side window. "I don't miss it one bit. Hey, you think them Jijis are already there, Captain?"

"Probably so, Colonel Brocket said they've got transportation now, so I'd think so."

"Well hell, there's your traffic jam," said Meeks.

"Once we get close, we'll pull over and do some recon," said Winters.

"Now that we've got radios, it'll be a heck of a lot easier to plan on the fly," said Scar.

CHAPTER 62

DETROIT LAKES MINNESOTA

Green sat in the lead Humvee with his young corporal, Josh Bassett, in the backseat as they headed to Detroit Lakes. He couldn't stop thinking how strange, his confrontation with Nunn had been. Green had never seen anyone act so bipolar. One moment, Nunn is arrogant and angry, the next he's defensive but then defeated. It had to be frustrating to admit you know what is happening is wrong, but there was nothing you could do about it. That defeatist attitude had to be because his bosses had kept him out of jail, and were holding that car over his head. Selling your soul. Hell of a price to pay. The idea sent a shiver up Green's spine

The surprise from their confrontation was that Nunn, for the first time, had actually shown some genuine concern. Green wasn't sure what to make of it, but he did appreciate the advice. Maybe things would be better between them in the future.

At least he had a real mission and hoped to work out some lingering hostilities. Colonel Nunn confirmed that the terrorists were in Detroit Lakes. The National Police had spotted them and said they were headed there, burning anything and everything in their path. This is what Green and his soldiers were supposed to be doing, defending American citizens.

An hour later, they had gone through a small town that had been set ablaze. This was a sure sign their enemy had been through. There was no one was around to question what had happened. They would just have to plow forward and find out for themselves.

"We're coming up on Detroit Lakes," said his driver.

"Take the next left, Sergeant," said Green, noticing some smoke coming from that direction.

The five Humvees turned into the town. Green keyed up the radio and ordered his men to arm the M2's. Corporal Bassett got up into the turret and racked the lever. They continued on North Shore Drive. Houses on the left had been built on the lakefront with an abundance of trees providing abundant shade to the neighborhood. A high school football field sat across the street. As they drove through this apparent tranquility, suddenly, two men, dressed in Arab garb and carrying AK-47's, strolled into the street. When they became aware of the Humvees, they turned and ran for cover.

"Fire!" ordered Green.

Bassett squeezed the trigger. The hail of lead caught both men in the back throwing them to the ground dead.

They pulled up to the dead men. Green hopped out, crept around the Humvee and checked the bodies. Definitely Middle Eastern. He rose and looked up the street.

Vehicles were coming straight at them.

He hustled back around to the passenger side. As he opened the door, he turned to discover even more vehicles coming from their rear.

Green growled. This was an ambush and they were in for a fight.

He grabbed the radio-mic. "We got Tangos in both directions. Back these trucks up."

The drivers scrambled the Humvees onto the lawns to form a fighting position. The soldiers fell out of the Humvees with weapons at the ready. The gunners remained in the turrets and let loose with the M2's, giving them cover.

The neighborhood exploded with gunfire echoing through the streets.

The enemy stopped about seventy yards away to abandon their vehicles and take up positions along the streets.

Green grabbed his binoculars to survey the battleground. Tangos had taken positions by the houses and behind several cars. He grunted because he knew they were in trouble. They were boxed in.

"Someone screwed up the intel on this one, Major," screamed Lieutenant Crick into the radio. "We've got a small battalion here."

Bullets snapped and whistled around Green as he took a final look through the binoculars. The enemy had taken casualties, but they had an overwhelming force. Crick was right, a small battalion.

"Sergeant," Green yelled at his driver. "Take a squad and clear those houses behind us." He looked up at Bassett. "How's it looking, Corporal?"

"We can hold them off for a while. They're very unorganized and their shots are chaotic, sir."

"AT4," ordered Green to the men on his right.

A private reached inside the Humvee as bullets bounced off the truck. Out came the deadly weapon. He pulled the pin before flipping up the iron sights and applying pressure to the trigger.

Green watched the rocket-propelled grenade slice through the air at almost three hundred meters a second.

It struck the enemies barricade dead-on. The explosion threw men up in the air killing them before they hit the ground. The remaining Tangos scurried away from the car as it exploded in a fireball.

Green's men let out with a hearty cheer. But their exuberance was short-lived as the enemy found new positions and threatened to overwhelm them with their superior numbers.

At some point, Green figured these guys would come at them all at once, and they would then be in a fight for their lives.

CHAPTER 63

The Shadow Patriots approached Detroit Lakes from the west side of town and stopped their trucks to decide how they should enter the city. As soon as they exited the SUV, they heard a familiar crackling noise in the distance.

"Is that gunfire?" asked Winters rhetorically.

"Damn terrorists must already be shooting up the place," said Meeks.

They moved to the front of the SUV and listened. Burns and Murphy joined them.

"Sounds more like a gun battle," said Scar.

"Think the townspeople are defending themselves?" asked Winters.

Meeks added. "Damn well ain't the cops."

"It's a heated exchange, whoever it is," said Burns.

"Got some .50 cal in there too," said Scar to Burns.

"Yeah…that's M2 for sure," stated Burns.

"We need to recon this right away. Scar, what do you think?" asked Winters.

Scar pulled out a map and placed it on the hood of the SUV. "Meeks and I can go to the east side, and let's have Burns and Murphy go west. There's a school here."

"Elliott and I can check that out," interrupted Winters.

Leaving the rest of the vehicles and men there to guard the north end. Elliott coasted their SUV down Roosevelt Ave toward the school while the others took off recon their flanks.

Winters rolled his window down and scanned the houses. He didn't notice any townspeople, not that he expected any. Everyone was either hiding or took off while they could. As they got closer, Winters held up binoculars. He found the source of the gunfire right away.

"Elliott, stop. They're at the end of the street," said Winters.

He handed him the binoculars.

"Yes, they are," said Elliott.

Winters keyed up the radio. "We've got Jiji's here. They're down by the lake."

"Nothing over here yet," said Burns.

"Scar."

"We've spotted them. We're moving in closer to see who they're fighting with," said Scar.

Elliott put the truck in reverse and parked on the side of the street. They both got out and hurried across lawns to get a closer look.

Moments later, Scar radioed in. "Captain, you're not going to believe who's in this firefight. It's that same major we took prisoner."

Winters and Elliott exchanged glances.

"Major Green? I thought they were all on the same side," said Winters into the radio.

"It doesn't look like they're on the same side today, cuz the Jijis got 'em pinned down. They've got nowhere to go."

The Shadow Patriots regrouped and huddled around a map of Detroit Lakes.

Scar pointed at the map. "Captain, they may have the major boxed in, but the dumb-asses left themselves wide open to get themselves surrounded. We should bring our people in the same way we just did our recon."

Burns added. "With their attention on the soldiers, we'll be able to sneak right up behind them, Captain."

Scar looked at Burns. "How about we come in on their flanks first? This will squeeze them into the center. They'll try to escape back up this way. Then we can ambush them."

Winters liked what he was hearing and with their new equipment and radios, he had little doubt they could save Major Green. He shook his head at the thought of having to save a man who was trying to catch him. At their last meeting he had told Green he had no doubt he'd have the pleasure of tying him up again. Winters was only joking but here they were.

Winters shrugged his shoulders. Life's full of ironies and coincidences.

The Shadow Patriots split into the three groups. Scar and Meeks took twenty men and headed east. Burns and Murphy took another twenty and headed to the west side. The rest stayed with Winters.

The gunfire echoed non-stop as Winters moved his men into position. They ran behind the houses and when they got near the school, everyone found a shooting position. Some inside houses, others behind bushes and fences. They positioned themselves all up and down the street and across the high school's parking lot.

"In position, Captain," said Scar over the radio.

"Give us another minute here," stated Burns.

When Burns was ready Winters gave them the okay to engage. Winters lay on the ground between two houses with Elliott and Nate. Their set-up was right across from a big wide-open parking lot. It was the perfect ambush site.

Winters' pulse increased as he tightened his grip around the Colt M4 the Canadians had given him. He was thankful for weapons and the training his men received in Canada. For the first time since they started, he felt like his men were ready for anything that came their way. The orderly way they moved into position showed their confidence had grown with the new skills they'd learned. Winters also noticed, for the first time, that his leg didn't start shaking in fear. He thought about what General Standish said to him about being thrown into a dire circumstance and finding out who he really was. He would find out today what that really meant.

Winters turned to Elliott when they heard their friends start firing. They nodded to each other.

CHAPTER 64

G reen ordered another AT4 hoping to put the fear of God in his enemy. He rolled his eyes knowing that these terrorists wished to die in battle. How else would they get their seventy-two virgins?

Regardless, he needed to thin their numbers as much as he could before they came in for a final assault. He only had twenty-five men against four to five hundred Tangos. Unfortunately, he just had a couple more grenades. He hadn't expected anywhere near these kinds of numbers and wasn't adequately prepared. A mistake that would haunt him. Though the bigger mistake was someone in the chain-of-command screwed up royally on the number of terrorists. He put that aside for now but would deal with it later.

Lieutenant Crick was on the other side of their perimeter firing down North Shore Drive towards Madison Avenue. The Tangos had spread multiple vehicles across the road blocking off any chance of escape. His sergeant fired their last remaining AT4's. The explosions reverberated through the air putting the barricade on fire. It stopped the firing down at that end for a few minutes but it picked back up again.

"Major, they've got an RPG," yelled Bassett from the turret as he spun the big .50 caliber around toward the threat. He let loose with a barrage of fire. Lead tore through the gunner, causing him to drop the launcher on the ground.

The young Corporal Bassett aimed at the launcher hoping someone else would try to pick it up. He didn't have to wait long before another Tango tried his luck.

A slight smile formed on Bassett's lips as he laid down a curtain of bullets. The Tango didn't even get to put his hand on it before a round blew his arm off. The man screamed in pain for help but none dared to expose themselves.

"C'mon, ya little bastards," dared Bassett.

"You got that handled, Corporal?" snapped Green.

"It ain't going anywhere, though I doubt it's operable now."

"Don't take any chances."

Bassett nodded and fired at the RPG. Bullets slammed into it, hurling it into the air. The launcher was torn apart and would no longer be a threat.

Green headed toward Crick and yelled up to the gunners. "Be on the lookout for RPG's."

"That's a game changer," acknowledged Crick.

"Yes, it is. But, they may have had only the one launcher. Why else would they have waited to use it?"

Crick nodded.

Green was satisfied with the assumption. They had fired their own at the enemy and it took a while for them to respond in kind, but still, they'd need to be ready. He hustled back over to Bassett.

"Got a large group of Tangos sneaking in through those trees," yelled Bassett as he turned the M2 toward them and sent a hail of lead at them. Hot shell casings tinkled the metal turret as tree branches snapped off and dirt kicked high in the air. A few Tangos screamed out as bullets ripped through them.

Their returned fire exposed the weak points in the soldiers' fortified position. Green fell to the ground as bullets hissed above him. His heart began pounding knowing he was inches from death.

A lull in the gunfire gave him the chance to tighten his position. He jumped up and ran to the lead Humvee. He threw it in drive and pulled it around the corner. This would force the enemy to fan out and make them work harder.

Picking up the binoculars he watched them fire at him. Rounds bounced off the armored vehicle. Their faces turned to frustration as they realized they were wasting ammo.

Green continued to watch them and estimated at least a hundred of them had gathered in the trees. They had the numbers to flank them. It wouldn't take them to long to realize that the houses by the lake would be an ideal position.

He keyed up the radio. "Lieutenant. Get a squad back into those houses."

"Roger that."

The soldier in the turret above him continued to engage, but the enemy was using the trees to their advantage. Green gritted his teeth watching them move in closer. His frustrations grew ten-fold when the gunner above him ran out of ammo.

"I'm empty, Major."

Green fought to control his temper. He took a deep breath and willed himself to relax. Slowly, he got his heart rate under control. Think. Think. He tilted his head thinking, if push came to shove, he'd get everyone back in the Humvees and try and plow through the barricades.

The radio squawked. It was Crick. "We've been overrun. We're peeling back. I repeat, we're peeling back."

Green grabbed the radio. "Bassett cover them."

"I'm on it."

Green turned and saw Crick and another soldier coming up the driveway. Each carried a man on his shoulders. They were just about back when Crick fell forward and dropped his man.

Green's eyes grew wide when he realized Crick had been hit. He threw open the door as bullets hit the Humvee. He squatted down and ran to Crick. He grabbed him by the back of his chest rig and dragged him back to the center of their Humvees while lead buzzed over his head.

"Get a kit over here," ordered Green.

Their medic rushed over and started to go to work on Crick. He was in bad shape and the color was draining from his face.

Green stared at his friend who was struggling to breathe. "Stay with us, David. Stay with us."

"Major!" yelled Bassett. "Major!"

"What?" howled Green.

"You hear that?"

"Hear what?"

"Listen. The gunfire. It's changed."

Green stood up and had to will himself to focus. It took him a couple of seconds to realize that Bassett was right. Something had just changed. "What is it?"

"There's new gunfire coming in behind them. Look, the bad guys are running away, sir."

Green raised his binoculars and scanned the area. The enemy was retreating. But why?

CHAPTER 65

Winters' eyes narrowed as the Jijis began running toward his position. They were in a hurry as their flanks were caving in on them. Their numbers started small but snowballed, just as he had expected. This was why he spread everyone out along both sides of the street. He wanted as many in their trap as possible before they opened fire.

More terrorists spilled into the street. Winters got as low as he could. His senses were on high alert and his heart pounded in his chest. The enemy was close enough he could see the lines on their hardened faces. He turned his attention back toward the parking lot across the street where a vast number of Jijis were running his way. Just another moment and they would open fire.

At least seventy-five rapidly retreating Jijis now filled the parking lot. The unexpected assault on their flanks had definitely thrown them off their game.

Winters looked at Elliott and Nate and mouthed NOW. He tightened his grip, leaned against the stock of his M4, took aim and squeezed the trigger.

For a split second, only Winters' shots rang through the air. A precursor of what was to come. A Jiji jerked his attention to Winters, saw the muzzle flashes and as if in slow motion, resignation registered on his face. He knew he was going to die. Bullets ripped into his chest as he dropped to his knees and fell forward.

Gunfire reverberated from all the Shadow Patriots weapons, and Jijis began dropping onto the street as the bullets rained down on them. The wounded screamed as they tried to crawl away. One pulled himself up in a sitting position, grabbed his gun and depressed the trigger. He instantly became a favorite target as bullets riddled his body, which jerked with multiple impacts and was kept upright longer than it should have.

The Jijis were confused and chaotically ran in different directions. Some started to return fire, shooting wildly at anything: trees, shrubs, or houses. Others formed a group at the school and piled into a car. It took off, leaving the rest of them behind. The car sped toward the gauntlet of Shadow Patriots with desperate men leaning out of the windows, rifles at bay, firing at anything and everything.

The car tore by Winters and he watched holes appear on the doors at a rapid pace as bullets penetrated the metal. He could barely see the driver, who was hunkered down low in the seat. A Jiji in the back window kept firing despite blood running down the side of his face. The tires blew out and the car crashed into a large oak tree. The delirious driver, bleeding, and shouting opened the door and stumbled out. He raised his AK-47 in a vain attempt to prolong his life. Several of Winters' men rushed the car, firing as they charged it. The driver fell back into the car as his blood spilled on the grass. The rushing Patriots stopped beside the vehicle and poured bullets into open windows at the mangled bodies inside.

The remaining group at the school took advantage of the distraction caused by the car. Thirty Jijis came storming up the street charging at the Shadow Patriots.

Winters saw them. "Guys!" he yelled pointing at them.

Bullets flew over their Shadow Patriots' heads keeping them pinned down in prone positions. The bad guys were heading straight toward them. Nate flicked the switch on his M4 from semi-automatic to full. He drew down on them and fired until he had emptied the magazine. Four of them fell dead. The Jijis spread out, as they got closer. Elliott and Winters were expending ammunition at a fearsome rate. Two more fell. The wounded didn't stop coming. Their faces were determined as they screamed "Allah Akbar." Nate grabbed another mag and slammed it in. Keeping the weapon on auto, he emptied it in seconds, taking down several more.

As the Jijis got closer, their bullets kicked up grass in front of Winters and Elliott. Their position was becoming vulnerable, but at the same time, the onrushing Jijis were becoming easier targets.

Winters yelled for Elliott to take the right side while he concentrated on the left. The bullets zipping over his head were unnerving. He forced himself to slow down and take better aim.

They methodically dropped the enemy one by one. There was less than half remaining when some of the other Shadow Patriots noticed what was going on and concentrated their fire at the charging terrorists.

Seconds later, it was all over.

Winters got up with his M4 locked against his shoulder while he inspected the enemy. Moans came from the dying Jijis. Bloodied bodies were strewn throughout the ambush site. He looked at his men and couldn't help but be proud of them. They came here to meet an enemy, not knowing what to expect and performed magnificently. His men moved confidently around the dying, removing their weapons and taking charge.

Some sporadic fire still came from Scar's position but soon stopped. Winters got on the radio to check on the outlying teams.

Scar reported in first. "We're all good here, a few got away, but we killed most of them."

"Same here," said Burns.

Winters and Elliott then hurried down the street to confront Major Green.

CHAPTER 66

As Winters moved down the street toward the soldiers, he passed the dead terrorists with a look of satisfaction on his face. He hated them for what they were and what they did to innocent people. Moving by a young one riddled with bloody bullet holes, he wondered what he might have become had he not been born in an environment where his only choice in life was to be terrorist.

Winters was anxious to hear why Major Green was in Minnesota. As he neared the soldiers, he could see Green had lost a couple of his men. He came to a group working on one who had taken a bullet in the chest. Blood spurted from the wound and cascaded onto the grassy ground. The men worked frantically trying to stop the bleeding. One of them screamed in vain for the dying man to hang on as he bled out and struggled to take his last breath.

Green took a deep breath and glanced at Winters, as he approached.

Winters spoke softly. "Major, I'm sorry for your losses."

Green acknowledged him with a nod.

"What's his name?"

"David Crick. He was my Lieutenant and my friend."

Winters looked sympathetic. "I am truly sorry, Major."

"Well, had you not shown up, it would have been all of us lying here on the ground, so I owe you a big thanks."

Winters didn't respond.

"How did you know we were here?"

Winters shook his head. "We didn't."

"Then why are you here?"

"Cuz we knew these guys were here."

Green gave him a confused look. "How did you know that?"

"I don't want to give away my sources, but some new friends of ours told us."

Green interrupted. "The Brits?"

"Yes, the Brits," said Winters impressed with his guess. "We were chased into Canada and that's where we learned of the terrorists' location. Question is, why are you here?"

"My commanding officer got intel that some terrorists were running around up here, and we came to engage them."

"You mean Colonel Nunn."

"That's right, Colonel Nunn."

"You didn't come here very well prepared. Didn't you know how many there were?"

"Our intel said around fifty lightly armed men."

Winters shifted his body. "Major, we knew how many there were when we fought them in Brainerd. We killed a bunch of them. We even lost ten of our guys in the process. As we were pulling out, the National Police came after us. They were in the area for a reason, which makes me wonder why you didn't know because the cops had to have known."

Green broke eye contact and shook his head. His thoughts were in overload trying to put the pieces together. He looked back at Winters. "You sure it was the National Police?"

Winters nodded.

"I don't know what to say. I can only assume someone in the chain-of-command got the intel wrong," rationalized Green.

Winters adjusted his hat. "Major, I find that hard to believe, especially when there is something else that you obviously don't know. My new friends up gave me the low down on some of the nasty things the National Government are doing. They even knew what the Patriot Centers were being used for. They've obviously been keeping things from you."

Green's facial expression transformed from uncertainty to anger when he started to realize the ugly truth.

"He set you up, didn't he?" asked Winters. "Colonel Nunn, he sent you up here knowing you'd be outgunned."

Green paused for a moment staring into the distance. "It would appear so. We got into an intense argument and I confronted him about what you'd told me. I went to the train station and saw those dead men in the pit. He didn't even try to deny it."

"He must have thought you'd do something about it."

"This whole thing is because of Boxer and his damn Patriot program."

"It was his idea?"

"Yes, the Patriot Centers were his idea."

"So, he is the one responsible for our friends getting killed?"

"He's also the one that chased you up into Canada."

"He's still here, then?" Winters asked with a heightened level of interest.

"Yes. Washington sent him here to catch you and knowing what I know now about these terrorists, he's probably here to keep an eye on them as well."

"Where's he at?"

"St. Paul."

"Really," said Winters turning to Elliott. "St. Paul."

"Are you thinking about paying him a little visit?"

Winters eyed Green to get a read on him before answering. "Would you have a problem with that, Major?"

Green shook his head slowly. "No, I can't say that I would."

"What about you, what are you going to do?"

"Don't know yet, but whatever it is, it'll involve Colonel Nunn."

"Well, Major, I think we'll be on our way unless there's something else you need from us."

"Just one thing."

Winters waited for the question.

"What's your name?"

Winters cracked a half smile knowing he had just made a new friend.

"It's Cole, Cole Winters," he said putting out his hand.

CHAPTER 67

ST PAUL MINNESOTA

The Shadow Patriots scavenged the dead for weapons and ammo and left them where they lay. There were too many to deal with, and they didn't have the time, so if anyone was still in town, they would have to bury them. After they got everyone loaded up, the Shadow Patriots headed south toward St. Paul.

Their spirits were running high from their overwhelming victory over the terrorists. What once would have seemed impossible was now a major coup for them. Winters dared to smile in light of what they had accomplished. For the first time, they had been a cohesive team. Each man performed well and no one had died. Their new equipment supplied by the Brits had been an essential factor in their success. He wondered how they'd gotten as far as they previously had without radios.

Winters sat in the front seat, looking out the window, and thought through what had happened to Major Green. The poor guy did his duty and followed orders like a good soldier, trusting his superior's orders to be in good standing. Never having to worry that, if put in harm's way, it was not for someone's personal gain or some kind of vendetta.

Winters could relate. The government had betrayed them as well by appealing to their patriotic duty to serve. Never in a million years would he have thought something like the Patriot Centers could have happened, but then the worst betrayals are probably like that…simply unexpected.

Scar and Meeks bantering in the back got Winters' attention. He listened in, as they were always entertaining.

"I can't believe this Colonel Nunn would set up his own man," said Meeks. "Talk about a dog eat dog world."

Scar laughed. "Man, that's what you call a demotion."

"Yes, I'm afraid we no longer need your services," Meeks started laughing. "So, if you could just step over to that trap door."

"Like some James Bond villain," said Scar.

"Yeah, yeah, like Blofeld," said Meeks.

"I loved Scaramanga," said Scar.

"Oh, of course, you do Scar…ah…manga," said Meeks dragging the last bit out.

Elliott looked in the rear view mirror to get in on the levity. "What about Jaws, best henchman ever."

"I liked Vesper Lynd," Winters offered.

Meeks pulled himself to the front seat. "She wasn't a henchman."

Winters raised his finger. "Well, no…but…she was very hot."

They all burst out laughing and started to compare and debate the hot Bond girls. They enjoyed the lightheartedness of the moment after the intense firefight they had so recently gone through.

They arrived on the outskirts of St. Paul and parked their vehicles off the road. Despite its size, Minneapolis/St. Paul had not suffered the devastation of a dirty bomb as other large Midwestern cities had. However, with food and fuel shortages, its population had been moving south along with most everyone else. Approximately one-fourth of the citizens remained. The National Police had a significant presence here, and they supported enough commerce to provide a livelihood for those who stayed.

Winters sent Bill Taylor, who was from St. Paul, with Scar and Meeks to recon the city. They would need to locate where the National Police Headquarters and, if possible, where Boxer spent his nights.

The next morning, after making some inquiries of the locals, they located the place Boxer had appropriated for his residence. He had taken over a large house owned by a wealthy lawyer. It stood on a sizeable lot in an older neighborhood which was boasted many thick, lush evergreens and oak trees. The three of them spent the night across the street watching the house to determine what kind of security he had. Scar noted he had four men on the inside and two patrolled the property.

Later in the morning, they showed up at the Shadow Patriots' makeshift camp outside the city to report to Winters. That afternoon, Winters, Scar and Meeks left for St. Paul. They drove as far as they thought safe and then parked the car in the garage of an abandoned house. They walked the rest of the way to Boxer's house. Scar took them across the street to the old Victorian house he and Meeks had stayed in last night. Looters had ransacked it, leaving busted up furniture strewn around, broken windows, and rotting garbage.

Four hours later, while Winters and Meeks were resting, Scar kept watching for Boxer to show up. Finally, a car pulled into the driveway. He looked through his binoculars and observed Boxer. Scar snapped his fingers to awaken Winters and Meeks.

"He's here?" asked Winters stretching his arms.

He and Meeks padded across the room to the broken window and watched as four men entered the house. Two remained outside patrolling the grounds.

An hour later, Winters led them through the back door to hide behind the bushes of the grand old home. As soon as the guard was out of sight, they bolted across the street. Scar positioned himself at the far end of the house, and the other two moved into the shadows of the tall oak trees.

The neighborhood was quiet enough you could hear the soft footsteps of the guard as he came back around. Scar grabbed his six-inch knife and waited for the guard to walk past him.

Like a leopard pouncing on its prey, Scar leaped out and threw his big arm around the man's throat cutting off his windpipe. He swung the knife around and shoved it into his stomach. He yanked it out and struck him again. The man went limp and Scar dragged the dead body into the hedgerow that lined the house. Moments later, the second guard rounded the corner and Scar repeated the move.

They then moved to the back door and found it unlocked. The door opened into a laundry room, which led to the kitchen. They padded through the house and into the dining room.

They froze when they heard voices coming from the living room. Scar motioned the other two to get on the other side of the doorway. The voices became more audible as they headed toward the kitchen.

A light flipped on and two men headed for the refrigerator. Winters' breathing all but stopped. He inched his knife out of its sheath. Scar did the same, while Meeks gripped the Sig Sauer 9mm. The gun would be a last resort, as they didn't want to alert the others in the house.

Scar peeked around the entrance-way to see where the men were. They stood at the counter by the sink, making sandwiches. A breakfast bar with four stools stood in the way of a direct assault.

Scar squatted down on his hands and knees. Winters followed. They both crawled across the floor to get in a better position. Meeks remained, standing guard. The two men were blissfully unaware as they continued to make sandwiches.

Winters' eyes began blinking rapidly and sweat beaded on his forehead as they inched closer to their prey. As soon as they reached the breakfast bar, Scar turned and signaled to Winters—go on three. He counted down with his fingers. Three...two...one. In a quick motion, he leaped to his feet and rushed them.

Winters followed, but as he came around the corner, one guard reached for his gun.

CHAPTER 68

DETROIT LAKES MINNESOTA

Major Green stayed in Detroit Lakes to help clean up the bloody mess, get the wounded patched up, and contemplate his next move. Green's state of mind didn't allow for much sleep that night. Besides mourning the loss of his friend Lieutenant Crick, he was incensed at Colonel Nunn. Everything Cole Winters had told him made sense. The whole idea of sending him up here was to make sure he was killed. He now knew the reason why, for the first time ever, Nunn had been respectful to him. He was planning his demise. Green slammed his fist on a table. The bastard.

He went back and forth, trying to decide what to do with Nunn. On the one hand, he wanted to march into Nunn's office, pull out his sidearm and assassinate him. On the other, justice would be the better option.

However, what kind of justice could there be? The government would more than likely protect him. He had little time to plan what to do because Nunn would soon be aware that he still lived.

After lunch, Green stepped onto the porch of the abandoned house he had stayed in last night. He saw some of the remaining townspeople milling around outside and talking to each other about what had happened the day before. A few children played together. These were innocent people doing no one any harm. They had survived a hard winter with limited power and very little food. Now they had been the targets of a dishonorable action perpetrated upon them for, God only knew, whatever selfish reasons. How did we come to this? How did the world become so helter-skelter that powerful people would murder the innocent in the United States? This kind of thing only happened in third world countries. This wasn't supposed to happen here.

Green's late father, a career soldier, taught him that the strong are supposed to help the weak. No matter what happened, you were supposed to choose the right and honorable thing. This was one of the reasons he had joined the Army. It offered him a way to live by a code of conduct that reflected his upbringing.

Green continued standing on the porch. He wished he could talk to his late father now because the man had always given him good counsel. His advice had gotten him through a rough period at West Point. When he was a Plebe, Green stumbled upon some fellow cadets cheating. He didn't know what to do. Should he not report the incident and carry the guilt of dishonoring the code, or risk the moniker of being a snitch forever. His father told him that sometimes doing the right thing, is the most difficult, but in the end, he had to be able to accept the Code of Honor.

So, he informed on them, and because of the deterioration of the caliber of cadets, he endured the stares and whispers for his remaining three years at the Point. He became an outsider and had few friends. It had been a painful experience, but he still had his honor intact, and that was all that matter.

Green walked off the porch toward his Humvee parked on the street. He hopped in and drove to where some of his men were still removing the dead. He rolled down the window. "Corporal Bassett, keep the men here till I get back."

Bassett gave him a knowing nod. "Stay alert, sir,"

The long drive back to the post gave Green enough time to reflect on Crick's death. He'd have to write to his parents about the incident. Still close to them, he would also have to take a trip to visit them the next time he was in Virginia.

Hours later, he reached the post, parked off to the side of the building that housed all the offices, got out, took a deep breath and walked inside. Nunn's personnel clerk was not there. Green looked at his watch. 1800 hours. He walked into Nunn's office and found him still at his desk, with a half emptied bottle of Scotch sitting in front of him. Nunn raised his head up and stared in obvious astonishment.

"Major, where have you been?"

"Colonel Nunn, you seem a bit surprised."

"We haven't heard from you since yesterday. We've been worried sick that something bad happened."

"I don't recall getting any calls from you. Why would that be?"

Nunn finished his drink and set the glass down. "What the hell's that supposed to mean?"

"You just said you've been worried something happened. Why didn't you try to contact me?"

Nunn didn't respond and looked down at the empty glass. He grabbed the bottle and poured himself another drink. He put the bottle down on the corner of the desk and nonchalantly reached for the desk drawer.

Green reacted quickly and with one quick motion, grabbed his Army-issued Beretta M9, and pointed it at Nunn.

"Don't even try and go for your gun, Colonel. I'd have no problem dropping the hammer on you right now."

Nunn moved his hand back on the desk. "So, how did you figure this all out?"

"Let's say a little birdie told me. Still, I held out some hope it wasn't true. That is, until just now."

Nunn snorted. "Yes, you would, wouldn't you? You never were very bright. Actually, I've always thought of you as more of a dumb-ass."

Green shook his head in disbelief. "Even now, with a gun pointed at you, you're still an arrogant prick."

"That's because I think so little of you, it just comes naturally to me. You're nothing but pencil pushing ass kisser," taunted Nunn.

"Yeah, well how's it feel to have a pencil pushing ass kisser get the drop on you? Must be an age thing, affecting your mind and reflexes. You're an old man who's still a Colonel. It must frustrate the hell out you being passed over for promotion all these years. Oh, and let's not forget your criminal background. How was that prison you were in, anyway?"

Nunn locked eyes with Green. "You're not half the man I am, Major."

Green fired back. "Thank God for that."

"So, what you got in mind, Major? You going to try and send me back to prison. Good luck with that one. It'll never happen. In fact, you'll be the one who'll end up in prison for pulling a gun on me," sneered Nunn.

"I'm not going to take you to the authorities. Hell, I wouldn't even know who to trust."

"That's right, you don't. So, what's your move, Major? You won't kill me. You don't have the balls for that."

"Killing you would let you off the hook. No, I've got something else in mind for you."

"And what would that be?"

"I'm taking you to Canada. I'm pretty sure British Intelligence would love to interrogate someone like you."

Nunn nervously moved back in his chair.

This bit of news had him rattled. The Canadians and the Brits would be interested in what Nunn could tell them. Not only were they worried about this war spilling over their border, but they also wanted to stay informed of the Government's overall plans. Green figured Nunn had plenty of information to share and he felt confident the Brits could get it out of him.

Nunn reached for his glass, his hand shook as he raised it to his lips and gulped the whole pour down.

"Now get up, Colonel," said Green still pointing his sidearm at him.

Nunn pushed his chair back, stood up and moved around the desk. Green backed up and bumped into the umbrella stand. When he turned to see where he was going, Nunn suddenly rushed him. The speed at which a man in his mid-sixties could move surprised Green when he felt a punch to the side of his gut.

Nunn grabbed for the gun with his right hand. The quick movement and Nunn's strength threw Green off balance as they fought for control of the weapon. The stench of Scotch vapors rose from the old man's breath stinging Green's nose. He collected himself and head-butted Nunn in the nose. Blood spattered and poured out of his nostrils, but it didn't slow the Colonel down.

Nunn pushed Green into the hallway. He stumbled and they fell backward with Nunn on top of him. The fall loosened Nunn's grip on the gun and Green took advantage of it. He called up all the strength he could muster to roll to the left.

Keeping a strict regimen of lifting weights had paid off for Green and he was able to push Nunn into the roll while taking control of the pistol.

He was now on top of Nunn.

With his arm now free, he swung the gun like a club across Nunn's temple. The first contact echoed as it crushed bone matter.

Green kept swinging.

All the frustration and pent-up anger he had suppressed came raging out of him. Again, and again, he hit Nunn until the old man stopped moving.

Green leaned back breathing in quick spurts of air. He looked down at the bloodied man and checked his pulse.

Nothing.

Colonel Nunn was dead.

CHAPTER 69

ST PAUL MINNESOTA

S car and Winters, with knives drawn, made a rush for the two guards who were making sandwiches. They were alerted by the noise of feet pounding across the floor. One instinctively reached for his gun. He was fast enough to have his piece drawn, but not fast enough to get off a shot before Winters plunged the knife into his stomach. The man dropped the gun and reached for his gut, he tried to scream, but couldn't get enough air. He fell to the floor next to the one Scar had taken out.

The two men turned when they heard another guard coming from upstairs, and they moved to the entrance of the kitchen to wait. Seconds later, a cop staggered through the doorway holding his neck. Meeks who had come up behind him had just sliced his jugular. The man fell, dead, onto the tiled floor.

They gave each other a firm nod before they hustled up the carpeted staircase. Upstairs was a long hallway, where at the end was an open door with light shining out. Winters led them down the hall and stopped at the entrance.

Inside were two men on the far side of a large room. They sat in beige theater recliners, facing a flat screen TV watching a movie.

Winters raised two fingers. He motioned for Meeks and Scar to check the other rooms. He placed his knife back in his sheath, drew out his Colt 1911, and walked into the room. He cocked the hammer back on the pistol. The clicking alerted Boxer and the other man.

Both turned their heads to see the gun pointed at them.

As Boxer's man reached inside his jacket, Winters squeezed the trigger and blew a hole in his head, splattering blood and skull fragments onto the chair.

"I've got six men guarding this place," cried Boxer.

"You did have six men, and he was your last hope," said Winters pointing toward the man slumped dead in the chair.

"What do you want?"

"I want you, Mr. Boxer."

"So, you know who I am. Who the hell are you?"

"I'm the man you've been chasing."

The answer took Boxer a moment to grasp. His eyes then got big as he realized who stood before him.

The shocked expression on Boxer's face stirred immense pleasure in Winters. His glare reflected his contempt for the man responsible for the killing of his friends back at the train station.

That night had been a turning point in his life. Would he flee or fight? He did both.

He was scared, so he ran. His friends were dead, and he had counted on them to lean on. He came back because he owed it to them. Killing the killers had given him a small degree of satisfaction, but now he faced the man who was responsible for it all.

"So, you're him."

Winters nodded.

"Back from Canada, I see."

"Yes, indeed. Learned a thing or two while I was up there."

"And what exactly did you learn?"

Scar and Meeks came into the room.

"We're good, Captain," said Scar.

Meeks looked at Boxer. "This is him? He doesn't look like much. Bit of a geek if you ask me."

Scar quipped. "Bet he got his ass kicked in high school."

Meeks smirked. "Oh, you know he did."

"Tie him up," ordered Winters.

Meeks and Scar grabbed the man, checked his pockets for weapons and sat him in a chair. Meeks left to find something to restrain him with and came back with a roll of duct tape.

"Duct tape, can use it for anything," chuckled Meeks.

Boxer wrinkled his eyebrows. "What are you going to do with me?" He asked in a high pitched voice.

Winters didn't answer right away and then spoke with an icy voice. "Seeing as you're responsible for the killing of what, hundreds, thousands, of innocent people, we're going to kill you."

"It wasn't me," Boxer whined.

"Yes, it was," retorted Winters.

"I was just following orders," he pleaded.

Winters pointed his gun at Boxer. "Isn't that what all of Hitler's men said."

"I'll tell you everything you want to know, just please don't kill me."

"How about you start with the Patriot Centers, they were your idea weren't they?"

"Sort of...mine and others."

"Why?"

"The Government wants to be in complete control of the country, but to do that, the Midwest had to be subdued. The East Coast had been easy to organize, but the Midwest has been a lot more difficult. It's bigger, more spread out, and the people are more stubborn and independent than we thought. The way they continued to protest, we were surprised to learn how leery everyone was of the new government. After the gun reclamation program failed, they realized they'd never be able to get everybody's guns, so we came up with the idea of, instead of getting rid of the guns, we'd get rid of the gun owners. So, we used the war, as an excuse to have you guys come in voluntarily."

Winters' mouth dropped open as the devastating truth burned through his mind. He turned to Scar and Meeks, both of whom were staring daggers at Boxer. "What better way than to tug at our heartstrings."

Scar gestured with his hands. "Yeah, come on, serve your country, we need you."

Meeks chimed in. "You know what they say, never let a good crisis go to waste."

"So, with fewer gun owners around," snorted Winters, "it'd be a hell of a lot easier to round up the rest of the citizenry."

"Bingo," said Boxer.

The three of them shook their heads in disgust.

Winters sat down in a chair trying to digest what he'd just heard. He didn't want to believe Boxer, but even though it made no sense, it actually did.

He remembered how, just last year, when the new government formed, it shocked everyone, when the President threw out the Constitution. Across the country, citizens started more protests to get their rights back. It was a sickening feeling that one day you could speak your mind and the next day, censorship was the rule. The gun reclamation program was the final straw for many. Knowing you would not be able to defend yourself against crime or what now looked like a tyrannical government was soul crushing.

However, all the hatred toward the government had changed the day China invaded California. Overnight, patriotism came back in style, sweeping the country, and everyone wanted to help drive out the foreign invaders.

Little did they know, the government was fighting two wars, one against the Chinese and the other against its own citizens.

What kind of people actually believe that the means justifies any action? He would never understand it, but then like the old man at the gas station had said, it doesn't matter the reason why, just that they're doing it.

Winters turned back to Boxer. "What about the terrorists?"

"They were brought here as a backup plan, in case something went wrong."

"Went wrong?"

Boxer spoke defiantly. "Yes...they're here because of you."

Winters looked confounded. "Me! What do you mean?"

"You and your rebels. These Patriot Centers were working perfectly, so well, in fact, we were going to expand them to include the entire country, but then you came along. Once you started putting us out of business, we needed to put our back up plan into action. So, with you making all this trouble, we had to go with Operation Sweep."

Winters raised an eyebrow. "Operation Sweep?"

"Total destruction, like Sherman's march to the sea. You didn't actually think we'd stop what we were doing, did you? You forced us to go and hire some very nasty people. People who really hate Americans, to do our dirty work. Not only are they expendable, but they'll also drive more citizens out. The citizens will then beg us to come in and protect them. That's where the National Police come in, to finish mopping up."

The three didn't respond.

"No, had it not been for you, our initial plan would have worked quite brilliantly. Taking advantage of one's patriotic duty to fight in the war had been easy."

Scar moved in and backhanded Boxer across the face, knocking his glasses off. "You piece of shit."

Boxer cried out.

Scar stepped back.

Boxer struggled to compose himself. "Think what you like, but we live in a different world now. It's every man for himself."

"Who orchestrated all of this? Who's your boss?" asked Winters.

"Lawrence Reed is my direct boss, but he takes his orders from Perozzi."

"George Perozzi, the billionaire?" quizzed Winters

"Yes."

"He works for the government?" Winters asked confused.

"No, but he has a definite influence."

"What kind of influence?"

"He spreads money around, it buys him favors."

"What kind of favors?"

"I don't know what his overall goal is, all I know is everyone kisses his ass, even the President."

"But what about the war effort?"

"It's a lost cause. In case you haven't figured it out, we're losing the war and there's nothing we can do about it."

Scar pulled his gun out of his waistband. "We ought to shoot this son-of-a-bitch right now."

Winters lifted his hand. "No, I've got a better idea."

Epilogue

TWO WEEKS LATER

The information Commandant Boxer possessed made him too valuable for an act of vengeance. Instead, Winters took him to Canada and handed him over to Colonel Brocket, who was more than happy to interrogate him.

Within a few days, Brocket felt confident they had gotten everything possible out of Boxer, allowing them to piece more of the puzzle together.

Major Green reported about the accident that had befallen Colonel Nunn. The colonel had gotten drunk in his office, and apparently stumbled hitting his head on his desk, killing him. They held a small ceremony at the post, cremated the body and flew the ashes to Washington for burial.

Based on information provided by Boxer and relayed to Green, he was able to round up the remaining terrorists. They had escaped to a nearby safe house. Once they were all in custody, Green immediately had them executed. It was a small act of retribution to help alleviate the loss of his men, especially his friend Lieutenant Crick.

While in Canada, Winters used the downtime to reflect. Throughout the whole ordeal, he had wanted nothing more than to be done with it, and then go search for his daughter. He had struggled with being the one everyone had relied upon and he doubted everything he did and the wisdom of those who had put him in charge. Winters had never seen himself as a leader. He had never been in such a position. In fact, he mostly avoided it, always feeling more comfortable being told what to do, and just being responsible for his own work.

He sat alone in his room and wrestled with these thoughts sitting alone in his room. One day, General Standish visited him and noticed his despair. After a few prodding questions, Winters confided in him. Standish understood and reminded him of their conversation about his destiny.

"Think about your actions at the train station. Your sense of duty to your fallen friends was stronger than the concern for your own life. These types of actions speak volumes about men, but even more for someone as humble as yourself. Your humility in what you did, was what the men saw and respected in you. Had you been a braggart, things would have been much different. You were the right man at the right time. This is why I say you are a man of destiny."

Winters came to realize he had sold himself short on what he was capable of doing. It bothered him knowing all these years, he could have done something more with his life. Been more of a leader in his career, the community and more importantly been a better father to his daughter. This disturbed him the most. Looking back, he realized he could have also handled things better with her. He now felt responsible for pushing her away and ultimately driving her off. He also felt sorry for her, that she had felt so alienated that she wasn't there for her mom when she passed away.

*   *   *   *   *

Winters drove a pickup truck to an abandoned store outside of Rockford, Illinois and pulled into the parking lot. He stepped out and extended his hand to Major Green.

"Major, it's good to see you."

"Likewise, Captain."

Winters leaned on the side of the truck. "I understand you've rounded up the rest of the terrorists."

"We did, thanks to you and Mr. Scarborough for getting that info to us."

"Well, you can thank British Intelligence for getting it out of Boxer."

"I'm just glad to be rid of them, and him."

"And your superiors, they bought the story of Colonel Nunn? And what do they say about Boxer?"

"Nunn was known for his heavy drinking, so it wasn't too much of a stretch. They figured it was you, who took Boxer. They still want me to do all I can to find you."

Winters smiled. "Yes, well good luck with that."

"This is why I wanted to meet with you. You've got some folks in Washington extremely pissed at you. They've started a massive propaganda campaign blaming your Shadow Patriots for the murder of Commandant Boxer, and the killing of defenseless men, women and children."

Winters shook his head.

"They're afraid of you and what you'll do next. They'll send more men and possibly more terrorists to eliminate you as a threat."

"It seems they'll stop at nothing."

"They'll do all they can to learn your identity. I'll keep throwing up roadblocks and feeding you whatever information I can, but at some point, they'll figure out it's me."

"I understand, but we'll worry about that when the time comes," said Winters firmly gripping the hand of the man who was once his enemy, but was now his friend.

Dear Reader:

The Shadow Patriots won the day.

Are you ready for a new adventure? Are the Shadow Patriots ready for their next move?

In a country at war with itself, there are good guys and bad guys. It can be hard to tell who's who and what their motivations are. Some are noble, while others are despicable.

The Patriot Centers are closed down, but Winters' next challenge will make closing them seem like a cake walk. He's going to need all the inner strength he can muster to lead the Shadow Patriots when a deviate activity is discovered.

Plans must be changed as they risk their lives to save the most vulnerable amongst us. But forced errors end with deadly consequences.

Who will survive?

If you enjoyed the first book in the series, you'll love _New Recruits_. The stakes are higher and the twists more surprising.

The other novels in the series:
2) New Recruits
3) Dark Maneuvers
4) Dark Toll
5) Innocent Shadows
6) Lost Shadows
7) Dark Justice – The final volume.

Made in the USA
Middletown, DE
10 March 2019